The Christmas Date

By B. N. Hale

27 Dates: The Series

The Dating Challenge

The Dating Secret

The Dating Game

The Christmas Date

The Valentine's Date

Table of Contents

Volume 20: The Lake Date

Chapter 1 8

Chapter 2 14

Chapter 3 21

Chapter 4 27

Chapter 5 34

Chapter 6 40

Volume 21: The Thanksgiving Date

Chapter 1 49

Chapter 2 55

Chapter 3 60

Chapter 4 67

Chapter 5 73

Chapter 6 79

Chapter 7 86

Chapter 8 91

Volume 22: The Brothers Date

Chapter 1 96

Chapter 2 102

Chapter 3 108

Chapter 4 115

Chapter 5 120

Chapter 6 126

Chapter 7 132

Volume 23: The Christmas Date

Chapter 1 138

Chapter 2 146

Chapter 3 151

Chapter 4 158

Chapter 5 165

Chapter 6 172

Volume 24: The Memory Lane Date

Chapter 1 179

Chapter 2 185

Chapter 3 191

Chapter 4 197

Chapter 5 203

Chapter 6 209

Volume 25: The New York City Date

Chapter 1 215

Chapter 2 221

Chapter 3 227

Chapter 4 234

Chapter 5 241

Chapter 6 248

Volume 26: The Distance Date

Chapter 1 254

Chapter 2 260

Chapter 3 264

Chapter 4 270

Chapter 5 276

Chapter 6 282

27 Dates: The Series...287

Author Bio...288

Volume 20: The Lake Date

Chapter 1

In the days following Jackson's proposal, Reed woke each morning with Kate on his mind. Before brushing his teeth or even getting out of bed, he grabbed his phone and sent a text with three simple words.

I love you.

Just typing the words sent a thrill into his chest, as did her response of four words. By the third day she beat him to it, and it quickly escalated into a competition to see who could send it first. The following week he set an alarm and woke at four in the morning—to find Kate had beaten him to it.

"I think it's time we proclaim me the victor of our little morning war," Kate said as she picked him up for classes. His car was dead again, but he didn't mind so much because it meant more time with Kate.

"What if I'm not ready to end the fight?" he asked with a smile.

"I am," she said, stifling a yawn. "Claiming victory at three in the morning was worth it, but I couldn't get back to sleep."

"Sorry," he said. "I've just never been able to say it to anyone before. I hope I'm not becoming too clingy."

She took his hand and smiled. "No, but I really would like to sleep."

"Then I concede defeat." He checked his backpack to make sure he'd brought his homework. "But I'm still ahead in the dating challenge."

"The last few dates have been a little different," she said. "You sure you want to continue?"

"I don't want to stop," he said, and then hesitated. "Unless you do."

"No," she said.

His eyes narrowed when he noticed her expression. Although neutral, there was a stillness about her features that suggested she had something to hide. She glanced his way and then quickly back to the road.

"You have an invite planned," he accused.

"I will not admit that."

"You *do*," he said.

"Maybe," she said, and sniffed. "Anything's possible."

She pulled up to the curb near the psychology building and pointed to the building. "You're early," she said. "You may want to take a stroll before you go to class."

"And what will I find?"

"How should I know?" she asked, and yawned.

"Wait," he said. "You said you've been up since three. Any other reason you might have been awake?"

She smiled brightly. "Have a good day!"

She leaned over to kiss him and then waited, her expression amused. Shaking his head, he grabbed his backpack and stepped out. As she drove away he walked around the building, and found the crowd.

Hundreds of early students were congregating at the corner of the building and staring at an object just out of view. Many had cameras out and were taking pictures, the angle of their phones suggesting it was large. He joined the crowd and turned the corner of the building, coming to a halt as it came into view.

At twenty feet tall, the tower of wood and paper had drawn a crowd. Boards had been painted black and lined with white until they resembled scorched logs that leaned against each other like a teepee. Streams of paper and red plastic fluttered from fans presumably placed within the structure, the combination obviously intended to look like a massive fire.

"Maybe one of the fraternities?" someone asked.

"I don't think so," a girl said, craning her head to look at the base of the campfire. "There's an invitation."

Reed threaded his way through the crowd until he reached the enormous campfire. When he stepped out of the crowd he looked up to the ball of white hanging on the end of a board, the front edge blackened until it looked like a toasting marshmallow. On the ground nearby, one piece of cardboard resembled a graham cracker, while another looked exactly like a giant Hershey's piece of chocolate. Next to the chocolate was a card addressed to him.

"It's Reed!" someone shouted, and suddenly a buzz of sound erupted from the crowd.

"It must be Kate's invite."

"But last week was Jackson's proposal," came the reply. "I thought it was his turn to ask."

Reed picked up the four-foot envelope and turned. "Does *everyone* know about my dating life?"

"Yes!" several girls chorused, and one added. "Everything is on Ember's blog."

Reed noticed that many of those present appeared tired—yawning just like Kate had. "And how many of you helped build this fire?"

10

There was a great shifting of feet and looking away, but several had broad smiles on their faces, unashamed at being caught. Reed laughed and ripped open the paper as the crowd surged closer to see the writing.

At a fire you'll be

If you'll be my date

For mallows by the sea

And kisses by Kate

The girls *ah*'d while the guys groaned. Reed merely smiled. It had been weeks since they'd done a big invite or date and he'd begun to wonder if—despite their decision—the dating challenge had come to a very quiet end.

One of his classmates stepped out of the group and put his arm around Reed. "I applaud you for your dedication to research."

Tall and a sporting a full beard, Caleb had started the same program with Reed, and they'd shared a lot of classes. He was a year older but had taken a liking to Reed's methods, even going on a few creative dates himself. It had helped him land his current girlfriend.

"It's not all research," Reed said.

"Just make sure you plan more than romance," Caleb said.

"Why do you say that?"

"Caroline and I broke up."

Reed grimaced. "I'm sorry."

Caleb shrugged and issued a wry laugh. "Turns out, creative dates were great at manufacturing romance, not so great at keeping one."

Caleb clapped him on the back and walked away, leaving Reed disconcerted. He shook his head in an attempt to dismiss the spark of doubt and gathered the envelope, taking it with him as he went to class.

11

Braving the well-wishers surrounding the fire, he pulled out his phone and called Kate.

"I assume we're going to have a campfire?" he asked.

"Whatever made you think that?" she asked.

He grinned and looked to the towering edifice of fake fire. "I found a not-so-subtle message."

A smile tinged her voice. "It took forever to set up, but I had help."

"There's no way you set that up with just the blondes and Jackson," he said.

"True," she said. "But I know you don't follow Ember's blog, so I posted an open invitation for anyone to help me."

"And people asked to help?"

"Hundreds," she said. "There were so many it was hard to get them to focus."

"I'm surprised so many were willing to wake up at three in the morning," he said.

"I did lose quite a few when I mentioned that part," she admitted.

"Well it's beautiful," he replied. "But we can't very well have a fire in the backyard."

"We won't," she said. "We're going camping."

"An overnight trip?" he asked, feigning shock. "You might take advantage of me."

"As much as I'd like that," she said, "we won't be alone. I decided it was time for a big group date with everyone. My roommates are coming and Jackson and Shelby will be there too."

"Sounds like fun," he replied. "Do you know anything about camping?"

"In Arizona," she replied. "But Tanner was an eagle scout here, so he said he knows where we can go. It was odd to see him so enthusiastic."

Reed smiled at the image of the normally quiet Tanner getting enthusiastic about a topic. "I look forward to our next date."

"We couldn't let the dating challenge die, now could we?"

"I'll see you later," he said. "I love you."

"I love you, too," she said.

When she hung up, Reed stared at the phone, wondering why he still felt disconcerted. Kate's comment about the challenge reminded him of what Caleb had said, and he wondered if the creative dating had become the foundation of their relationship. If it had, then it begged an obvious question.

What would they be without the challenge?

Chapter 2

In the days after they got the invite, Reed couldn't shake the question. Like a sliver under his finger, it nagged at him as they packed for the trip. Most of them didn't have gear, so they had to borrow sleeping bags and tents, many of which came from Tanner.

"Just how many sleeping bags does your family have?" Ember asked, eyeing the tower of equipment.

"My family provided most of the gear for my troop," he said. "Plus I have four older brothers."

"How many are eagle scouts?" Reed asked as they picked up a box of supplies for dinner.

"All of them," he said.

"I earned my wolf," Jackson said proudly.

"Like when you were six?" Shelby asked, shouldering a pack.

"Yep," he said.

"Er, that's nice," Tanner said.

Reed hid a smile and gathered up a pair of tents, joining Kate as they left her house and piled the gear in the back of Jackson's truck. His own car had been deemed unsuitable for a drive into the mountains, so they would be riding with Ember and Tanner in Ember's jeep. As they loaded tents, another car parked on the street and Marta got out dressed in jeans and a plaid shirt.

Jackson walked by and smirked. "Nice shirt."

"We're going camping," Marta said. "What are you supposed to wear?"

"Normal clothes," Jackson said.

"And that's normal?" Shelby asked, pointing at Jackson's shirt, which said, *I'm Batman.*

"Hey, it could be true," Jackson protested.

"You're missing a few billion dollars," Reed said with a laugh.

"I'm Bruce Wayne before Batman," Jackson said.

"Ha!" Ember said, walking into view carrying a pair of camping chairs. "You're closer to Robin than Batman."

"Still a superhero," Jackson said.

Kate pointed to the truck. "We'd better get going or we'll be arriving after dark."

Tanner dropped the last of the pile into the bed of Jackson's truck and nodded. "We've got all the matches, kitchen tote, Dutch oven supplies, and—"

"I love it went you talk nerdy," Ember said, going up on her toes to kiss him.

He flushed and opened the door on her jeep. "You ready?"

"Let's go," she said. "I've brought two sleeping bags that zip together."

Tanner flushed bright red. Jackson laughed aloud and clapped him on the back. "Let's go camping!"

Reed and Kate climbed into the back of Ember's jeep with Brittney, while Marta joined Jackson and Shelby in his truck. Directed by Tanner, Ember took the lead and headed out of town. As they left Boulder behind, Tanner described their destination.

"I went to Clover Lake to get my camping badge," he said. "It's a couple hours away, but it's beautiful. It's not one of the popular places to camp, so we'll probably have the place to ourselves. Jackson's going to stop and pick up the trailer with my canoes."

"You have more than one?" Brittney asked, sitting on the other side of Kate.

"Well I have mine," Tanner said, "and each of my brothers have one. It was our gift when we got our Eagle."

"I'd rather have a car," Reed said.

"That's just because your car is junk," Ember said.

Kate grinned. "She has a point."

"It's still moving," Reed said, and then amended. "For now."

The jeep accelerated out of the neighborhood. Ember swerved around a slow moving car and sped up, crossing two lanes of traffic to make the next corner.

"Your car moves about as well as a turtle," Kate said.

Betrayed, Reed looked to her. "Hey!"

"It's true," she said, her expression sheepish.

Reed laughed sourly. "It's not dead yet."

"You should put it out of its misery," Brittney said. They all looked to her and her face turned pink. "Sorry."

Brittney asked Tanner about his time as a boy scout. He launched into a description of camping trips with his brothers and hiking across mountain ranges. The way he described it made Reed wish he'd been in scouting.

"Were you ever a scout?" Kate asked when the conversation shifted.

16

"I wanted to," he said. "But my dad thought I should play a sport."

"What did you play?" Tanner asked.

"Football."

"You were a football player?" Kate asked.

"For one season," he admitted. "It wasn't my finest moment."

"What position did you play?"

"The bench," he replied.

She laughed and shook her head. "No, seriously."

"Seriously," he replied. "I played a few positions but spent most of the time out of the game."

"Why didn't you mention it before?"

"Do *you* like sharing embarrassing moments?"

She gave a small smile. "Probably not. But you're athletic."

"Don't patronize me," Reed said.

"It's true," she said, a touch of pink lighting her cheeks, her eyes flicking to his torso.

"Truthfully, I like to play lots of different sports, but nothing really stuck." He smiled and put his arm around her. "I shared an embarrassing moment. Now it's your turn."

"Do I have to?" Kate asked.

"Are you going to leave me hanging?" Reed asked.

She sighed and then relented. "I was on the swim team."

"Really?"

"Did pretty well too," she said. "But I didn't care for the early morning practices."

"You woke up early enough to build a bonfire for me," he said with a smile.

"I wake up when I have sufficient reason," she replied. "Speaking of which, thanks for doing all this for us, Tanner. We never could have gone camping on our own."

"My pleasure," Tanner replied, his attention on the paper map in his lap.

"Do you need a compass?" Ember asked.

"Already have one," Tanner replied absently.

Ember glanced to the back seat and caught Reed's eye, and they shared a smile. Tanner was an unusual guy, but it was clear Ember liked his oddities. Reed had to agree, and was grateful he'd set them up.

"What are we doing tonight?" Brittney asked, clinging to the door handle as they turned onto the freeway, the jeep's tires squealing.

Tanner shook his head and gestured to Kate. "I'm just in charge of the equipment. Kate has the activities planned."

Kate answered a few questions but kept her answers vague, obviously with the intention to surprise Reed. He smiled and leaned back, enjoying the spectacle of the others attempting to glean information from his girlfriend. It was nice not being the only one left in the dark.

The highway took them north, winding through endless desert and patches of trees. Northern Colorado contained few towns, and the emptiness had a stark sort of beauty, the kind that made Reed want to watch the vista roll by.

It had snowed when Aura had arrived but the cold had left with her. Autumn had returned and the air was warm, likely the last warm spell before the harsh winter blanketed the horizon in snow. Until then, the season resisted, pushing for one last day of heat before temperatures plummeted.

In late afternoon they pulled off the highway and followed a gravel road into the mountains. Uneven and rough, it took them out of the valley into a series of winding canyons, rising until they plunged into a dense forest.

Light flickered across the jeep as they passed beneath the boughs, the illumination just beginning to fade as the sun crept toward the mountain. They crossed a small stream that gurgled its way under a bridge, the rocks adding a cadence that filled the trees with music. Reed opened the plastic windows and the others followed his lead, filling the jeep with the scent of pine.

Beyond the stream they came to a sign that directed them up a side road, and Ember eased the jeep into the narrow road. Hardly more than two ruts cut into brush, it climbed up the slope and deeper into the trees. Half an hour later the road crested a ridge and descended into a valley.

A glittering lake greeted them, its curved edges resembling a four-leaf clover. They all praised the view as Ember brought them to a halt in a clearing close to the water. Reed stepped out and gazed on the beautiful seclusion. The air carried the scent of dirt and trees, the combination inspiring a sense of openness.

Jackson's truck pulled in behind them and the three of them piled out. Jackson turned a circle next to the truck, for once at a loss for words. Marta too seemed struck by the beauty. Reed found Kate at his side and reached for her hand, his smile one of awe.

"This place is incredible," he said.

"It's better than Tanner described," Kate exclaimed.

Ember walked to the edge of the lake, her hands on her hips. "It'll do," she said with a firm nod.

19

Brittney and Marta shielded their eyes and pointed to a hawk surveying them from above, while Shelby simply closed her eyes, a small smile on her face. Reed turned to Kate and pulled her into his arms.

"Do you ever cease to amaze?" he murmured.

"I'm glad you like it," she said, leaning in to kiss him. Her eyes sparkled with anticipation. "But the night is young."

Chapter 3

Tanner took charge and quietly directed the others to place the gear around the camp. Much laughter ensued as the group attempted to erect tents and prepare dinner, which Kate revealed would be tinfoil steak, potatoes, and Dutch oven pie. Reed managed to get his tent set up and then helped the girls with theirs.

He was highly conscious of the sideways glances from the blondes, and realized it was because he was going to be sleeping in a tent alone. On the outside Kate seemed unperturbed but he sensed a touch of tension to her laughter and he wondered if it was for the same reason.

Tanner surveyed them until they had things well in hand and then nodded. "I'll get started on dinner."

"How did he get his tent set up so fast?" Marta asked, eyeing Tanner's immaculate tent.

"He's a literal boy scout," Ember said.

"Boy scouts don't have a body like that," Brittney said.

Ember smirked and eyed him. "He's a little quiet, but I think I'm starting to like that."

"He does seem oddly immune to your fire," Kate said.

Ember snorted in agreement and called out to him. "Are you going to use flint and steel to start the fire?"

Jackson poked his head into view, his expression incredulous. "He's a boy scout, not a mountain man."

"Well how should I know?" Ember said. "It's not like I run around starting fires."

Reed leaned over to Kate as they set the last pole in place. "We should be grateful she doesn't do that," he whispered.

Kate grinned and they tied the rain guard on top of the tent. Then they stood back to admire their handiwork. Reed thought it looked lopsided but it was standing, as were the rest of the tents—except for Jackson's and Shelby's, which looked like a tent carcass, its poles sticking up like ribs.

"Do you need help?" Brittney asked uncertainly.

"I think we're good," Jackson's voice came from inside, followed by Shelby's giggle.

"Duct tape isn't part of tent construction," Tanner said.

"Was that a joke?" Marta asked.

Tanner's lips twitched. "Maybe."

Ember laughed and joined him where he was setting up a tent of logs in the fire pit, a circle of stones left by a previous camper. Tanner's tent of logs looked better than Jackson's actual tent, and when Reed pointed out the distinction, Jackson merely laughed. He and Shelby appeared a moment later having changed into swimming suits.

"You're going swimming?" Reed asked, shocked. "It's October. The water will be freezing."

"Have to do our swim check to use the canoes," Jackson reasoned, making Shelby giggle again.

"I never said that," Tanner said.

Jackson waved airily and walked with Shelby to get a canoe. "Anyone else for a dip?"

22

Reed looked to Tanner, but he motioned to the fire, which was just beginning to lick its way into the wood. Tinfoil packages were stacked on top of the cooler and a Dutch oven rested nearby.

"It'll take time to get the right coals," he said. "You have time to enjoy the lake."

"Are you sure?" Kate asked.

"Don't tip the canoe," he said, frowning at Jackson's and Shelby's excitement. "Getting a submerged canoe out of a cold lake is not an experience I would like to repeat."

Reed and Kate exchanged a look and then stepped to the trailer. They each took an end of a canoe and followed Jackson and Shelby to the rocky edge of the lake. Kate got in first and eased it out before gingerly stepping in and pushing off.

"Is it supposed to feel unstable?" Kate asked as the boat tipped precariously with every motion."

"It's perfectly fine," Jackson called, and leaned both ways, nearly swamping his own canoe.

Shelby cried out in surprise and used her paddle to hit the water, sending freezing drops splattering across Jackson's chest. He gasped and sucked in his breath. Then his eyes glowed with the challenge and in seconds white water blasted between them.

Reed carefully paddled away from the ice-water duel. Their canoe glided across the still water, sending ripples arcing back toward the shore. The sun had half submerged itself behind the mountain and the colors were just beginning to change, the sunset reflecting in the pristine waters of the lake.

"This is beautiful," Kate said.

"I've been camping before, but this . . .?" He shrugged, unable to complete the statement.

Marta and Brittney launched another canoe and paddled out onto the water, also avoiding the still furious battle between Jackson and Shelby. They canoed out toward the middle of the lake, where Reed and Kate sat with their paddles across their legs.

"We should do this more often," Marta exclaimed, sweeping her hand at the towering mountains.

"It depends on how long Ember and Tanner stay together," Kate said, glancing back to shore. "We don't really have the equipment on our own."

"I think they're good together," Brittney said.

"They do," Kate said. "But the average life expectancy of Ember's relationships is probably three months."

"I like him," Brittney said.

"What do you think?" Marta asked, looking to Reed.

"Me?" Reed asked.

"Your thesis is on relationships, isn't it?" Marta asked.

"Sort of," Reed said, reaching down to touch the water.

"Well," Marta asked. "Do you think they have a chance of staying together?"

"My research doesn't really extend to long-term," Reed said wryly. "And Ember is far from a normal case."

They all smiled at that and Kate dipped her paddle in, keeping them from drifting away. "You must have a guess of whether certain couples will work out."

Reed thought back to Caleb's comment and wondered again if the romance inspired by his creative dating was all false. He wanted to voice an opinion but doubt assailed him and he gave a wry laugh.

"I don't think anyone can know that."

Kate's eyebrows briefly pulled together in confusion, but a hawk soared across the lake, drawing Reed's gaze. Majestic and beautiful, the bird glided above them, its reflection crossing Marta's and Brittney's canoe.

As they explored the exterior of the lake, Reed frequently felt Kate's eyes on him but pretended not to notice. He had no qualms about discussing his thoughts with Kate, but he couldn't identify the source of the doubt. Until he did, he didn't want to risk making Kate think his feelings had changed.

"Look!" Brittney called, pointing to a deer darting away from the lake. Another deer followed and the graceful creatures bounded away.

The sun continued to set, the shadows gradually stretching across the lake until the water turned opaque. Curiosity had taken Marta and Brittney in a different direction, while Jackson and Shelby had retreated to the fire on the lake's edge to warm themselves after swamping their canoe.

Reed and Kate drifted near the center of the lake and both spoke in soft tones, as if afraid to break the peace that now gripped the valley. The sun was no longer visible but the shimmering red and orange poured over the mountainside, the colors reflected in the mirror of glass on which they floated.

Peace permeated the lake, with even the animals growing quiet at the approach of twilight. Unwilling to dip his paddle into water, Reed breathed deep of the cooling air, shivering at the supreme wonder the sight instilled.

With great care he shifted in his seat until he faced Kate, but her eyes were on the sky, where stars began to sparkle, their light growing brighter as the iridescent sky gave way to darkness. She looked at Reed, a wondering smile playing across her features. Kate's green eyes glimmered with emotion, her dark hair hanging against her shoulder, curving over her collarbone in an enticing arch. Her eyebrow lifted under the scrutiny.

"What?" she asked.

"You're just beautiful."

She chuckled softly. "I think you mean this place is beautiful."

"It is," he said. "But that's not what I want to watch."

"It's just the date," she said, but her smile was pleased.

Her words recalled Caleb's comment and Reed shook his head, both to disagree and discard the seed of doubt. "*You* are beautiful."

"You're not so bad yourself," she said. "But as much as I'd like to kiss you, I really don't want to end up taking a swim."

He smiled and motioned to the shore. "Ready to leave the lake?"

"Not yet," she said. "Not until it's dark."

Reed smiled and agreed, and together they relished the final seconds of a flawless moment. Between Kate, the abnormally warm fall, and the stunning sunset on the lake, he found himself struck by the profound sense of serenity.

The scene was marred by the seed of doubt that had wormed its way into his skull, and again the question arose. What would they be without the dating challenge? He recognized the doubt would not fade and resolved to speak to Kate about it. But not now. Not when the last seconds of a perfect moment begged to be enjoyed.

Chapter 4

"Dinner's ready!"

Tanner's voice echoed across the dark lake, finally breaking the spell. Reed and Kate paddled their way to the shore, arriving just after Marta and Brittney pulled their canoe from the water.

Reed climbed out and dragged the canoe out of the water, the hull scraping across the rocks. He balanced the end but it nearly tipped when Kate stepped out, and she laughed and caught his hand.

"I got you," he said.

"You think?" she asked with a laugh.

"I do," he said.

"Will you stop kissing and come to dinner?" Jackson called.

"Coming, *Mom*," Kate called.

"Don't talk back to me, girl!"

Reed laughed and took her hand, walking with her toward the delicious smells wafting their way. They claimed the last seats on the log next to Brittney. Then Reed noticed Jackson and Shelby were in pajamas.

"Are you ready for bed?" he asked.

"It didn't make sense to change twice," Jackson said.

Dressed in pink flannel pants and a unicorn/dragon shirt, it looked like Jackson had borrowed Shelby's pajamas, but Reed knew them to be his. Jackson endured the teasing with a smile, unperturbed that his clothes were brighter than the fire.

The flames crackled beneath the logs. Tanner had separated the coals to the side and used the bed of heat to cook the tinfoil packages. The firelight reflected off the metal and illuminated the faces of those around the fire.

"You look like a teenage girl," Ember said, but her smile took the sting from the insult.

"These are my favorite pajamas," Jackson said, feigning offence.

All eyes turned to Shelby and she nodded. "It's true. He'd wear them every night if he could."

"Do you really want to marry this guy?" Ember asked Shelby.

Shelby smiled and looked him up and down. "Every morning I wake up and laugh."

"I do my best," Jackson said.

Reed stood and opened the cooler, searching the assorted drinks until he found a lemonade. He glanced to Kate and she smiled knowingly, indicating she'd anticipated his favorite drink. Collecting a root beer for Kate, he handed it her, and at Jackson's request, tossed him a beer. Others clamored for drinks and he served them all before resuming his seat.

"Thanks for the drink," Kate said.

He reached the bottle out to tap hers. "I live to serve."

"I thought you said dinner was ready," Marta said.

"It is," Tanner said, and used a pair of tongs to remove the packages of tinfoil.

As Tanner loaded plates, Shelby passed them to each of the group, pointedly giving the smallest to Jackson. She grinned as she passed him the plate in a flourish, and offered a plastic fork and a knife.

"A small portion for the little girl in the group."

"I may have the figure of a teenage girl," Jackson said, "but I have the appetite of a teenage boy."

Shelby laughed and switched plates, and Jackson's frown turned into a smile. Reed accepted his plate with a nod of gratitude. Balancing the plate on his knees, he pried open the tinfoil with his knife and fork, releasing a plume of steam and the scent of seared meat.

Steak sat nestled with potatoes, onions, and carrots. Spices darkened the gravy that spilled onto the plate in an enticing swirl. He breathed deep, hunger spiking. The others looked equally as excited and were quick to dig in.

"I'm *starving*," Marta said.

"This looks incredible, Tanner," Reed said.

"Kate put the dinners together," Tanner said, nodding to her.

She waved aside the murmurs of appraisal. "Tanner cooked them. And he did the pie."

"How's that coming by the way?" Brittney asked, craning for a look at the Dutch oven.

Tanner stood and used a metal rod to lift the lid, filling the campfire with the smell of cherry pie. Amidst a new round of smiles and praise, Tanner examined the dessert and pronounced it nearly finished.

"Where'd you learn to cook in a Dutch oven?" Shelby asked.

"My grandpa," he replied, resuming his seat and balancing the plate on his knees. "He was a scoutmaster for twenty years and even earned the Silver Beaver award."

29

"Is that better than my wolf badge?" Jackson asked.

Tanner grinned. "It's an award for a lifetime in scouting."

"So a year isn't enough," Jackson said. "Too bad."

"Tell them what he did," Ember said.

"He was in World War II," Tanner said, "and served on the Pacific front during the war. He had several military awards but I didn't learn about them until after he died. He's the one that taught me to be a scout."

"Sounds like a great man," Kate said. "With the way you cook, he'd be proud."

Tanner shifted, obviously uncomfortable with the attention. "I think credit for the night goes to Kate for setting up the activity."

Kate smiled and accepted their gratitude with a nod. "Things have changed a lot in the last year," she said. "I figured it was time to get us all together."

"It certainly has been an interesting year," Reed said.

"It has," Kate agreed. "But our little dating challenge has brought Jackson and Shelby into our life, as well as Tanner. I don't think I ever imagined it would have such an impact."

"Which was your favorite date?" Marta asked.

Reed and Kate exchanged a knowing look and she smiled. "Isn't it obvious? The one where we kissed for the first time at the Festival of Lanterns."

"What about you?" Shelby asked Reed.

"Our bad date," he said.

"Really?" Kate asked.

"Anyone can make a creative date fun," Reed said. "But it takes someone truly gifted to have fun on a terrible date."

"So now I'm gifted?" Kate asked.

He grunted in amusement. "You didn't need me to tell you that."

"Ugh," Ember said. "You two make me sick sometimes."

Reed grinned and leaned over to kiss Kate, the act nearly sending their food into the dirt. Ember groaned again while the others laughed. When they parted Kate's expression was smug, eliciting a smile from Reed.

The conversation shifted to other camping experiences, and Brittney talked about camping with her parents and sisters. Marta spoke of sleeping in the backyard when she was a kid, but that was the closest she'd ever come to the woods.

"There was *one* tree," Marta said with a smile.

Deep in the woods and sitting around a campfire, the stories seemed more vivid and enthralling. Firelight flickered across their faces as they talked and laughed, and Reed was surprised to realize how much he'd come to care for the group of friends.

Prior to meeting Kate, he'd had many friends, but few that he would have considered for a weekend camping trip. Since he and Kate had begun dating for real, he'd gotten to know each of Kate's roommates and was surprised to realize just how much he valued the relationships. Kate's roommates had become more than friends—and now they were akin to sisters.

Ember now asked him questions about dating and Tanner. She reminded him a great deal of his sister, Natalie. But Jackson was even more of a brother to Ember, and the two teased each other incessantly, frequently eliciting laughter from the group.

Reed's eyes settled on Brittney. Over the last few weeks Brittney had begun texting him about career options. In return, Reed had requested her help in the kitchen, and the unassuming girl had taught him more about cooking than his own parents.

Marta, too, had become essential to his life, as was her extended family. Reed and Kate ate dinner every week at Marta's family restaurant and he loved talking to Marta's mother. Reed had helped Marta apply for grad school and they'd talked for hours about programs, college, and post collegiate life.

"You've been really quiet," Kate murmured, pulling him from his thoughts. "What are you thinking about?"

They'd finished the dinner and the pie, their plates long since put into the trash. The fire had been rebuilt once already, and was just beginning to weaken again. A chill had crept into the air and Reed shivered.

"Just thinking about how close we all are," he murmured.

Her smile was soft as she surveyed the talking group, the atmosphere warm and comfortable. "We're family," she said.

"Family," he said, smiling.

He kissed her on the forehead just as a strange rumble came from the dark trees. He instinctively turned but didn't see anything in the darkness. A moment later he heard it again, a shuffling and a snapping stick. He turned and blinked to clear his vision of the firelight—and spotted a shape moving in the shadows. The sense of peace hardened into concern.

"Tanner?" he called. "Do you know what that is?" he pointed toward the shape.

Everything went quiet and they all followed Reed's gaze. Then the shadows shifted again and Reed's eyes widened, shocked by the size of the shadow. There was a sharp intake of breath from someone on the other side of the fire.

"Everyone get to the cars or up a tree," Tanner said, his tone quiet, urgent.

"What, is it a bear?" Marta asked, already on her feet.

"Worse," Tanner said, rising and pulling Ember toward her jeep. "That's a moose."

Chapter 5

The huge beast rumbled, and Tanner hissed for them to move slowly. His heart thumping against his ribs, Reed caught Kate's arm and eased away from the fire, nearly tripping over the log they'd been using as a bench. Closest to the jeep, Tanner and Ember worked their way behind it, but the moose was next to the truck and swaying side to side.

"The trailer," Brittney hissed, and she and Marta climbed into it, both wincing when the steel creaked.

Reed took a step toward the trailer but the moose advanced, cutting off that route. Another step and it was in the pool of light from the fire, revealing its enormous antlers. Reed sucked in his breath and drifted to a nearby tree.

"Reed!" Jackson hissed.

He looked up and spotted Jackson and Shelby already in the branches, with Jackson's hand extended down to him. He grabbed Kate around the waist and lifted her up, where she caught Jackson's hand and scrambled into the safety of height.

Swallowing his fear, Reed eyed the moose as he reached for his roommate's hand, grabbing it just as the beast turned and spotted him. Both sides froze, and Reed gauged the gap, wondering if he could climb high enough before an antler hooked him and knocked him free. Jackson heaved him upward, yanking him into the branches.

Hooves thudded across the ground as the moose charged but Reed was already scrambling for height. The relief was so sharp that he laughed, and it spread to the others. His eyes found Kate.

"You okay?" he asked.

"There's a moose at our campout," Kate exclaimed. "No, I'm not okay."

He grinned at her voice and looked to the others. A glance revealed everyone was safe, but the moose trotted around the camp and tree, moving to the water before returning to sniff around the fire.

"It's a bull," Tanner called. "Probably coming to the lake to eat aquatic plants. It's part of their diet."

"How long before it leaves?" Brittney asked, her face twisted with fearful fascination as she huddled on the trailer.

"I don't know," Tanner called. "Moose can be unpredictable."

The moose paused to sniff at Jackson's plate, which still contained a few bites of steak. Jackson grunted in irritation. "If he eats the meat, is that cannibalism?"

"It was steak from a cow," Shelby said in exasperation. "Not a moose steak."

"So?" Jackson asked. "It's still a cousin, right? And eating a cousin is still cannibalism."

"Will you stop talking about cannibalism!" Ember growled, making them all laugh.

The moose cantered about, rotating around the truck and trailer and back. It passed the fire and briefly disappeared into the trees before trotting next to the jeep. Tanner and Ember were huddled inside, but she'd left the top down, so they just had bars and the windshield for cover. Then it paused next to Jackson's tent.

"It doesn't know what your tent is," Reed said.

"I told you we should have set it up right," Shelby said.

The moose dropped its head and sniffed the tent, catching a pole with its antler. It tossed its head in an attempt to dislodge it, sending the

35

tent soaring through the trees, spilling sleeping bags from the open doorway.

"Aw, man," Jackson called. "Can we please shoot it?"

"Even if we had a gun, that would be a bad idea," Tanner called.

Brittney's voice came from the trailer. "Isn't your motto to *be prepared*?"

Reed snorted a laugh and Jackson grinned. "She's got you there," Shelby said.

The moose jogged around the camp, pausing at each spot before stopping at the tree. Reed swallowed as it cast back and forth, peering into the branches. That close, Reed could have reached down to touch the antlers.

Jackson pointed upward and Kate climbed to a higher crook, vacating space for Reed to reach up and grab the branch. Just as his fingers coiled around the wood, the moose began to paw the ground. Reed froze, his eyes on the huge creature. Its ears lay flat and it and lowered its head, pawing the ground like it was about to charge.

"Most charges are bluffs," Tanner's voice reached Reed's ears.

"It doesn't feel like a bluff," Reed called back.

The beast lowered its head and Reed seized the opportunity, scrambling upward just as the moose raised its head, the antlers clattering off the branch he'd been sitting on. Precariously balanced between Shelby and Jackson, he watched the moose.

"You should move that fast on the court," Jackson murmured.

"Really?" Shelby asked. "Now?"

"What?" Jackson exclaimed. "I'm nervous."

Abruptly Ember ducked into the darkness of the jeep. There was a fumbling inside the jeep as if she was searching for something. The next moment she reappeared and checked the ammunition on a .357 Magnum.

Reed's eyes nearly burst from his skull as he watched the tiny woman nod in satisfaction and then raise the huge pistol. Then Tanner noticed his girlfriend was armed and his expression turned to shock.

"Who gave that girl a gun," Shelby breathed.

"Where did you get that?" Tanner demanded.

"I keep it in the car for emergencies," she said matter-of-factly. "I think this qualifies."

"She brought a cannon," Jackson said.

Reed recalled the date where Kate had taken them to a shooting range. It was a few months ago, but the guy at the range had said he wasn't teaching Ember anymore. Apparently thinking the same thing, Jackson leaned down.

"I thought she didn't finish her class," he said.

"Me too," Reed said.

Kate shook her head. "Ember went back and managed to get her concealed weapons permit. I didn't know she'd bought a gun."

"What kind of a gun is that?" Brittney cried, causing the moose to trot over to them. It sniffed at the edge of the trailer, causing Brittney and Marta to climb under the last canoe. Huddling just out of sight, Brittney pointed to it. "Are you going to shoot it?"

"Don't shoot the thing," Tanner said, his voice desperate. "It will charge your jeep." He reached for the gun but her eyes flashed dangerously.

"Always keep your distance from a girl with a gun," she said. "And I wasn't going to shoot it."

She pointed it into the air and braced. Reed had time to plug his ears before she pulled the trigger, the report echoing like thunder off the mountains. Startled, the moose bolted into the trees, the sounds of its passage quickly fading.

"Have you lost your mind?" Tanner demanded. "You can't just take that thing around with you!"

Ember expertly unloaded the remaining bullets and checked the chambers, looking all the while like a child checking the tube of a bazooka. Then she turned on Tanner. Although her voice was mild, the intensity to her eyes set him back.

"I have a permit," she said.

"Where do you conceal a gun that size?" Shelby called.

Ember tried to resist but smiled without taking her eyes off Tanner. "Can we return to our fire now?"

Tanner began to laugh, the sound rolling off him as he cautiously wrapped his arms around Ember. When he spoke his voice was filled with admiration.

"You're stunning, you know that?"

"Yes," Ember said with a smile, and then kissed him.

Laughing at the sheer absurdity of watching a tiny redhead scare off a moose by firing a giant gun, Reed extricated himself from the branches and dropped to the ground. Then he reached up and helped Kate down. Jackson and Shelby joined him and they hurried to their tent.

"Did anyone bring duct tape?" he asked as he lifted the torn pieces.

"I have some," Tanner replied, climbing out of the jeep.

"Now he's prepared," Kate murmured.

38

Reed stifled a smile and helped Jackson pick up the torn pieces of his tent. Despite its appearance, it wasn't in terrible shape, and with a little duct tape they did manage to get it standing once again.

"I need a drink," Jackson said.

"There's some tequila in the cooler," Shelby called.

Jackson found the bottle and poured himself a shot. As the others resumed their seats around the fire, he held it aloft and waited for the others to similarly raise their bottles. His expression turned solemn.

"To the moose."

"To the moose!" they chorused, and Reed took a drink from his bottle of lemonade.

Chapter 6

Tinged with relief and amusement, the conversation focused on their sudden danger and Ember's scaring the beast away. Then Marta frowned and gestured to Tanner, who was sitting behind the cooler opening several packages.

"What are you making?" she asked.

"The smores," he said.

"With tinfoil?" Reed asked.

Tanner smiled and held up a waffle cone. Instead of ice cream, he added marshmallows and chocolate chips, as well as peanuts and caramel. Then he wrapped it in tinfoil and carefully placed it on the bed of dying coals.

"Smores in a waffle cone?" Shelby asked.

"I was going to save it for tomorrow night," Tanner said, "but I think after our visit from the moose we could all use a treat."

They lined up to make their own and Reed chose caramel, chocolate, and pretzels to go with marshmallow. Wrapping it as Tanner indicated, he placed it on the coals and sat back. A moment later Kate joined him.

"Where'd you learn that?" she asked, motioning to the tin-wrapped cones.

"My grandpa," Tanner said. "He was always doing crazy stuff for my grandma."

"The original creative dater," Jackson said.

Reed grinned but glanced at the woods. He noticed the others did as well, and as they ate the strange yet delicious dessert the entire group remained on high alert, with the exception of Ember, who looked unnervingly calm. Reed supposed that if he had an enormous gun within easy reach, he probably wouldn't be worried either.

The tension gradually faded and Tanner assured them the moose was unlikely to return. Still, when the fire died and the group trickled off to bed, Reed noticed Ember sneaking her gun into her tent. She caught him looking and smiled.

"It's not loaded," she said.

"I trust you," Reed replied.

Ember smiled and nodded. "Thanks."

As the others yawned and left, Tanner killed the dying fire with a bucket of water, plunging them into darkness. Reed stood, reluctant to end the night. As if sensing his thoughts, Kate caught his hand and used her head to point to the water. Donning his coat to ward off the chill, he picked his way to the edge of the lake and they took seats on a dead log.

"Tonight's been a little intense," Kate said as Reed wrapped a large quilt around both of them.

The air had cooled considerably, as if winter snapped at the heels of a departing autumn. Reed gazed across the still lake, which now reflected the stars and moon, once again struck by the tranquility of the place.

"The moose was certainly exciting," Reed agreed. "But I still can't believe that girl has a gun—let alone a gun that size."

"She finished the class shortly before our marathon date."

He swept a hand at the slumbering camp. "It's surprising how much time we've all spent together but there are still things we don't know."

41

She cast him a sideways look. "I'm glad you say that, because there's something I wanted to ask you."

"I have a question for you, too," he said.

"You first," she said.

He hesitated. Then he grimaced and said, "What would we be without the dating challenge?"

"What do you mean?" she asked.

"I just wonder what we'd be without it."

Kate snuggled deeper into the blanket and leaned her head on his shoulder. "If I had never asked you out and issued the challenge, would you have asked me out at a second time?"

"Probably not," he said. "I was attracted to you too much, and I found that frightening."

"The challenge did bring us together," she said. "Without it, we never would have had a chance."

He did his best to keep his voice neutral. "I love you, but I worry that emotion has been created because of our dates. That without them . . ." he shrugged, unwilling to voice the rest of the thought.

"Where's this coming from?"

Beneath the blanket her hand threaded into his and he was suddenly grateful she hadn't responded with hurt and anger—which she still might. But for now she seemed merely confused and curious.

"I have a friend that tried the creative dating thing," he said. "He ended up dating a girl for a few months but couldn't maintain the sense of romance, and when it was gone they fell apart."

"And you think that will happen to us?"

"No," he said, "but it made me worry. Our challenge means a great deal to me, and not just because it's with you. I enjoy the game of it, the attempts to top each other and the new surprises. I feel like you're always thinking of me and I'm always thinking of you, but I know there will come a time we can't keep doing the challenge. When that day comes, what will we be?"

She leaned against him, letting her dark hair fall down his shoulder. The silence lasted for several moments and he vacillated between regret at voicing his fears, and fear over what she would say. Had he just made a terrible mistake? Had he sowed a sliver of doubt that would ultimately doom their relationship?

"I don't think what I feel was manufactured," she finally said. "But I can see where you're coming from. We've already shared a lifetime of romantic moments, and it can't continue forever."

"That's what I'm worried about."

"I've already gotten more than I ever thought I deserved," she said, "so I understand your worry."

"You do?"

"How can I not?" she asked, her eyes meeting his. "But watching Jackson and Shelby since their engagement has made me notice something I hadn't seen before. They love to play basketball together, and in that way it's not unlike our challenge. It's their game.

"But it's not the game that keeps them together," she continued. "When the whistle blows and the game ends, they want to spend time together. They crave it more than the sport, more than the competition, more than anything. I think it's the reason he proposed, because Shelby was the person he couldn't live without."

"So you think that's us?"

"I hope so," she said, her smile tentative. "I know I miss you when you're at class—which I know is ridiculous. Even though I'm going to see you in an hour, I never want to say goodbye, or see you walk away.

43

And that's the reason I love you, because our game is fun, but I live for my time with you."

"I feel the same way," he said, relieved. "But I was just afraid it was because of the challenge."

"I like the challenge," she said. "But I love you."

He smiled and released a breath he'd seemed to have been holding for days. "That settles my question," he said. "What's yours?"

Her expression turned reluctant. "I'd rather not say."

"I shared mine," he said. "It's only fair you share yours."

"Another time?" she asked.

He shook his head and swept a hand at the lake, shifting the blanket and letting cold in. "When else could we have such privacy?"

"We shared our fire with a moose," she said. "It's hardly private."

"True," he said, now curious. "But your attempt to change the subject has been noted and rejected."

She snorted and looked away, and after a moment looked back. "My question is about sex."

"Oh."

"I'm sorry," she said, the words seeming to tumble from her mouth. "I just don't understand. We're months past the point I would have slept with you and I care about you more than anyone I've ever dated—"

"—really?" he asked. "Even Jason?"

She glared at him. "Your attempt to change the subject has been noted and rejected."

He laughed lightly, the sound floating across the lake. "It was worth a try."

Her smile faded. "Do you want that? Do you want that with me?"

"Of course I do," he said, struggling for a way to explain.

"Then why wait?"

The question hung in the air. He could see the doubt reflected in her gaze, the worry, the fear. All at once he saw it from her perspective. He said he loved her but refused to cross the physical line that proved it, leaving her uncertain.

"Sex changes relationships," he said slowly. "I saw it in high school, college, and in my research. I think it creates an attachment that goes much deeper than physical, and if that attachment is broken, people are broken. It's not visible on the surface, but it makes it harder for them to create the same level of attachment again. I want to be with you, but I *love* what we have, and I don't want it to change—not yet."

"So you're afraid to be with me?" she asked.

He chuckled. "When I see you, fear is not the emotion I feel."

She flashed a faint smile and leaned against him. "I love what we have too," she murmured. "But I want more of you."

"And I want more of you," he replied.

For several moments the silence stretched between them and Reed felt an odd ache in his chest. He realized the desire to share all of himself was growing, and was not going away anytime soon . . .

—A sudden rumbling came from just behind them. Loud and sharp, it sent them scrambling away from the log and Reed spun, hoping the moose had not returned. Instead of a large beast it was Jackson.

"Are you serious!" Kate asked, holding her chest. "I thought the moose came back!"

"You should have seen your faces," Jackson crowed.

Reed's heartbeat thundered in his skull and he stabbed a finger at his roommate. "What are you even doing up?"

Wiping the tears from his eyes, Jackson gestured to the woods. "Nature called and then I heard you two talking. I couldn't resist. I would say I'm sorry but . . ."

"You're not," Kate said flatly.

Ember's tent unzipped and her head poked out. "It's two in the morning! Don't make me come out there!"

Jackson's laughter faded and his expression turned to abject fear. "We woke the dragon!" he hissed, and tip-toed back to his tent.

Reed chuckled, the sound irritated rather than amused. "I can't really blame Jackson for being so happy."

"He did get engaged," she said sourly. "But we can still spike his beer with onions, right?"

"Without question," he replied.

Her smile was positively devious and they slipped into the campsite. Reed was not normally the type for such an act, but tonight with Kate, he relished squeezing an onion into Jackson's beer bottles. They washed their hands free of the stink and then he walked her to her tent.

"Goodnight," she said softly.

"I love you, Kate," he said.

"I know," she replied. "And I'll try to be patient."

He smiled and leaned down for a final, lingering kiss. Then he turned and made his way to his tent. Once inside, he stripped and pulled on warmer clothes, shivering until he was snug inside his sleeping bag. But as late as it was, sleep did not come quickly, and he stared at the empty space at his side.

He'd slept near Kate on a number of occasions, especially on the Marathon Date, but tonight was the first time he felt alone. He suppressed the urge to text her and invite her to his tent. The desire was not so easily dampened, but as he wrestled with emotion a new idea came to mind. He might be alone now, but when they finally did come together, it would be all the better.

Volume 21: The Thanksgiving Date

Chapter 1

With a drink in hand, Kate threaded her way through the crowd to one of the arena entrances. Descending the steps, she joined Ember on the third row. Brittney and Marta arrived just moments later.

"How soon does the game start?" Brittney asked.

"We've got a few minutes," Ember said, gesturing to the clock above the hoop. "The players just came out."

Kate scanned the group and spotted Shelby among the uniformed players. The lower arena was packed, with people filing into the upper seats. Although the game was not part of a tournament, it felt official. Cheerleaders armed with t-shirt guns roamed the sides of the court and the jumbotron was in full swing, the video showing the stats of the starting players.

The annual game was a highlight for many of the students, and allowed non-NCAA players to play in a game against the campus in Denver. Although it had originally started as a friendly competition between the two campuses, it had gradually become known as the UC Brawl.

"Shelby was pretty excited she made the team," Brittney said.

"Not as excited as Jackson," Kate said.

"At least he gets to help coach," Ember said, pointing to the bench.

In true Brawl tradition, the girls picked guys as their coaches, and at the men's Brawl the next week, the players selected girls to coach. Jackson and two others had been nominated as the coaches this year and they stood with several of the girls. Painted all in gold, Jackson looked like a gilded statue, his abs sparkling with glitter. Denver's colors were also black and gold, but the coaches were dressed in black, matching the host of Denver students that had made the drive for the game.

"Where's Tanner?" Kate asked.

"Working," Ember replied with a grimace. "He couldn't get the night off."

"Sure he's not afraid now that he knows you carry a gun?" Marta asked.

Ember smirked. "He has been reluctant to ride in my car."

"That's because it's equipped liked a tank," Brittney said.

"You should think about getting a gun of your own," Ember said, her eyes on the players just starting to warm up.

"We don't need one," Kate said, and then smiled. "We have you for protection."

Ember laughed and pointed to the empty seat next to Kate. "Where's Reed? I thought he was coming."

"He said he had to meet with his advisor after class," Kate said. "Something about his internship in January."

"*And introducing, the Boulder starting lineup . . .*"

The announcer's voice rumbled throughout the arena, galvanizing the golden side of the crowd. Kate was grateful for the interruption. Reed had called to let her know he was running late, and she'd heard worry in his voice. He'd said it was just concern about the meeting with Dr. Caldin, but she suspected there was more.

"SHELBY!" Ember bellowed, causing the tall blonde to look up and smile. She waved to them and then dribbled the ball to the hoop.

"I like having her in our group," Brittney said. "She brings up our group's athletic average."

50

"And average height," Marta added.

A whistle blew and the players jogged to their benches, Boulder in gold, Denver in black. Shelby stood by Jackson as he issued final thoughts and encouragement, his serious expression contrasting with the glitter adorning his body.

The whistle blew again and the players took their positions. Kate didn't know the positions well, but did know that Shelby was a guard. As tall as she was, she was only average height on the court, and Kate noticed the player opposite her was taller and larger.

The whistle blew a third time and the ball went up, and Shelby rushed onto defense, struggling to keep up with number 17. The two fought for the ball and Shelby lost, the ball bouncing off the backboard and into the hoop.

Ember cursed while the Denver crowd cheered. Shelby was quick down the court and threaded a gap, catching a high pass and laying it in to put points on the board. Number 17's aggressive play knocked Shelby to the floor and she was awarded a foul.

As the first quarter passed Kate marveled at how Shelby managed to stay in the game. She was outmatched, both in size and skill, but refused to quit. She and 17 didn't touch the ball on every play but they fought every time, two warriors on the court battling for supremacy.

Kate had attended several of Shelby's games over the last few months and she'd always been graceful and dominant, staying even with Jackson despite the inch disparity in height. But here she was inferior in every way except for grit.

"I've never seen Shelby struggle," Brittney said.

"That's what I was thinking," Kate said.

"Look at Jackson," Marta said.

Kate followed her gaze to see Jackson pacing in front of the bench, his gold glittered features twisted in anger. He looked like a glitter bomb

51

set to explode. A moment later they called a time-out and another player took Shelby's place, losing the next three contests against 17.

As Kate watched the game, she marveled at Shelby's ability to fight against a losing tide, that despite a near certain loss against her opponent, an inner will compelled her to rise to the challenge.

Her thoughts shifted to Reed and his meeting with Dr. Caldin, and the worry again settled into the pit of her stomach. He'd said he was likely to get at least one of the two internships—but what if he didn't get either? What if he graduated but had no future because of her? What if he had to leave the state? What if he went across the country? Could they stay together? Could they stay together without the challenge?

She glanced at the empty chair at her side, her worry mounting. She checked her phone but he hadn't sent a message, suggesting he was still talking to Dr. Caldin. What was taking so long? Was it just her imagination?

She took a sip of her Sprite and tried to shake the sense of foreboding. Brittney noticed her tense posture and made a comment about the game, assuring her that Boulder, down by six, would rally after the half. Kate smiled and nodded, hoping it was true.

Half time was called but still no Reed. As her friends talked about the game she pulled out her phone and sent a quick text, asking if everything was okay. There was no response for several minutes, each second tightening the knot in her gut.

Everything's fine. I'll tell you after the game.

The vague text did not reassure. She wanted to press him for more details but her courage failed her. **When will you be here?**

Fifteen minutes, he said. **I just left Dr. Caldin's office**.

You were meeting with him for an hour. I'm worried.

Too long to explain in a text.

"Everything okay?" Marta asked.

They were sitting alone, the other two going to refill drinks before the second half began. At the base of the arena, a guy in gold was trying to shoot backwards free throws for a chance to win a year of free pizza, drawing laughter and groans from the spectators.

"Just worried about Shelby," Kate managed. "She's getting pummeled."

"I know," Marta said. "But 17 already has four fouls. Two more and she's out of the game."

"How many does Shelby have?"

"Three," she replied.

Ember and Brittney returned just as the game resumed. The second half ticked by and Kate counted the fouls, rising to her feet when 17 got her fifth. Clearly upset, the girl tried to hack Shelby on the next play, sending her skidding across the floor. Shelby was helped to her feet by her teammates, and Kate noticed a smile on her face.

"Shelby goaded 17 into a foul," Kate said in surprise.

"A girl after my own heart," Ember said.

"I thought you would have just hit the girl," Marta said.

"That too."

A time-out was called and, as in previous breaks, the announcer called for a contest from a spectator. Ember elbowed Kate, dragging her from her thoughts. Then Kate looked up and realized it was her face on the jumbotron.

"It's your seat they're calling," Marta said excitedly.

"... *please come to the floor!*"

53

Kate stood and uncertainly made her way down the steps. She'd seen hundreds of such contestants make their way down the court for a contest and always wondered what it would feel like. Excitement warred with nervousness and she felt the weight of thousands of eyes.

Shelby caught her eye and gave an encouraging nod, and then Jackson walked out to greet her. Blinded by the light and swell of noise, she looked up into his glittered face and spoke nervously.

"Is this for real?"

"Everyone gets lucky sometimes," Jackson said.

"What do I have to do?"

"Hit a three pointer from each end of the court," he said, and then pointed to a giant box being wheeled out on a cart. "If you do it in twenty seconds you win what's in the box." Jackson grinned and handed her a basketball. "Good luck!"

Chapter 2

Kate bounced the ball as she waited for the clock to start, but that failed to release the excess energy. She swallowed, the dryness in her throat thick and making it difficult to breathe. She was highly conscious of the thousands of spectators, and wondered if they wanted her to succeed . . . or fail.

Her jaw tightened. They'd picked the wrong girl. In the midst of her swirling emotions she looked to the hoop and took her place on the three point line. Next to her was a rack of balls, allowing her to shoot at will before sprinting to the other side of the court. She wanted to win. She needed to win—to fight the doubt that had pooled in her stomach.

Twenty seconds appeared on the clock and she reminded herself it was just like shooting hoops with her brothers in the driveway. But it wasn't, and when the buzzer went off she shot the ball. To her dismay it sailed by the hoop without making contact.

"It's supposed to go through the hoop!"

Ember's voice somehow pierced the din and Kate released a muttered curse. Then she grabbed another ball and shot again. The clock above the hoop kept counting down, the seconds dwindling remarkably fast.

She reached eleven seconds and missed her fourth shot. Then sank her fifth. Shocked and relieved, she turned and sprinted for the other rack of basketballs at the opposite end of the court. Dimly she heard Jackson shouting at her but she only had eyes for the clock, for the six turning to five. At best she'd have two or three shots. Better make them count.

She picked up a ball and sent it sailing toward the hoop. Not bothering to wait, she grabbed another as the first *clanged* off the rim. The second felt good but she grabbed the third, launching it just before the buzzer sounded. In quick succession two sounds followed, the *swish* as two balls sank through the hoop.

She stared at the bouncing balls and then suddenly all the roar of the crowd engulfed her and Jackson was at her side. He picked her up and spun her about, shouting at the top of his lungs, plastering her with glitter.

She screamed, her voice barely audible as the spectators cheered their approval of the resounding win. Then the announcer's voice overpowered the tumult and Jackson set her down next to the large box.

"What did I win?" she asked breathlessly.

"What did you expect?" he asked.

The announcer's voice changed pitch, revealing a smile as he called, "*And please welcome to the court, our very own, Reeeeed Haaaanseeeen!*"

As the box opened and Reed appeared, Kate burst into a surprised laugh. Dimly she heard the announcer say she'd won her very own date, but her attention was on her boyfriend, whose expression was smug as he climbed free of the box and stepped to her.

"What do you say, will you be my date this Friday?"

"How can I say no to all this?" she asked, sweeping her hands at the court and crowd.

He wrapped his arms around her back and pulled her into a kiss, and the announcer rightfully assumed consent for the date. When they parted a whistle blew and the players took to the court. Jackson jogged out and personally escorted them across the court.

"You have glitter on your chin," he said to Reed.

"I wonder where that came from," Reed said.

"Who knows," he said with a smirk.

Reed walked Kate back to her seat and Kate glared at the blondes, who all looked rather smug. She sat down and leveled an accusing finger at them but before she could say a word, Ember raised her hands.

"What did you expect us to do?" she asked.

"They were rather willing to support me," Reed said.

Kate turned on him, a smile on her face. "I can't believe you did all this just to ask me on a date."

"You've had your share of public invitations," he said. "I figured it was my turn to prove I'm still in the lead."

"Excuse me," a voice said. They turned to a girl dressed in black sitting behind them. "Did you really do that just to ask her on a date?"

"I did," Reed said, glancing at Kate in amusement. Then he briefly explained the challenge.

"But you're actually dating, right?"

"For a few months now," Kate said, smiling.

The girl shook her head and sat back. "I wish more guys did stuff like that."

Reed shrugged and flashed his easy smile, his expression almost apologetic. "We're just having fun."

She looked to Kate. "Don't let him slip through your fingers, girl."

"I won't," she replied.

They turned back to the game and Kate marveled at the shift in what she'd felt over most of the game. Just having Reed at her side did wonders to alleviate the worry that had risen in her stomach, and she wondered if it had all been her imagination.

"Did you really have to meet with Dr. Caldin?" she asked in an undertone.

"I'll tell you all about it after the game," he said.

Her worry returned, her stomach twisting anew. When he spoke his features were a shade tight, his eyes on the game as if he didn't want to meet her gaze. It was a rare reluctance that could only indicate bad news—news he didn't want to share in front of the blondes.

The final minutes of the Brawl were a testament to endurance. Both teams were exhausted and fouls were committed. With only one foul remaining, Shelby was still in the game, and her new opponent was not as good as 17, who fumed on the bench, helpless as Shelby rolled around a Denver player and stepped into a jumper, bringing them to a tie.

"It's going to be close," Ember said, her voice nervous.

"Hasn't Denver won the last few years?" Brittney asked.

"Four in a row," Marta said. "But their campus is bigger."

The seconds drained down and points were gained on both sides, until one of Shelby's teammates sank a three to tie the game again. Six seconds left. Despite Kate's fears, she was on the edge of her seat as the Boulder team set up a full-court press, waiting for the inbound pass. The girl faked low and lobbed it over a Boulder student, but it tipped off her outstretched finger and wobbled toward Shelby.

Shelby whirled around the girl guarding her and scooped it up, darting to the hoop and bouncing it off the glass as the seconds bled away. It rolled around the rim and then dropped into the net, the buzzer echoing over the court.

Kate leapt to her feet and cheered with Reed, shouting Shelby's name as the final score changed. 86–84. The sea of gold fans were also on their feet, roaring and stomping their approval of the finish.

Jackson rushed through the court and picked up his fiancé, spinning her in circles as 17 glowered on the bench. Other players and coaches milled about while spectators began filing out of the arena. Kate and the rest of the group descended to the arena and tackled Shelby, who was flush with excitement at the narrow win.

"Great game," Kate said, hugging the taller girl.

"It was the coaching," she said.

Jackson's smile was as bright as his costume, and Reed carefully slapped him on the back, avoiding the bulk of the glitter. As the blondes moved in to congratulate the pair, Kate and Reed said their farewells and followed the exiting crowd. Raucous gold-dressed Boulder students left in a wash of golden clothing, carrying them outside the building. Kate wanted to speak but the words failed her. He too seemed without words, and although he held her hand, remained silent.

Winter had descended upon Boulder in all its fury. The last few weeks had seen the temperatures drop into the teens and snow dusted the ground, with flurries drifting down from the sky. Undeterred by the freezing temperatures, the victorious Boulder students left the arena, likely to continue celebrating the Brawl victory in the local bars.

They reached the car and Reed fumbled for his keys, letting her in before circling and getting in the driver's seat. He started the car but they sat in silence until she frowned and turned to face him.

"I can't take it anymore," she said. "What did Dr. Caldin say?" Reed met her gaze and she saw the weight in his eyes, so she braced herself for the answer.

Chapter 3

"I didn't get the first internship," he said. "And the second doesn't look promising."

Reed said the words dully, as if they did not matter, as if the shock was too much for him to register a response. She grappled with the knowledge that his future—once so bright and promising—had crashed and burned because he'd decided to stay with her.

"What else did he say?" she asked, mechanically putting her hand on his arm.

"We spent an hour looking up other possibilities, but it's just too late," he said.

Now the frustration came, burgeoning up like lava from a volcano. He clenched his fists and his expression tightened. For Reed, who never expressed such finality, to speak with so much force left her shaken.

"I never thought I would be in this position." He continued staring out the window without seeing the snow drifting onto the hood. "I built everything on my resume and I'm a perfect candidate for almost any program—internship or doctoral, but it's just too late."

"Because of me."

His eyes widened and he looked to her. "That's not what I'm saying."

"But it's what I hear," she said softly. "You had the perfect career path and I've screwed it up."

"Kate . . ."

"Say all you like," she said. "But you chose to give up your dreams to be with me."

"Maybe I had a new dream."

"You say that, but what are you going to do, deliver pizza for the next eight months while you apply?"

"I like pizza," he said.

She didn't smile at his effort at humor. "I can't ask that of you. Someday you're going to make an incredible psychiatrist, and broken couples need you—my parents needed you."

"I can wait," he said.

"No," she said. "We both know that a year of working fast food and no classes will hurt your application."

"So what if I can't get into the upper programs," he said, his voice firm. "My grades don't exactly expire."

"No," she said. "I want you to call Dr. Caldin and see if you can still go to internship in New York."

"I'm sure it's too late on that."

"It's only been a few weeks," she said. "And they're probably still trying to find someone to fill your shoes."

"Kate," he said. "I don't want to go."

"I'm not letting you stay."

Her stomach churned with regret but her features had gained a calm confidence. He'd given up everything for her, and now it was her turn. Come what may, she needed to support his dreams for the very reason he was willing to give them up.

"If I ask Dr. Caldin if it's still an option, will you let it go?"

"I'll wait," Kate said, folding her arms.

Reed snorted and pulled out his phone. He typed out a brief message and then looked to her. "Feel better? I doubt we'll hear back anytime soon."

"Just promise me that if it's a possibility, you won't give an answer without talking to me."

He held her gaze for several moments and then consented with a nod. Putting his car in reverse, he backed out and followed the line of cars out of the lot. After several minutes he asked about the game, the quiet question tacitly asking if they could change the subject.

The conversation lightened but the weight remained, and then she allowed a small smile. "I still can't believe you hijacked the Brawl to ask me on a date. How did you pull it off?"

"I actually can't take credit for this invite," he said. "It was Shelby's idea to use one of the time-outs, and Jackson convinced the organizers to let me do the invite."

"How'd he do that?"

"He said I was going to propose," Reed admitted.

"He *what?*"

"It was the only way the athletic department would go for it," he said. "He didn't tell me until after he'd done it."

The sudden adrenaline at the prospect of a proposal cooled into mixed emotions and the obvious question. "Won't he get into trouble for lying?"

"Probably," he said. "But he just smiled and said he could handle it. I got the feeling he was going to blame me, and say I chickened out."

"Did you?" she dared to ask.

He glanced her way, his easy smile amused. "If I was ever going to propose, it wouldn't be like that."

Her heart fluttered but she didn't dare consider the prospect of a future with Reed. "So tell me about our date. Are we moving it because of Thanksgiving?"

"Jackson and Shelby are saving for a big honeymoon so they decided to stay here for the break. They invited all of us and they're even cooking a turkey."

"You mean they asked Brittney to cook the dinner," she guessed.

"They did," Reed said with a laugh.

"Ember was thinking of going home for the week," Kate said. "But Marta's family is here, so I'm sure she'll join us."

"She won't be with her family for Thanksgiving?" Reed asked.

"Their family does lunch," she said. "And Marta will love the excuse to get out of their afternoon tradition of watching home movies."

He cringed. "Why are home movies so terrible to watch?"

"I think it's because watching our past selves is embarrassing," she said.

The conversation about their upcoming date had cooled her worry regarding his future, but it had settled into the corner of her thoughts like an anchor. She'd expected the burden to be painful, but instead it was oddly sobering, as if it was time for them to face something serious. She just hoped they could weather the coming storm.

"You okay?" he asked.

"I think so," she said. "But can we not talk about it for now?"

He cast her an appraising look. "Are you sure?"

"Yeah," she said.

They were at a stoplight so she leaned over and kissed him on the cheek. Then she leaned her head against his shoulder. He seemed caught by surprise and did not speak until the light changed and he had to drive.

"What was that for?" he asked.

"I'm sorry this is so hard for you," she said. "But I'm here, and I think we can figure it out."

"I thought you didn't want to talk about it."

She smiled. "No more. I promise."

"Then thank you," he said.

She smiled and they fell to talking about the Thanksgiving break. Their big date might have been Thursday, but they had already planned on spending the bulk of the week together. After the hectic class schedule and Reed preparing to defend his thesis, she looked forward to the calm before the end of the year.

The weekend passed in a flurry of snow that mounted into a blizzard. Twelve inches of snow dumped on the city of Boulder in the two days before Thanksgiving, clogging traffic and making the roads treacherous. The group opted for building a snow fort that quickly devolved into a snowball fight.

Kate laughed her way through the next several days, grateful for every moment that Reed was at her side. Many times she saw the tension return to his features as he waited for a final verdict on New York, and she did her best to distract him.

After a mercifully clear night, Thanksgiving morning dawned with a stunning sunrise, which Kate watched from her window. Reed has said he wanted to pick her up early and so she'd risen before dawn.

Brittney's door opened and she padded down the stairs into the living room. "What are you doing up?" she asked.

"Reed's coming to pick me up," Kate said.

Brittney paused on her way to the bathroom, her expression uncertain. "Is everything okay? You've been a bit off the last few days."

"How so?" Kate asked.

"I can't put my finger on it," she said. "What's up? Is there a problem between you and Reed?"

Kate smiled and shook her head. "No, everything's fine."

Ember folded her arms, her worried expression softened by a yawn. "Then what is it? I keep seeing you looking at him like it's the last time you'll see him."

"Do you think we could survive a long distance relationship?" she asked, abruptly deciding to speak her thoughts.

"Why? Is he going somewhere?"

Kate briefly outlined what they faced, and that they were still awaiting the final call on whether Reed's internship in New York would happen. Brittney's expression of concern deepened until Kate finished, and by then the sun had crested the horizon to bathe the city in golden light.

"We should hear any day now," Kate finished, trying to keep her worry from her face. They should have known by now.

"You don't sound worried," Brittney said.

"Maybe I just think we'll be okay," Kate said.

"Sometimes people only come into our lives for a season," Brittney said, reaching out to put her arm around Kate. "I know you love him. But he might just be a season."

"I hope not," Kate said as Reed's car appeared on the street and pulled into the driveway. "Because I don't want it to end."

"Good luck," Brittney said.

Kate grabbed her coat and hat. "I'll see you at dinner," she said, and slipped out the door.

Chapter 4

Kate exited the house just as Reed stepped out. She waved him to stay inside and walked to the passenger door. Bundled up against the freezing temperatures, he reached across to open her door, but she grabbed the handle first.

"It's freezing," she said, shivering as she settled into the passenger seat.

"I could have opened it for you," he said.

"Got to be faster next time," she said with a smile.

She leaned into the heat coming from the vent, grateful the fickle fan had not decided to quit today. He carefully backed out onto the icy road and then drove through the nearly empty streets of Boulder.

"No questions about what we're going to do?" he asked.

"Nope," she said. "I've learned to trust your instincts."

"It only took ten months," he said.

"Any word from Dr. Caldin?" she asked.

"He said he would call by tomorrow," Reed said.

She removed her glove to hold his hand. "So what are we doing today?"

"There it is," he said.

Her smile widened and she gestured to the car. "Your fan is blowing better than normal."

67

"That's because the fan is new," he replied.

"Really?"

He nodded. "Remember Roman, Marta's cousin? I mentioned the problem to him and he fixed it with a part from a junkyard."

"You found an organ donor for your car?"

He laughed and nodded. "That we did."

"I'll have to thank him next time I see him," she said.

The traffic was sparse as he drove through the sleepy morning toward downtown. Snow and ice had finally been cleared and Kate marveled at the piles lining the street. More snow covered houses, the white resembling frosting that dripped into icicles that twinkled in the early light. They pulled off the main road and she looked away from the view to the ice skating rink.

"Ice skating?" she asked.

"It's a staple in normal dating," he said.

"After all the big dates, we're going to do something normal?"

"It might be a little different," he said with a smile.

She felt a familiar thrill crackle in her heart, and recalled the date where they'd played pool golf. They left the heated car behind and made their way to the entrance. The posted hours said it would be closed on Thanksgiving but the door was unlocked, and he walked inside.

Their footsteps echoed off the benches where eager skaters would don their skates. A wall of windows out onto the ice rink, which lay dark and empty. She raised an eyebrow to Reed but a figure appeared in the doorway to the booth.

"You're right on time," he said.

"This is Caleb," Reed said. "He started working here a few months ago but I've known him for years. We're in the same program."

Caleb smiled and offered his hand, which Kate accepted. "It's a pleasure to meet the one that snagged him. Taking him off the market has made life bearable for the rest of us."

"I do what I can," she said. "Thanks for doing this for us."

"No problem," he replied. "I have to study over the holiday and this place was quiet. Give me a minute and I'll get your skates."

He asked their sizes and returned with skates for them to try. She expected figure skates but they were hockey skates, which Caleb explained were usually easier, with no toe pick getting in the way. Once they were laced up she carefully walked to the door and pushed her way into the freezing arena.

"Have fun," Caleb said, and disappeared into the booth.

Kate pointed to the ceiling. "I think he forgot the lights . . ."

The lights came on, but instead of a flood of white, the arena shined with twinkling stars. Colored lights brightened and dimmed, turning the ice rink into a dance hall. Then the music began, a soft song that inspired a smile.

"May I have this dance?" Reed asked, extending his hand.

"You may," she said.

They stepped onto the ice and she pushed away from the wall. It had been years, but it came back quickly, with each push more confident than the last. She glanced to Reed and found him skating comfortably at her side.

"You already knew I could skate," she guessed.

"Ice skating isn't very fun if you just stumble about," he replied. "But alone on a rink filled with light and music?" He swept his hands at the empty rink, the solitude adding to the enchantment.

69

"You're pretty proud of yourself," she said.

"I've always wanted to do a date like this," he said. "But I never had a connection at the rink. I actually talked to the previous manager a few times but he refused. I think he hated romance."

"Last time I skated was in junior high," she said. "At Kristen's and Beth's birthday party."

"Twins?"

She nodded and watched her skates glide across the ice, slicing a line between two spinning snowflakes. The sound of the steel scraping the ice did not mar the music, and instead added to the sense of magic.

"What about you?" she asked. "Last time you skated?"

"Two years," he said. "Here. I tried to bring a date who liked to rollerblade but she didn't transition well. She tripped me and I smashed my face on the ice. We spent the rest of the date in the ER, where I got nine stitches."

"I remember you mentioned that," she said. "Yet you still bring me on such a hazardous activity?"

He chuckled. "Your roommates said that at one time your mom wanted you to figure skate."

"That never happened," she said. "A fact I'm grateful for."

"Your mom sent me a video."

She cringed. "I told you, watching our past selves is embarrassing."

"You were good," he said. "And adorable in that little tutu and pink hat . . ."

She groaned at the memories of the gaudy outfits her mother had insisted would wow the judges. They didn't, and she'd finally convinced her mother to pick a more normal sport. She would have burned the videos but her mom had guarded them like they were made of gold. Then her mom had discovered Google cloud and Kate realized she'd never be able to eradicate them from existence.

"When this is over, I'm calling your mom for embarrassing photos," she said.

"There are none," he said.

She pulled out her phone. "Let's find out, shall we?"

He laughed and skated closer, forcing her to shove the phone back into her jacket pocket. They were roughly in the center, where spotlights illuminated them amid snowflakes and stars spinning across the walls and ice.

"Just don't ask her for the one where I fell asleep in a box."

"Now that's the one I want," she said.

He laughed in chagrin and pulled her into a kiss. Wrapped in layers of warmth, it was the kiss that filled her with heat, and she remained in place until their sliding skates pulled them apart.

"I don't think this tops your last date," she said. "Or mine."

"Perhaps," he said. "But sometimes the simple dates are the best."

She couldn't argue with that and spun a slow circle, relishing the curve of the skate under her leg. Seized with a desire for speed, she released his hand and accelerated, casting a challenging look back as she sped away. He grinned and pursued, and for several moments they raced across the open ice.

She'd been on a rink alone before, but never with a guy, and she enjoyed the freedom the emptiness permitted. She could skate anywhere, curve and spin, and know he was with her. The sense of unity with Reed was exhilarating.

A favorite song came on and she returned to him, catching his hand and skating along the wall. His eyes sparkled with amusement, drawing her in. She leaned closer but the distraction caused her skate to tip . . .

71

—Her skate caught the side and yanked her body to the ice. She went down, hard, bruising her knee and scrapping her hands on the ice. Their legs intertwined, Reed tripped over her and rolled onto the ice.

"Not again!" Reed called out.

She burst into a laugh but lay in place, staring at the beautiful ceiling. "Well that was embarrassing."

"I just figured you wanted me on my back," he said.

She laughed again and tilted her head to look at him. He lay nearby, his eyes on her. "You okay?" she asked.

"I think I bruised my ego," he said.

"You and me both."

"I still want the kiss, though."

She smiled and rolled over on the ice, kissing him briefly before Caleb called out from the edge of the rink. "It's a family rink. Can you keep it G-rated?"

Reed laughed and waved to him. "Will do."

Kate groaned and sat up. "You know, if I knew all it took to get you on your back was ice skating, I would have taken you sooner."

He rolled onto his knees and gingerly stood. Then he helped her up. She winced when she put pressure on her knee but gave an experimental bend. He raised his eyebrow so she nodded.

"I'm okay."

"Ready for more?"

She smiled. "Always."

Chapter 5

They skated until Caleb said he had to leave and then reluctantly left the ice. The frigid air had failed to pierce the warmth Reed inspired, and they skated to the door with their hands intertwined. They exited and removed the skates, donning shoes that now felt strange to her feet.

"That was wonderful," she said as they climbed into the car.

"Even the fall?"

"Even the fall," she replied with a smile.

He pulled onto the street and drove them back to his apartment. After they parked in the empty driveway he led her into the empty interior. They'd been together here numerous times, but this time the solitude felt more intimate, and she had to stifle a surge of nervousness.

"What are we doing here?" she asked, glancing at his bedroom door.

"Cooking," he said. "We're having Thanksgiving dinner at your house later, but we have a few things to contribute to the meal." He pulled out a pair of aprons and handed one to her.

"The challenger?" she asked, reading what was written. Then she saw his apron and laughed. "The professional dater? Did you have these made for us?"

"Consider it a souvenir of this date," he said.

She tied the apron around her back and put her hands on her hips. "How does it look?"

"Sexy," he replied with a smile.

"What are we cooking?" she asked.

"Dessert," he said, reaching into the freezer to pull out two cartons of ice cream.

"Ice cream with Thanksgiving?"

"It's Jackson's tradition," he said. "I convinced him to let us prepare part of it."

"How does one prepare ice cream?" she asked.

He reached into a drawer and pulled out a spoon. "What does anyone do with a frozen block of ice? You carve it."

She laughed and accepted the spoon as he placed the two cartons on plates and peeled off the cardboard. Then he gathered other knives, forks, and spoons so they had an assortment of tools.

"I never thought I'd learn ice cream carving on a date," she said.

"We're going to carve several," he said, setting a timer on his phone. "Ten minutes before these go back into the freezer. Then we'll get out the next set."

Kate examined the block of mint chocolate chip with a critical eye, as if she knew anything about sculpting. Then she shrugged and leaned forward, digging her spoon in and removing a portion.

"Jackson has done this forever," he said. "He claims his family does it every year but his mom refuses to acknowledge it as a tradition."

"What are you making?" she asked, glancing at his cookie dough sculpture.

"I have no idea," he said, flashing a lopsided smile. "Usually by the end I just try to make it look like something. Jackson's surprisingly good."

"What does Shelby think of this tradition?"

"She wants to get him into pottery but Jackson refused. He said he only works with edible mediums."

Kate grinned, imagining Jackson standing indignant at the question. "I really like them together."

"Ready for our game?"

"We've been dating for months," she said. "Don't we already know everything about our pasts?"

"We know quite a bit," he said. "This is not a game where we share our pasts. This is a game where we share our futures."

She raised an eyebrow, to which he used an ice cream covered spoon to point at her. "It's called 'someday I'd like to'."

"Ah," she said. "So I could start by saying, someday I'd like to go to Disneyworld."

"Exactly," he said. "And you've never been to Disneyworld?"

She shook her head. "California, yes. Florida, no."

"That's something we will have to remedy," he said.

"Sounds like a great date," she said, "but I want to hear yours."

"Someday I'd like to snowboard in the Alps."

"I already knew that," she protested.

"Fine," he said, and then examined his sculpture. "Someday I'd like to go to Hawaii."

"I've been there," she said. "But I was just ten, so it doesn't really count."

"Your turn," he said.

"Someday I'd like to swim with sharks."

75

He paused. "Really?"

"I find them fascinating," she said. "And the idea of swimming in a cage with sharks seems incredible."

"Most people *don't* want to be food," he said.

She grinned and gestured to him, indicating it was his turn. When the ice-cream began to melt they put it into the freezer to harden while they tried another pair of flavors. As she started on a dragon out of Rocky Road, the game pushed into more amusing ambitions.

Reed admitted he wanted to grow out his hair and play the guitar, just once, while Kate described wanting to learn another language. The game gradually grew more serious, with both sharing what they wanted out of career and family.

As they talked, she began to wonder if he'd come up with the game specifically for her, and specifically for this date. With them still waiting for the final call regarding New York, she wondered just how far he was willing to push the game.

"Someday I'd like to have five kids."

"Five?" he asked. "Not four?"

She shook her head. "Five. I'd like the girls to outnumber the guys."

"And if there are more boys?"

"Then the girls will have more brothers to watch out for them," she said.

"What if they're *all* girls?"

"Then my husband will just have to deal with six women in the house."

She watched his expression, attempting to gauge his response. He'd initially expressed surprise at her choice in somedays, and now cast her quizzical looks. She returned his glances with a look that said, *it's your game.*

"Someday I'd like to have four kids," he said. "And I don't care if they're boys and girls—except I'd like to have at least one boy so I can name him after Jackson."

"And if they're all girls?" she asked, returning his question.

He grinned. "Then Jackson will have a little girl named after him."

"Someday I'd like a wedding on an island."

"How exactly do you do that?" he asked.

"I don't know," she said with a shrug. "I just know I want it on an island. Somewhere that you can see for miles and miles while the sun is setting."

"Sounds beautiful."

"I think you mean expensive," she said.

He grinned. "That too."

"Someday I'd like to go into space," Reed said, and pointed to the rocket he was shaping out of ice cream.

"For your wedding?"

"Perhaps the honeymoon," he said.

"Someday I'd like to have a star named after me," she said.

"Do they actually do that?"

"Jason talked about doing it for Shelby when you were with Aura, and I thought it was cute. Besides, the idea that someone will one day visit Katelandia made me smile."

The conversation shifted to their sculptures, which were not ideal but also not a total melted mess. She didn't attempt to steer the

77

conversation back to marriage and family, and instead pondered the purpose of the game.

At first she'd thought he wanted a casual peek into the future, but as the conversation had continued she'd begun to wonder if he had a deeper intent. Their relationship had always been open, but she felt a rare hesitation about asking what he intended. With the real potential of him leaving in weeks, why had he chosen to focus on a game about their future?

"Your dragon's wing is melting."

"Your turkey is melting," she retorted.

He grinned and pointed to the freezer. "We should put these away before all our work is gone."

He picked up his plate and walked to the freezer. She followed and placed hers next to his, balancing them against the other four ice-cream sculptures crammed into the tiny space. When he closed the freezer she found herself against him and impulsively wrapped her arm around his back.

"Someday I'd like to not worry about my future."

He brushed a hair behind her ear. "Someday I'd like to show you how much I care for you."

Her heart fluttered in her chest and she marveled that even after all this time, he still had the power to elicit such attraction. She leaned up on her toes to kiss him, and let the contact wash away her lingering doubt.

Chapter 6

They gathered up their sculptures and walked them to the car, carefully placing them on a tray so they could drive to Kate's house. On the way they talked about the upcoming meal and she tried to squash her worries regarding the game. And failed.

The way he'd spoken reminded her of a boyfriend in high school. Although brief, her relationship with Carter had been intense, and she recalled being stunned when he'd ended it. His family was moving and he'd said that awaiting the inevitable breakup was just too hard. A week later he was with Wendy Hornock, whom he'd dated until he actually moved.

She knew Reed enough to know he wouldn't break things off and jump into another relationship, but he *would* try to protect her from heartache. The way he'd spoken, with such finality, made her question if he would break things off in an attempt to prevent her being hurt by his departure.

Reed picked up on her doubts and cast her several searching looks but she managed to set her doubts aside. After everything they'd been through, Reed loved her, and she loved him. He wouldn't just leave. Right?

They parked in the driveway and he reached out to grasp her hand. "I'm sorry."

"For what?" she asked.

"I had hoped a game about our future would lighten the mood, but it appears I grossly underestimated the situation."

"Nobody bats a thousand," she said.

79

"Are you sure there isn't something else you want to talk about?" he asked.

His blue eyes seemed to pierce her soul like a searchlight, but before she could speak a knock at the window made her turn. Ember had parked next to them and she'd knocked on Kate's window.

"You coming in or not?" Ember called.

Kate wanted to stay in the car and talk, but if Reed and Kate did not join them, Ember would bombard her with questions until she cracked.

"Coming," she said with a sigh.

They got out and Reed helped carry the ice cream sculptures. Tanner grabbed two of them while Ember opened the door to the house. Kate stepped inside to be assaulted by the smells of turkey roasting and spices baking. A pumpkin pie lent a delicious cinnamon to the air and Christmas music washed over those in the room.

"How'd they come out?" Jackson asked, rushing over to examine the sculptures. He frowned. "What's this one?"

"A turkey," Reed said.

"Your bird from last year was better," he said before stepping to Kate. He raised an eyebrow. "Is this supposed to be a dragon? For Thanksgiving?"

"I thought you'd like it," she said.

He grinned. "I love it. We'll get these out after dinner. How was the ice skating?"

"Great . . ."

Jackson was already gone. Taking the sculptures with him, he returned to the kitchen where Shelby and Brittney were working on the turkey that had just come out of the oven. The two were locked in deep conversation as Brittney explained the intricacies of turkey baking, while Jackson bustled about, doing as ordered.

Marta sat on the couch drinking a glass of wine, which she raised to the new arrivals. Ember removed her coat and sank onto the couch, accepting a glass and the bottle from Marta. Tanner declined the offer.

"I'll see if they need help in the kitchen," he said.

"I wouldn't," Marta said. "Those three have been quite stubborn about letting anyone else in the kitchen."

"You don't seem to mind," Reed said.

Marta smiled and raised her glass. "Let's just say I'm enjoying the holiday."

Kate grinned and took a seat as Reed removed his coat. She settled in to watch the parade as Ember took a seat on her other side. Reed glanced her way and then braved the kitchen in order to put the ice cream in the freezer. Then he began to set the table.

Their table for four would not be enough for all of them, so Jackson had 'borrowed' a table from the athletic department. Kate volunteered to help set up but Reed waved her back into her seat, so she smiled and relaxed.

With the second table set up, Reed began to set the places and Kate surreptitiously watched him. With Brittney, Jackson, and Shelby in the kitchen, and Ember and Marta in a debate over the hottest guy in the marching band behind the snoopy float, Reed worked in silence. He responded to questions, but his usually light demeanor was absent. Their eyes met and Reed smiled faintly, still trying to reassure her. On impulse, Kate stood and joined him.

"I got it," he said.

"I know," she said. "But I'm here to help."

She picked up a glass and put it at the head of the plate, the proximity making their hands brush. He paused and met her gaze, and for an instant she saw the ocean of worry in his gaze. His entire life hung in the balance, and he'd been waiting since last Friday for an answer. She smiled at him and he nodded, accepting her offer to help, and not with the dishes.

"I'll get the silverware," she said.

They worked together to finish the table, placing the last of the glasses just as Jackson removed the turkey from the oven and placed it on the table. The crispy skin, the scent of roast meat, the pile of stuffing, all inspired hunger, eliciting a chorus of compliments.

"That looks amazing," Marta said, rising to her feet.

"Well done," Ember said.

Jackson smiled proudly but motioned to Shelby. "My beautiful fiancé did the turkey."

"It's true," Brittney said, placing a bowl of mashed potatoes on the table. "She's a natural."

Shelby leaned over to kiss Jackson. "I had help," she said.

"It looks delicious," Reed said.

They took seats around the table and Shelby asked if they could pray. Ember folded her arms and nodded. "A meal like this deserves some words of gratitude."

Shelby nodded and said a brief prayer before they all dug in. Food was passed around and plates piled high, and Kate noticed Reed momentarily seemed to forget the impending phone call.

"If I knew Jackson cooked like this," Reed said, his words muffled by potatoes, "I would have made him cook an actual dinner once in a while."

"What's wrong with cold cereal?" Jackson protested.

"I like cold cereal for dinner," Shelby said. "But not every day."

Ember leaned over to Brittney, and lowered her tone. "Negotiations have begun between the two parties. But who will blink first."

Jackson used a turkey leg to point at Shelby. "Four nights a week."

"Two."

Jackson snorted. "Three. Final offer."

Shelby smiled. "One."

"You can't go the other way," Jackson protested. "That's not how this works.

"Zero."

"Two!" Jackson said, panicking.

"Well played," Kate said with a laugh.

"She is the captain," Reed added.

Jackson consented with a sigh, and then consoled himself with turkey. Kate watched the banter with a smile on her face and noticed Reed did as well. She leaned over and whispered in Reed's ear.

"They were always my friends," she said. "We needed the three of you to become a family."

"We needed you too," he said. "*I* needed you."

She squeezed his hand. "What was last Thanksgiving like?"

Shelby heard the question and began to laugh, and pointed a finger at Jackson. He looked bewildered as Reed tried to change the subject, but Shelby had already outed Jackson, and his expression turned haunted.

"The great spider war of 2017," he said.

"The what?" Ember asked, looking between them.

"Don't," Reed warned, but Jackson was already talking.

"The three of us were having dinner with Shelby's brother," Jackson said. "I remember it so well, the potatoes, the green beans, even the turkey—not as good as this one but it was still a turkey—all looked so delicious. Then we saw it . . .."

"Saw what?" Marta asked when Reed groaned.

"The spider," he said. "It was as large as my hand and sitting on top of the turkey—JUST LIKE THAT!!!"

His pointed—at the giant spider sitting on the turkey. Kate jumped, as did Brittney and Marta. Ember released a strangled shriek and picked up her plate, smashing it on the turkey with so much force the plate broke in two. Kate flinched and nearly fell over but Ember wasn't finished.

She grabbed a serving spoon and began to beat the turkey. Meat and bones flew in all directions as screams filled the room. Reed ducked behind the table, his laughter matched by Jackson and Shelby, who'd fled into the kitchen. With bits of turkey splattering her form and dotting her hair, Ember finally came to a stop, her chest heaving.

"I think it's dead," Marta said dryly from behind the ottoman.

Ember lifted the broken plate and poked at the mangled spider. Then her eyes narrowed and she leaned in. Kate looked to Reed and he nodded, confirming what Ember had just discovered.

"A *toy*," Ember said.

"It's my family's tradition," Shelby said in a small voice. "We try to scare each other at Thanksgiving."

"I. Don't. Like. Spiders," Ember said, her voice soft, dangerous.

"At least we know the turkey's dead," Jackson reasoned.

Ember swiveled to face him, her hand snatching out to grab the handle of the spoon in the potatoes. Jackson's eyes widened but she was already rearing her arm back. He tried to protest but it was too late.

"Ember, don't, I was just—"

He ducked, and the potatoes splattered across Shelby, causing everyone in the room to freeze. Shelby began to laugh and reached for a piece of meat that had flown away from the beating of the turkey and raised it to throw.

"You want a food fight?" she asked.

"Shelby, I'm sorry," Ember said. "But he deserved it—"

The turkey flew and slapped Ember in the face, falling down her chin and sliding off her chest to *plop* on her shoes. Her features contorted and she stared at Shelby. Kate saw what was coming and dived for ammunition just as the kitchen exploded with food.

Chapter 7

The fight was fast and dirty, with potatoes, green beans, even sweet potato pie flying in all directions. Only Brittney remained above it all, and hid behind the fridge shouting at others to stop.

Kate grabbed the remains of the potato on her plate and sent it soaring at Reed. Caught off guard, he turned to stare at her, the potato covering his ear and neck. She burst into a laugh—as a glob of green beans struck her in the side of the face. Marta's laughter replaced her own as she quickly dived behind the ottoman, only to be struck by Jackson, who was also hiding behind there.

"Look out!" Reed shouted.

A pile of stuffing splattered Kate's arm and chest, bouncing off her to strike Reed. They gathered the remains of their plates before hurling them into the mix, both striking Ember, who still stood in the middle, leveling food in all directions. Turkey juices dripped down her shirt, while potatoes stuck to her jeans. A glob of cranberry sauce was in her hair, and she pulled it free to throw at Reed, splattering his hair and part of the wall. Then she reached for the miraculously untouched pie.

"NO!"

Brittney's bellow brought everyone to a halt, and she stepped out from behind the fridge. She glared at all of them, her gaze sweeping the group until settling on Ember, who seemed surprised.

"Not the pie," Brittney said.

Kate slowly stood and surveyed the food covered room. "Perhaps we did take it a little far."

They all turned at a sudden jangle at the door. The knob turned and Tanner strode him, his attention on the bowl of fruit he carried under his arm. He began to talk as he carefully began to remove his coat.

"I made it back early," Tanner said, and then noticed the room. His eyes took in Ember, who'd suddenly gained a very devilish gleam.

"Ember," he warned, scrambling backwards.

"Welcome to Thanksgiving," she said. She picked up the bowl of potatoes and scooped out the remaining food into her hand.

Tanner retreated but slipped on the porch and fell into a snowdrift. Trapped, he could only watch in horror as Ember dropped the entire pile on his face. Then she stood and laughed. Kate cautiously joined her at the door and saw Tanner wiping the food off his face, his features twisted in shock.

"Time for ice cream!" Jackson said brightly.

Everyone groaned, to which Shelby stabbed a finger at him. "You promised we could eat the sculptures after shopping."

"I don't recall agreeing to that," Jackson said.

"Later would be better," Tanner agreed, wiping potatoes off his chin and tasting it. "Nice job, Brittney."

"Shelby did the potatoes," Brittney said. Then she turned to the group and folded her arms. "You made the mess. You clean the mess. Then you can go shopping."

"Okay Mom," Jackson said with a smile. "But I call the dragon."

The group set to work cleaning the room, and Kate scrubbed the walls as Reed did the floor nearby. His smile had returned and she considered the mess worth it. The girls took turns cleaning up in the bathroom, while Ember needed a full shower to get clean. An hour later the mess had been gathered onto the kitchen sink.

Jackson surveyed the pile of dishes and food with distaste. "My old nemesis," he said. "Dishes."

Kate laughed and motioned to Reed. "Why don't we clean up while you shop?"

"You don't want to shop?" Shelby asked. "I thought you liked Black Friday shopping."

"I'm not in the mood to fight the crowds this year," Kate said. She glanced at Reed and raised a questioning eyebrow.

He shrugged and nodded. "Neither am I."

Shelby shook her head uncertainly. "Maybe we can do the dishes before—"

"Too late," Jackson said, already putting on his coat. "They offered, and I accept."

"Are you sure?" Brittney asked Kate.

"Of course," Reed said.

The group exchanged looks but at Kate's urging they departed the table and donned coats, moving considerably slower than prior to the lavish meal and food fight. Kate noticed Jackson lean over to Reed and ask if he should stay and help with the cleaning.

"Would you rather do them?" Reed asked.

Jackson snorted and shook his head. "Why do you think I eat cold cereal for dinner?"

"I thought you liked the cereal," Reed said.

"That too," Jackson said.

They said their farewells and the others departed, leaving Kate and Reed alone in the kitchen. Reed stepped to the sink first and turned on the water. When she protested, he merely smiled and pointed to the table.

"Why don't you finish putting the food away while I wash."

"There's not much food left," Kate said with a laugh.

For several moments they worked in companionable silence. They'd often done dishes together, especially when he'd been sleeping on their living room floor, but today was the first time they cleaned up after a holiday.

She found herself imagining a life with Reed, of them being married and sharing holidays, cleaning up after their friends had departed. She paused in gathering the napkins and looked down at her finger, wondering what it would look like with a ring.

The image faded as she recalled the seriousness of their earlier conversation, and the trickle of fear returned. Why had he played a game about their future? Did he mean to use her own wishes against her? Other guys might leave, but Reed would never leave unless he thought it was best for her.

"Are you okay?" he asked.

"Just thinking."

"About what?"

"You," she said. "And the game from earlier."

"Do you have another Someday?"

She stacked the plates next to the sink and turned to him. Noticing her expression, he turned off the water and hurriedly dried his hands on a nearby towel.

"What?" he asked.

"Are you going to break up with me?"

She blurted the question, the doubt spilling from her lips before she could stop it. Reed seemed stunned, and stared at her. She fought to keep her fear at bay but her heart began to crumple, folding inward as he continued to stare.

Chapter 8

"*That's* what you're worried about?" he finally asked. "That I was going to break up with you?"

"You wanted to play a game about the future when you might be leaving the state," she said. "I know you wouldn't end things for yourself, but you would do it if you thought it was best for me. You could say you wanted me to have my Somedays and—"

"Kate . . ."

He caught her hands but the words continued to tumble from her lips. Afraid of what he would say, she looked down at their intertwined hands, the words coming faster and faster. She swallowed and wiped at her mascara, annoyed that it was running across her cheeks. Was she crying? She'd wanted to hold her ground, look flawless so if he left it would be the image he would always remember.

"I understand if you have to go but I don't want you to. I want you to stay with me, to be with me. I can't imagine a life without you and don't want things to end—"

"Kate," he said, the softness to his tone finally cutting through her rising despair. "Here or there, my heart stays with you."

She finally met his gaze and saw a smile on his face. His blue eyes lit with compassion and a touch of amusement, as if he found the prospect of breaking up utterly absurd. A spark of hope ignited in her chest.

"You're not breaking up with me?"

He laughed, the sound light and amused, before he engulfed her in an embrace. "You don't end things with the one you love because life gets hard. Unless I have it wrong . . ."

"No," she said, relief and guilt coloring her tone. "I'm sorry, I just thought—"

"Doesn't matter," he said, leaning down to kiss her.

His lips washed away her lingering fears and she snaked her arms around his back. Then a thought crossed her mind that made her retreat and examine Reed with new eyes.

"If you didn't do the game to break up, why did you do a game about the future?"

"With all the doubt hanging over the internship, I thought it would be fun to talk about the things we wanted out of life."

"Your timing is usually good," she said. "But today, not so much."

"Hey," he said, indignant. "Maybe I wanted to know your Somedays so I can plan new dates."

"Still a failure," she said, sniffing.

She smiled to take the sting from her words, and realized that waiting for the phone call had gradually added pressure. Reed's game hadn't been the cause, but it had inadvertently pierced the wall of fears and doubt she'd locked away.

"I'm sorry," she said. "I didn't realize how worried I was about the call. I thought we'd know by now."

"Me too," he said. "Even if it was a no, I'd rather know the answer than sit and wait."

She picked up a napkin and wiped at her eyes. "Look what you've done to me," she said with a small laugh.

He feigned a wounded expression and then reached to the water. Dipping his hands into the stream from the faucet, he flicked water at her. Droplets scattered across her face, neck and shirt, the chill startling her to silence.

"It wasn't me that misread the game," he said.

She glared at him and then reached for the water, flicking him back. He laughed and wiped his face before leaning into kiss. The phone rang twice before they heard it, and then he dried his hands and reached into his pocket. Then abruptly his smile evaporated and he straightened.

"Dr. Dickson," he said. "I didn't expect a call from you."

"Sorry to interrupt you on your holiday . . ." a new voice came into the room. "But I knew you would want to know as soon as possible."

"Yes, thank you," Reed said, raising his hand and running it through his hair.

Kate stood frozen, her hand gradually emptying of water. Their eyes met and she saw the hope and worry in his gaze, and it reflected her own fears. She dumped the remaining water and dried her hand to reach for his.

". . . have not filled the internship. If you are still committed, we'd love to have you here in New York . . ."

Relief and sorrow battled for dominance, and Kate fought the surge of emotions. She was relieved because Reed hadn't lost his future because of her. But the sorrow was sharp and bitter.

"I understand," he said.

"You'll have to start in January . . .," Dr. Dickson said, his voice barely audible to Kate. "On the 15th. Are you sure you want to accept?"

Reed looked to Kate, and after a moment she realized he was waiting for her. Gathering her courage, she nodded. Reed measured her resolve for a moment and then answered Dr. Dickson, his words quiet yet echoing like a cell door shutting.

"I'll be there."

". . . be in touch after the holiday with the details . . ."

"Thank you, Dr. Dickson. Enjoy your holiday."

"You as well, Mr. Thompson."

Reed hung up and stared at the phone. The silence lasted until abruptly the front door swung open and Jackson darted into the house. He collected an object from the corner of the room and exited without noticing Reed and Kate's rigid posture.

"Forgot my wallet!" he called, and then the door shut.

Kate took a deep breath and slowly released it. "I guess you're going to New York."

"I guess I am," he said.

Kate realized their time together had just been put on a deadline. In seven weeks Reed would be leaving for New York, and their relationship would change forever.

Volume 22: The Brothers Date

Chapter 1

Reed packed the last of the clothes on his bed and zipped the suitcase. He'd wanted to pack the previous evening, but after he'd defended his thesis his friends had wanted to celebrate. Kate had dropped him off after midnight and he'd been too tired to pack.

He hadn't been on a trip since Jackson had unceremoniously kidnapped him back in August—and he hadn't been able to pack for himself. Although this trip would only be four days, he'd packed for more. After all, it would be the first time he met Kate's family in person.

He stepped into the living room and glanced out the window. The sun was just touching the horizon, peeking into view as if promising a day of light. The streets were empty as were the sidewalks, and Boulder slumbered.

Driving to Arizona would take all day, but the prospect of hours alone with Kate banished any lingering fatigue. He checked the time on his phone and then strode to the door. Then Jackson's door swung open and he appeared dressed in pajamas, his hair in disarray.

"Did you wake up just to see me off?" Reed asked.

"I was hungry," Jackson said with a yawn. "And it just happened to be when you were leaving."

Reed smiled and nodded his gratitude. The morning after Thanksgiving, he'd told Jackson and the others about his acceptance to the internship in New York. Hearing that Reed would be leaving in just a few weeks had been a surprise, especially to Jackson, who'd already been planning on spring together.

Over the last two weeks, Jackson had expressed a marked increase in efforts to spend time together. He denied it, but Reed realized Jackson was going to miss him. He'd refused efforts to find a new roommate, claiming, "I'll find one."

"Cereal?" Reed asked.

"Out," Jackson said mournfully.

"I bought some Thursday," Reed said with a smile. "Check above the fridge."

Jackson lit up like a kid finding a bonus gift at Christmas and retrieved the box of Life. Grabbing a bowl, he filled it up before adding milk. As he chewed, he blissfully held up the box as an offer.

"Kate told me to be hungry," Reed said. "I suspect she has breakfast planned."

Jackson swallowed. "Are you not doing your big date? I can't recall an invite."

"Our date is the road trip," Reed said, taking a seat opposite him.

"Are you ready?" Jackson asked. Reed gestured to his luggage, at which Jackson shook his head. "Are you ready to meet her family?"

Although he still felt the weight of his impending departure, the prospect of a weekend with Kate sounded incredible, and for the moment his flight to New York was held at bay. He'd met families before, so he wasn't concerned.

"I think I'll be fine," Reed said.

"You aren't just some guy Kate is dating," Jackson said. "You love her, which means her brothers are going to be protective."

"That sounds like a warning."

"It is," Jackson said. "You're going to have to watch your back."

Reed frowned. "You never told me what it was like meeting Shelby's family."

"Weird," he said. "She's the only athlete in a family of nerds. They kept asking me questions about a book series called Game of something."

"Don't you mean Game of Thrones?"

"I thought it was Game of Bones," Jackson said, his expression haunted.

Reed grinned at the image of tall Jackson sitting at a table with Shelby's skinny younger brothers, somehow appearing inferior despite his size. In most settings Jackson was the consummate leader, but in such an environment he was like bacon on a vegan's table.

"Have you ever seen an episode?"

"Never," he replied. "But everyone in her family is an enormous fan. It appears that I'll need to watch some to be assimilated."

Reed smiled. "I don't think I'll need to watch a show in order for Kate's brothers to like me."

Jackson poked him in the chest. "Exactly. They're military," he said. "And Kate is their *only* sister."

He frowned again. "What do you mean?"

"You're going to need more than a show to impress them." The doorbell rang and they both looked up. "Like I said," Jackson said. "Watch your back."

Reed laughed and stepped to the door. "I'll be fine."

"Don't say I didn't warn you," Jackson said, reaching for Reed's bag.

Reed accepted the suitcase and swung the door open. Kate stood on the porch dressed in her warm coat and beanie, her green eyes sparkling with anticipation. Reed donned his coat and grabbed his bag, joining her on the porch.

"Ready for a road trip?" she asked.

"More than I can express," he said.

She smiled and gestured to her car. "Your date awaits."

He grinned and rolled his bag down the steps. His feet crunched over the salt placed on the walkway to melt the latest snowfall, and he put the bag into the back seat of the car. Then he motioned to the driver's seat.

"You want me to take the first shift at the wheel?"

"Not a chance," she said. "You already knew what was coming so an invite was pointless. The least I could do was plan a better date than Thanksgiving."

"That's not very fair," he said, climbing into the passenger seat. "Thanksgiving wasn't my fault."

"It was my fault," Jackson called from where he stood in the door. "At least the food fight part."

"Jackson's right," she said with a smile. "But this time, I'm in charge."

"Should I be worried?"

"Not about me," she said. She waved at Jackson and then got into the car. As she backed out of the driveway, she added, "My brothers are another matter."

"You said they'd like me," Reed said.

"I did," she replied. "But you'll have to earn it."

Her comments mirrored Jackson's warning, and for the first time a touch of worry tightened his chest. They'd been dating for four months now and visiting her family carried a certain connotation. Still, he had a thirteen hour drive to figure it out.

"You said to come hungry," Reed said, "so I hope you have breakfast in mind."

"In the back," she said, gesturing to the back seat. "Open box number 1."

He looked behind his seat and found four boxes stacked neatly, each showing a number. "Just how many surprises do you have in store for me this weekend?" he asked.

"Several," she said with a smile. "But my brothers insisted on taking you out tomorrow night. I suspect they have their own plans."

The worry returned and he considered its source. He'd met countless parents but never felt such trepidation. Was it because he found her family intimidating? Or because his relationship with Kate had become so close?

He reached for the box and placed it on his lap. Inside he found a series of smaller boxes, along with one larger than the others. Noticing they were all labeled with letters, he reached for the first, a small, oblong carton. Inside he found a large car charger with ports for a USB and a plug.

"What's this for?" he asked.

"Box B," she said.

He plugged in the car charger and then opened the largest box. To his surprise he found a small toaster that gleamed in the early morning light. He held it aloft and looked to Kate, who smiled and pointed to the charger.

"Plug it in," she said.

"Am I going to find bread in C?"

"Maybe," she replied, her tone mischievous.

100

He opened the third one and found bagels, plain and blueberry. The fourth contained cream cheese. He grinned as he dropped the bagels into the toaster and began making their breakfast on the road.

"How did you even come up with this?" he asked.

"Brittney got me this charger last Christmas and I've wanted to use it forever." Kate checked her mirrors before pulling onto the freeway. "This seemed like a good time."

"This is epic," Reed said, watching the toaster work its magic on his lap. "Much better than a bowl of cereal."

"The car wouldn't run a fridge," she said. "So I had to be creative."

When the bagel popped up he grinned and reached for the cream cheese. "So, bagels for breakfast?"

"Nope."

He paused in spreading the cream cheese. "What do you mean?" he held up the bagel for emphasis.

"Three meals," she said. "Seven courses each. Bagels are just a part of breakfast."

Reed's gaze dropped to the remaining cartons within the box. "You planned a *21 course* day?"

"Welcome to the road," Kate said, motioning to the open road stretching away from them. "It's going to be quite a ride . . ."

Chapter 2

"You can't be serious."

Kate's response was positively giddy. "Why not?"

It was after five and they'd been driving for just over ten hours, with four hours to go. Throughout the day they'd had everything from fruit to hot steamed corn, and a variety of cheeses. Reed couldn't imagine what lay in store for dinner, but his expectations were exceeded when he'd opened up the latest box and found what lay inside.

A Panini machine.

"Are we really going to make panini's?"

"You're the chef," she said. "I'm the driver."

He pulled out the small cookie sheet and set the Panini machine next to the package of meats and cheeses. An entire tomato and a head of lettuce were also present, and he gestured to the variety of ingredients.

"The grill is officially open," he said. "What would you like?"

"Turkey with Pepper Jack cheese, lettuce and tomato," she said. "And add some mushrooms."

"Coming right up," he said. He plugged in the Panini machine and prepared her sandwich, even buttering the edges of the bread so they would toast better.

"Did you always know you were clever?" Reed asked, his tone tinged with admiration.

Kate cocked her head to the side. "I don't think I ever thought of myself that way."

"Well you are," Reed said. "This proves it. How many people would have come up with such an inventive date?"

"We haven't even gotten to Phoenix yet," she said, and yawned.

"Why don't you let me drive," he said. "You've been in that seat all day."

She seemed to hesitate, and glanced to the boxes in the back seat. All were now empty, suggesting her surprises were about done for the drive. She motioned to the Panini machine and relented.

"Why don't you make your sandwich and eat. Then I'll pull over and I'll trade you."

"Done," he said.

He quickly prepared his sandwich. While it cooked he looked out the window at the setting sun, which kissed the mountains to the west. Yellow was just beginning to fade to gold, with red streaks appearing across the horizon.

Rocky foothills stretched to the mountains in both directions, trees dotting the slope, their canopies covered in patches of snow. They'd crossed into Arizona and the blanket of white had given way to warmer rocks, the reddish hue distinct to the region.

"This place is beautiful," he said.

"My brothers and I would come this way to camp," she said. "We're close to the Grand Canyon, you know."

"You think they'll be okay with me?" he asked.

The question had nagged him since they'd left, but he'd managed to keep it subdued until now. She glanced his way before returning her eyes to the road. She seemed uncertain of her answer until the Panini

103

machine beeped and he used a fork to extricate the sandwich. The scent of melted cheese and seared meat filled the car.

"Can this be a tradition?" Reed asked, smiling.

"Deal," she said.

He put her sandwich into the machine while his cooled and then began to eat, tempering the heat with the bottle of lemonade left over from the afternoon. He wanted to press her on his question but her expression indicated she had not forgotten.

"My brothers have always been hard on the guys I dated," she finally said. "Bake most of all."

"He's the oldest, right?"

Kate nodded. "Orin is the youngest of the three, and the most likely to be on your side. Tyler will probably be okay with you, but I haven't talked to him much, so I'm not sure."

"So Bake's the one I need to convince?"

"I wish I could say it will be easy," she said, "but I don't think so. He got to Phoenix last night, so they will have had the whole day to plan for your arrival."

"Should I be worried?"

She flashed a faint smile. "Probably."

He chuckled and shook his head. "Usually a guy has to worry about the dad."

"My dad won't be there," she said. "He'll probably Skype in sometime on Sunday, but for tonight and tomorrow it will just be my brothers and my mom."

Recalling Bake was a marine—with a penchant for knife fighting— Reed released a sigh. "Please tell me that whatever initiation they have planned, it won't involve sharp weapons."

"It might," she said with a laugh.

Reed joined in the amusement as he finished his sandwich and Kate pulled at the next exit. The road was empty, so he set the tray aside and got out. When they'd traded sides, he settled into the driver's seat and checked his mirrors before crossing the road and accelerating up the onramp.

The freeway stretched away, rising and falling as it followed the contours of the road. Kate savored her sandwich while they continued to talk about her brothers. Instead of worry, it was a quiet dread that settled into his stomach, not unlike the feeling he had prior to a test he had not prepared for.

Darkness overtook them and he turned on the headlights just as they passed a sign indicating Phoenix was three hours away. Shortly after, Kate asked if she could sleep for a moment and he acquiesced with a nod.

"I'll wake you up if I get tired."

"Thanks," she said, and reclined her chair.

Reed listened to her gradually fall asleep, his thoughts drifting to their time together. He glanced her way and watched her twitch, and resisted the urge to brush a stray hair out of her face. She slumbered next to him, serene and beautiful.

As the miles rolled by, he marveled at how much he cared for Kate, how much their lives had merged. He loved her, but that word didn't seem adequate to convey what he felt. And in just a few weeks he was going to leave.

He grimaced and wiped a hand across his face, wondering again if there was any other option. Short of giving up on his career, he could not stay with Kate. For the first time he legitimately considered other career choices.

He glanced at Kate and his heart burned. At the same time, the prospect of relinquishing his career felt wrong. Was there no way he could have both? No way they could be together? He examined the depths of his feelings for Kate but found no bottom, and he realized that of the two, it was Kate he desired most.

He shifted lanes to pass a semi, and light briefly filled their car. Kate shifted onto her side and reached out for his hand, murmuring a question to see if he was okay. He quietly assured her he was fine and she returned to sleep.

One year. That was the length of his internship. But could they endure a year apart? Prior to meeting Kate, he'd considered studying long-distance relationships, and read some on the topic. The statistics were not encouraging, and for good reason. Couples that spent time apart rarely survived because time was nearly always essential to a stable relationship.

But he wanted both, Kate and career. He'd wrestled with the choice off and on since Thanksgiving and once again came to the same conclusion. He hoped they could survive a year apart. He hoped.

She woke up an hour outside of Phoenix and they talked their way into the city. He made no mention of his concerns and shoved them aside by telling himself this weekend was about meeting Kate's family.

Wending their way through the evening traffic, they pulled off the freeway and dived into the endless neighborhoods of Phoenix. In the midst of a forest of houses, she directed him to pull into a large, two-story home with palm trees lining the driveway. He parked on the side of the long drive and got out to stretch.

"Ready?" she asked.

"No," he said. "But I'll be okay."

They retrieved their bags and walked up to the front porch. Wide and aged, the house had a small porch next to the garage. Rocks and cacti were in lieu of grass, and only the palm trees offered shade. The air had cooled considerably and Reed shivered, grateful Kate did not notice the motion.

He followed her into a spacious living room with a large television. To the left, a kitchen, recently redone, boasted oak cabinets and marble countertops. He'd expected her brothers to be waiting and was not disappointed.

Kate's three brothers sat in the living room dressed in full combat fatigues, right down to the paint across their faces. Guns littered the room, filling the space with the scent of oil and steel. The largest of the brothers sat in the recliner, sharpening a knife, the cold scrape of the blade on the stone sending a chill down Reed's back.

"Katie," he said with a smile, his eyes flicking to Reed. "We've been waiting for you . . ."

Chapter 3

"Bake," Kate said, her tone filled with disapproval. "What do you think you're doing?"

Baker was huge, his body built like a cement truck—one that ate stone and steel for breakfast. His hair was short but not shaved, and his eyes seemed to harbor the potential for violence. He didn't respond to the question.

"We're just cleaning our guns," Tyler said innocently.

Thinner than Baker but equally as tall, Tyler had dark hair and a darker complexion. His eyes were the same as Kate's, the green sparkling with mischief as he spoke. There was an amused intelligence about him that suggested leadership, and Reed recalled that he was in the Air Force.

"Why the fatigues?" Kate asked.

"We just got back from paintballing," Orin said.

"I don't see any paint," Kate said.

Orin snorted with laughter. "There wouldn't be any on us."

The youngest brother, Orin, had gotten Baker's width without the height. He was the brick next to Baker's bulk, but the smile on his face was easy, as if it came quick and often. Reed hoped that Kate was right, that Orin would be easiest to win over.

"Kids with toys," Baker said, flashing a smile that again made Reed want to shiver. "They couldn't hit us if they tried."

Kate released an explosive breath and leveled a finger at them, but Reed caught her elbow and spoke first. "I appreciate the welcome," Reed said. "But I'd prefer to get the execution over with. Would you rather shoot me outside so we don't get the carpet bloody? Or perhaps you prefer the knife for a clean kill?"

He looked to Baker and smiled.

And waited.

Tyler managed to hide his smile but Orin failed. The youngest laughed outright, the bark of amusement punctuated by the clatter of steel as he put the gun on the table. He glanced at Baker, but the eldest betrayed no hint of a smile.

"You'll see which I prefer by the end of the night," Baker said.

"*Bake*," Kate snapped.

Baker glared at his sister but Kate did not retreat, and ultimately it was the special forces soldier that did. He rose to his feet and gathered up his gun, his muscles making it clear that he was the weapon.

"Fine," he said. "I won't kill him."

"Can we include maiming in that promise?" Reed asked.

This time Tyler did laugh, as did Orin. Baker's lips twitched as he looked down on Reed, his towering posture intimidating even without the weight to his green eyes. He shrugged like the question didn't matter.

"I'll consider it."

Bake turned to the door, swinging it open just as a flustered woman came up the steps. Her hands were full and at first she didn't notice the open door, almost tripping when she saw Bake standing at the opening. Kate leaned over to Reed as her mother entered the house.

"Bake always knows when someone's coming," she said.

"He has ears like a cat," Tyler said as he passed.

"Except he would kill the dog that tried to sneak up on him," Orin said. He gave Reed a meaningful look and then swept his mother into an embrace. "Hey Mom, how was work?"

"Grading papers," she said, hugging her middle son, "took me longer than I wanted." She caught sight of Kate and leapt to her, hugging her fiercely. "When did you get in?"

"Just before you," Kate said. "This is Reed."

"It's a pleasure to have you," she said, turning to him.

"Lisa," Reed smiled and leaned down to hug her. "It's great to meet you in person."

"It's about time Kate brought you home," Lisa said. "How was the drive . . ."

Her eyes swept the room, her voice fading as she registered the way her sons were dressed and the armament on the coffee table. She rounded on Baker, who still stood by the door, and her features darkened with disapproval.

"Do you have to do this with *every* guy Kate brings over?"

"You've done this for others?" Reed asked, his tone wounded. "And I thought I was special."

"We're just showing him how we treat all guests," Baker said, shutting the door and hugging his mom.

"You only do this to guys Kate has dated," she said, her scolding tone at odds with the warm hug. "Do you remember what you did to Jason? I've never seen a boy so white."

Reed looked to Kate, and she mouthed, *I'll tell you later*. Then Tyler stepped in and hugged his mom. Lisa, still berating Baker for the display, embraced her son and then swept her hand at the living room.

110

"I'll give you ten minutes to clean up this mess—and take that face paint off. You're not going to war."

"We'll have it done by dinner time," Baker said.

Unperturbed, Baker responded like a tiger tolerating the chattering of a monkey, and motioned to his brothers. The trio set to work putting away the guns while Kate followed her mom into the kitchen. Reed would have liked to stay and try to bond with her brothers, but decided he'd pressed his luck enough and went with Kate.

"And get the groceries from the car," Lisa called.

"I'll get them," Reed said.

"Me too," Orin said.

Lisa tossed her keys to Reed and he walked out the front door, Orin falling into step beside him as they strode to the car. The moment the door shut Orin released a low chuckle, the amused sound fading quickly in the warm Arizona night.

"That was fun to watch," he said.

"What?" Reed asked.

"Bake's been threatening Kate's guys since we were kids," he said. "And I've never seen one stand up to him like that."

"I didn't stand up to him," Reed said, opening the door and reaching for the grocery bags.

"You didn't cower in fear," he said. "And to Bake, that's the same thing."

Reed paused and looked to Orin. "Are you saying I just poked a bear with a stick?"

"Maybe," Orin said with a smile. "I like you already, but maybe that's just because I'm excited to see what he does to you."

111

"It can't be that bad."

"Tommy Jones liked Kate too," Orin said. "He was a bully in the sixth grade that didn't take no for an answer. Bake sent him home with two black eyes—him and his friends." Orin gave Reed a meaningful look and then walked to the front door.

Reed had thought his blunt humor might have gained a measure of respect from Kate's oldest brother, but now he wondered if he'd taken the wrong track. Still, it was already done, so the best he could do was forge ahead. Hopefully it wouldn't get him killed . . . or maimed.

They carried the groceries in and Lisa set to making dinner, a pile of tacos that Kate's brothers devoured with frightening speed. Reed managed to catch two before they were gone. Orin and Lisa sat on the ends while Baker sat across from him. Reed got the impression Tyler usually took that seat, but Tyler had subtly shifted the chair, offering it to Baker. He threw Reed an amused look as he placed Bake across from him, and Reed realized that Tyler also wanted to see what Baker had in store.

Baker's looks aside, the dinner conversation was light and amusing, and the brothers kept their threats veiled. It seemed they wanted to behave themselves while their mother was present, and she dominated most of the conversation.

Lisa skillfully shifted between talking about Kate and Reed, and Baker's deployment. Tyler talked of his upcoming advancement in rank while Orin joked about moving up the chain of command at his mechanics' shop. Throughout the meal, Baker watched Reed, his expression inscrutable. They'd cleaned off the face paint and both Tyler and Orin looked normal. Baker didn't need the war paint to be intimidating.

As they cleaned up dinner Lisa gestured down the hall. "Your room is all set up for you and Reed," she said. "It's a queen bed, so you should be comfortable."

Kate shifted her feet. "Is there another place Reed could sleep?"

112

"Why?" she asked, distracted by putting the food into the fridge.

Kate looked to Reed but he merely shrugged, uncertain of how to proceed. The brothers weren't looking at him but he felt their eyes on his back, and hoped they couldn't tell he was sweating. Keeping his face unperturbed, he continued drying the plates.

"We actually don't sleep together, Mom," Kate said.

Although she'd lowered her voice, all activity ceased in the kitchen, with Tyler holding a plate half dried in his hands. Orin stood at the sink, the water draining away, forgotten. Lisa looked up at Kate in surprise.

"What?"

Kate looked about the kitchen, at her brothers finally brought to silence. Lisa's question hung in the air as all awaited Kate's response. Then abruptly she straightened and spoke in her normal voice, displaying the courage Reed had come to admire.

"Since our nonexistent sex life is of such interest to you, we need a place for Reed to sleep. Is that a problem?" Her challenging gaze swept her brothers and settled on her mother.

"Of course not," Lisa said, her eyes flicking to Reed and then back. "I'm sure you can sleep in—"

"My room," Baker said, drawing all eyes to him. He smiled. "Tyler and Orin are both in the other bedroom, so it only makes sense."

"Am I going to wake up in the morning?" Reed asked.

Baker laughed lightly but sidestepped the question. "I'll take good care of him."

"Are you okay with that?" Kate asked.

Reed managed to keep the nervousness from his voice. "Don't worry. My life insurance covers death and dismemberment."

As Tyler and Orin laughed, Baker nodded. "Then it's settled."

113

Kate looked to Reed and he smiled reassuringly, unwilling to speak. It was late, so after cleaning up dinner they all got ready for bed. Reed brushed his teeth between Tyler and Bake, and never had he felt so small. Then he spoke with Kate until after eleven, finally kissing her goodnight before entering Baker's lair and claiming the air mattress. Without a word Bake turned off the light and climbed into bed, his entrance making no sound in the darkness.

"Good night," Reed said.

There was no response, and Reed struggled to fall asleep. The absolute silence grated on his ears and he resisted the urge to flee. He considered himself brave, but realized that bravery had never been tested.

Until now.

Chapter 4

Deep into the night, the fatigue of the day finally claimed him, and he dreamed of being chased through an endless house. He woke frequently and tried not to fidget. Every motion seemed to scrape loudly against the sheets, and the rubber of the air mattress groaned. No sound came from Baker's bed and he wondered if he was even asleep, or was he pointing a gun at Reed's head.

He tried to shake his fears by telling himself they were irrational, that Baker would never actually hurt him. Baker wouldn't murder him in his bed, the bullet passing through his body and puncturing the air mattress. It wasn't logical. But logic too, was afraid of Baker.

Shortly after one in the morning, a heavy hand settled on his shoulder. He woke to the sudden fear one gains in the presence of a predator, and found Baker's face just inches from his own. The combat paint had been reapplied, making his features terrifying in the darkness.

"Get up," he said.

"Is the grave dug?" Reed asked, yawning in spite of his fear. "Or do I have to dig that myself?"

Bake bared his teeth in a smile. "Let's go, Valentine. Time to see if we let you into the family."

Reed rose to his feet and glanced at Baker's bed. Although he could have sworn the big man had gotten in the night before, it was made and looked unused. He wondered if he'd moved without waking him but realized Baker was used to going undetected when his life depended on it. Avoiding Reed would have been laughably easy.

He was led into the living room, where the dim light allowed him to see Tyler and Orin, already dressed in black and their faces painted. Even in the gloom, all three moved like the darkness was an old friend.

"What's going on?" Reed asked.

"Quiet," Tyler said. "Do you want to wake them?"

"Yes," Reed whispered. "I could use a bodyguard."

Tyler grinned and handed him a set a clothes. "Get dressed, quickly."

Reed took a step toward the bathroom but Orin leaned against the wall, blocking the way. "No time for privacy," he said.

Reed shrugged and removed his shirt to don the black, long sleeved shirt. Then he pulled the pants on over his basketball shorts. When finished, Orin closed the gap and told him to close his eyes while he applied streaks of black to hide his features.

Bake watched the entire thing from the shadows by the door, his large frame somehow finding refuge in the darkness. When Reed was properly ready, he was led out the front door and to Tyler's car, which proved to be a large truck able to fit them all. Reed expected the back seat, but instead he was directed to sit in the front.

"Where are we going?" he asked.

"We'll infiltrate the target's location in thirty," Baker said, pointing to the clock.

"And what do we intend for this target?"

"He's going to get shot."

Reed's heart sank at Baker's smile. "And who will be doing the shooting?" he asked.

"You, of course," Tyler said from the back seat.

"A felony isn't really what I wanted to get this weekend," he said.

Bake merely snorted and pulled into a parking lot in the seedier side of town. Parking behind a warehouse where the shadows hid most of the truck, he climbed out and surveyed the empty lot. Reed exited to the sounds of shouting and breaking glass, both coming from a bar across the street. A siren wailed in the distance and then faded.

The back of the parking lot abutted a strip of trees, the ground around them filled with trash and broken beer bottles. In any other setting Reed would have felt uneasy, but it was his companions that inspired fear.

Tyler and Orin got out and each had two guns in their hands. The bulbous top indicated they were paintball guns, but the larger size and sleek look suggested they were more powerful than the average variety. Orin handed one of the guns to Reed.

"I hope you're a good shot."

"Kate has helped improve that," Reed said ruefully, trying to keep the relief from his face. At least it wasn't an actual gun.

"Let's go," Bake said, holding a paintball gun that dwarfed the others. "He usually exits the club at two."

As they walked into the trees Reed asked, "How long have you been watching this guy?"

"Two weeks," Orin replied. "Had to get ready for tonight."

"You spent two weeks preparing for tonight?" Reed asked. "I'm flattered."

"You should be," Tyler said.

"Are you going to tell me who this guy is?" Reed asked. "I prefer to know who I'm shooting."

"We won't need to tell you," Tyler said.

117

Reed frowned but Baker barked an order for silence as the trees thinned. Ahead was another parking lot, this time on the side of a structure. Bright neon lights flashed, pulsing in the darkness in garish pink and green. Baker put his hand out to keep Reed from stepping out of the shadows.

"This isn't the type of place you just walk into," he murmured.

Reed accepted the warning with a nod and slipped behind a tree to examine the structure. Wide and squat, the structure boasted peeling paint and grimy walls. The parking lot had seen better days, the painted lines all but vanquished by the multitude of cracks. There were no windows at all, and when he lifted his gaze to the sign he understood why. A garish image of a woman stood, the sign indicating it was a strip club.

"What are we doing here?" Reed asked.

"Your target should be out in the next few minutes," Bake said, and motioned to the gun. "If you're any good at all, you won't have any problem hitting him from this distance."

"What if I don't want to?" Reed dared to ask.

"I think you will," Tyler said. "You can practice on the garbage can."

Reed frowned again and followed Tyler's direction to set up his stance, taking aim toward a dingy trash can sitting at the side of the lot. They said he should hold the gun against the tree for stability and directed him to shoot the can a couple of times to gauge his shot. He reluctantly did so, and was surprised by the recoil of the gun. To his amazement he hit the trash can, and Tyler gave an approving nod.

"Kate always was a good teacher," he said.

"Aim at the door," Baker said. "When you see him, you're going to want to hesitate. Don't."

Reed lowered the gun and slowly shook his head, swallowing against the sudden surge of fear. "I'd really like to gain your respect, but I don't want to randomly shoot someone you don't like."

"This isn't someone *we* hate," Baker said. "It's someone *you* hate."

Reed blinked in surprise, but before he could ask, Tyler stabbed a finger to the door. "There he is."

The three brothers lined up on trees remarkably fast, and against his better judgment Reed turned and readied himself. The door had opened, allowing raucous music to escape the club. A man had stumbled outside and braced himself against the wall to puke on the ground. Large and broad shouldered, he wore a dirty letterman's jacket, likely from high school. Six men followed him out, all stumbling and laughing. One clapped him on the back and made a comment that drew more laughter from the men. Then he stood and wiped his mouth, bringing his face into view.

Reed went rigid, shocked to find that he recognized the man. It had been nearly four years, but his face was etched into Reed's memory. The last time he'd seen him, he'd been sitting behind the steering wheel of a black mustang just before Aura had gotten into the car. The man they'd brought Reed to shoot was the same one that had put Aura into a coma.

Tim.

Chapter 5

Reed stared at Tim but imagined him in his car, his voice as he shouted at Aura to hang up, that he was fine, that he wasn't drunk. The profanity was punctuated with a horn, and then a massive *crunch*. Then silence.

"You should not have brought me here," Reed said, his voice rough. "You don't understand."

"We know all about Aura," Tyler said.

"Then why did you do this?" Reed demanded, rounding on them. "How did you even find him?"

"I tracked him down because I was curious," Tyler admitted. "He's been in Phoenix for a few months now, but spends most nights here." He gestured to the strip club, his lip curling in disgust.

"He and his group of loud mouthed friends brag about the girls they've dated," Orin said. "And he's mentioned Aura, more than once."

Reed clenched his fist in anger and shot him a look. Tim was still outside the club, a beer bottle in hand as talked to his friends. He waved it about, his voice echoing back to the woods as his drunken friends chattered like monkeys.

"Why did you bring me here?" Reed demanded.

"We needed to know you could defend Kate," Bake said. "Things look like they're getting serious and we had to be sure."

"And you thought this would work?" Reed asked, his tone scornful as he held up the paintball gun.

Bake grunted in irritation and shot Tyler a look. "I told them we should have brought the taser."

"It wouldn't matter," Reed said, dropping the gun and starting down the slope.

"Reed," Orin hissed. "What are you doing?"

Reed ignored him, and strode down the slope, his eyes fixed on Tim standing with his friends. He didn't know what he was going to say or do, but he couldn't just hit him with paint. Tim deserved worse. He deserved to hurt.

"Tim!"

Tim turned, his bleary eyes bloodshot and red rimmed. He smirked as Reed advanced upon him and took a step to greet him, sauntering like he was lord of the cronies. The others followed and one licked his lips in anticipation, revealing yellow teeth.

"We want entertainment and a crazy kid shows up," Tim said, tossing the bottle to shatter against the wall.

"How *dare* you," Reed snarled. "How dare you speak Aura's name after what you did to her."

Tim came to a halt and squinted at him, blinking in surprise . . . and then recognition. "Reed?"

Reed closed the gap and stabbed a finger into his ribs. It wasn't hard, but it sent him recoiling backward. Taller than Tim, Reed glared down on the quivering man, the force of his expression holding them all at bay.

"You're a cockroach, Tim, an insect unworthy of the trash it feeds on. Aura kept thinking she could make you better, that she could *save* you, but look at you now, a quivering waste of a man."

Reed advanced again and Tim retreated, flinching like the words were physical blows that left him reeling. He stumbled, desperate to

121

escape Reed's condemnation, the alcohol in his veins causing him to tumble backward. Then abruptly the shame and guilt on his face turned to anger and he stopped.

"You don't know me," he sneered. "You don't know what I've been through."

"You think I don't?" Reed demanded. "You're here because guilt is eating you like a cancer. Alcohol and obscene pursuits may dull the pain, but it never goes away. What you don't understand is that your guilt is just getting stronger, and when you finally look at what you've become, you're going to shatter."

"You weren't driving the car," Tim sneered, closing the gap, his nostrils flaring. "You think you can judge me? I killed a girl and look at me." He swept his hands wide. "I don't even care."

"Aura woke up," Reed said.

His voice was quiet, but a wealth of scorn infused the words. Tim stood still, the blood gradually draining from his face. Relief appeared on his features, and then he began to tremble, and all at once he crumpled. He collapsed to the ground, tears quietly leaking from his eyes as he endured the agony he'd tried to suppress for four years.

"I didn't kill her?" Tim's voice trembled with a desperate hope.

"No," Reed said. "You just took four years of her life away. Four years from the best woman you will ever have the privilege of knowing. I could have hurt you tonight, but I don't have to. The pain you feel right now will haunt you for the rest of your life." He knelt and looked him in the eye. "And you deserve it."

Tim's mouth opened and closed but no sound escaped, and tears dripped down his dirty cheeks, spilling onto his jacket and darkening the leather. The ring of friends, frozen in drunken surprise, began to shift their feet, and Reed suddenly noticed the glint of steel, of knives in hands.

"Come on, Tim," one growled. "What's wrong with you?"

122

On his knees, Tim didn't move, he just cried silently. Another friend grimaced, revealing gaps in his teeth. He brandished the knife like it was a sword and inched forward, his eyes looking to his companions as if they would add to his courage.

"I think it's time we had our entertainment," he said, licking his lips.

Reed turned about and realized he was surrounded. The circle of Tim's friends began to drift closer, eager to punish Reed for what he'd done to Tim. Then one growled and recoiled, a splotch of red paint appearing on his neck. Another snarled as green paint slammed into his arm, and he dropped his knife with a curse. Then paintballs filled the parking lot. Reed expected Tim's friends to run, but they were either too stubborn or too drunk, and several charged.

Reed twisted as a fist swung past him and retreated, accidently stepping into the reach of another. The fist came from his side and he flinched, catching the blow in the jaw. He saw stars but instinctively swung back, punching him in the gut. A knife glinted nearby, but suddenly Baker appeared.

The man lunged at Baker, but the big man twisted on cat's feet, catching his wrist and rotating it until the joints popped. Then he plucked the knife from his hands and threw it into the garbage can. The man's shriek ended when Baker kicked his legs from under him and sent him to the unforgiving pavement.

Baker calmly advanced to the next and ducked the hasty punch, putting him down with a short blow to the neck. Another man came at him with a knife and he twisted, catching a knife from the ground and deflecting the blade with ease. Then he darted in and used the hilt to strike him in the skull. As he collapsed, Tyler and Orin appeared, and the trio leveled the remaining opponents. The three brothers put them down almost lazily, avoiding blows and landing their own.

Reed wiped at his mouth and his hand came away bloody. He wanted to laugh but the smile hurt, so he nursed the split lip as Kate's brothers turned from the unconscious forms and joined him.

"What about him?" Orin asked, gesturing to Tim, still crying on the ground.

Baker shrugged. "What about him? Reed hurt him more than we ever could." Then he smiled and put his arm around Reed's shoulders, guiding him from the parking lot. "Do you mind walking me home? It's a tough neighborhood."

Reed laughed, the sound ending in a wince. "It was my first fight," he said. "And without you all I'm pretty sure I'd be dead."

"To be fair, without us, you wouldn't have been here in the first place," Tyler said.

"Your tactics were poor and your hand to hand combat skills may be zero, but we can change that," Orin smiled.

"He's got what matters to us," Baker said.

Reed glanced back at Tim. In the midst of unconscious forms, it was him that was broken. Reed wanted to be angry with him, but the only emotion he felt after the fight was pity, and he shook his head as he left the scene behind.

They returned to the truck and drove back into town, the ride considerably less hostile than before. Tyler found him some napkins from a fast food meal and Reed pressed them against his lip. Blood had dripped onto his shirt, which was dirty and torn where someone had grabbed the collar.

Bake parked in the driveway and they walked to the door. It wasn't even five and the sky was just beginning to lighten, illuminating the rocky front yard and the cactus next to the front door. It seemed like weeks since he'd driven thirteen hours to arrive.

Reed yearned for the welcome embrace of sleep. Chuckling like school kids sneaking out, Tyler and Orin eased the door open and the foursome crept inside. Baker entered last and quietly shut the door. Then he straightened and faced the corner of the room, muttering a curse.

The light clicked on to reveal Kate sitting on the couch.

Chapter 6

The four of them froze, and Reed abruptly realized how absurd they looked. They were dressed in black, their faces painted like they were going to war. Reed wore the worst of the fight, but they were all dirty.

Kate's eyes swept across them and widened when she spotted Reed's bloodied lip and torn shirt. She rose to her feet and closed the gap in an instant, raising a hand to his face. He winced as her fingers touched his lips.

"I'm okay," he said. "Really."

Kate's eyes sparkled with anger and she turned on Baker. "How could you do this to him?" she snapped.

Baker raised his hands to placate her. "It wasn't us," he said.

"It kinda was," Orin said, disappearing into the kitchen and returning with an ice pack from the freezer. "We did take him to the strip club."

Kate's eyes widened again, her voice going up an octave. "You took him to a *strip club?*"

"Kate . . .," Reed began.

Kate shoved his hand away and stepped to Baker, whose amusement only served to heighten Kate's fury. The look on her face would have shaken mountains, but Bake remained in place, his arms at his sides.

"I cannot *believe* you would be so *stupid*," she growled. "I thought we were close, that you were my brothers—but brothers don't do this—brothers don't hurt the one I bring home—"

"Kate," Tyler said, his tone exasperated.

"—and you," she rounded on him. "You've always been the smart one and I *trusted* you. I trusted you to treat him with a *tiny measure* of decency—but you have to take him to a *strip club and BREAK HIM?*"

"It's not what you think," Baker said.

"Then *explain it to me*," she shouted, "before I take your knife from you and give you a scar to remember."

Baker laughed at the threat but it was the wrong move, and Kate reared back and slugged him in the gut. Unprepared for the assault, the blow sent him back a step, more in surprise than pain. Then he looked at Kate.

"That actually hurt," he said.

"The next one will hurt more," she snarled.

Reed reached out and caught her arm. "Kate," he said. "Seriously, it's okay. They took me to the parking lot of a strip club to shoot a guy with a paintball gun. They wanted me to prove I could protect you."

Orin was laughing. "Saying it out loud makes it sound really stupid."

"It *was* stupid," Kate said.

"It was not the best of our ideas," Tyler said, his tone conciliatory. "But we had a reason. We took him to Tim."

Her eyes widened in recognition and she turned to Reed. "The Tim that put Aura into a coma?"

"The same," Reed said.

127

"And they took you to shoot him . . .?" she folded her arms and glared at Baker, who shrugged.

"I didn't," Reed said. "I only talked to him."

For the first time since their arrival, Baker laughed. "I never thought I'd see words do so much damage, but Reed left him crying on the ground."

"You hit him?" Kate asked.

Reed wasn't sure if she was proud of him or disappointed, but she looked into his eyes with a rising concern. He shook his head and sought to assuage her concerns.

"I hardly touched him."

"Then how did he end up on the ground?" Kate asked.

"And crying," Orin supplied.

Reed shot him a look and then turned back to Kate. "I just talked to him. That was all. Honest."

"That's when the fight began," Orin said helpfully.

"Fight?" Kate's anger was rapidly returning.

"Relax," Baker said. "They only had a few knives and—"

Reed had seen videos of a nuclear bomb detonating back in high school. The mushroom cloud rising into the sky, the buildings shattering from the furious expansion of heat and fire. He recalled wondering if anything could match such fury.

"YOU GOT REED INTO A KNIFE FIGHT?!"

Baker actually retreated a step and cast about to his brothers, but Kate stomped toward him with rage wafting across her frame. Tyler made to intervene, but Kate threw him a look that made him snatch his hand back. Reed leapt between Kate and Baker.

128

"As much as I'd love to see you prove you're stronger than your brother," Reed said, "I've already had my first real fight and I don't really want a second in the same night."

"But—"

"I know," he said, stepping to block her path when she tried to pass him. "But they thought they needed me to prove I wasn't a coward."

"He wasn't," Baker said, poking his head into view. Kate's eyes flashed dangerously and he retreated again.

"I'm okay," Reed said. "I really am, and in a way, I'm glad I had the chance to talk to Tim."

Her eyes narrowed and Reed realized he was risking her anger shifting to him, so he stepped in close and cautiously wrapped his arms around her rigid frame. He gave a tentative smile which she did not return.

"My brothers are still stupid," she said.

"That's always been true," Orin said with a smirk.

"If they promise never to get me into a fight again, will you let it go?"

He held her gaze, using all his powers of attraction to soften her anger. Although totally justified, her indignation threatened what he'd gained from the evening, and he didn't want Baker or the others to respond in kind.

"Please," Reed said.

She finally looked to Baker and her eyes narrowed, to which he held up his hands in defeat. "I promise not to get him in a life-threatening situation again." She continued to glare at him until he sighed. "I promise not to get him into another fight."

"And no knives," Tyler added, drawing her gaze.

129

"Unless we're teaching him blade fighting," Orin said. When she glared at him he shrugged apologetically. "Then knives are kind of required."

Kate swept her brothers with a gaze as if measuring their commitment, and Reed marveled at how much alike they all were. He'd never seen Kate so furious and deep down he found it intimidating, and awesome. She could have been angry *at* him, but she'd been angry *for* him.

"Fine," she relented. "But I reserve final judgment until I've heard the whole story."

Orin smiled and said brightly. "Anyone else ready to go back to bed? It's been a long night . . ."

Orin's voice faded when his mother strode into the room. Her hair was in disarray and she wore a bathrobe over her nightgown, but she took in the room at a glance, her eyes settling on Reed. He held his breath, expecting another detonation, but instead she shifted to face Baker.

"Sit," she commanded.

"Mom," he groaned. "It's already resolved. Kate's good and Reed's hardly hurt at all."

"Your sister may have forgiven you—"

"I haven't," Kate said, but Lisa continued as if she hadn't spoken.

"—but I want to know exactly what my boys did to my daughter's boyfriend."

"It's late," Orin said. "Can't we talk after we've had some sleep?"

"You should have thought about that before you kidnapped the first really decent guy Kate has brought home—and then brought him back half dead."

"He's fine," Tyler said. "He doesn't even need stitches . . ."

130

She looked to her middle son and he sighed and took a seat. Orin and Baker exchanged a look and sank onto the couch. Reed hid a smile at the image of three war-painted boys awaiting a scolding from their mother.

"You can go, Reed," Lisa said, her voice considerably softer. "Kate can take care of that lip for you."

"Make sure they tell you all about the knife fight," Reed said.

Orin and Tyler glared at him but Reed merely smiled and inclined his head. Baker regarded him with the same inscrutable expression from before, but this time there was a different emotion in his gaze.

Respect.

Chapter 7

As Lisa demanded answers, Kate and Reed escaped. Kate stopped in the kitchen to get a towel, which she got wet in the sink. Then she motioned him down the hall to the backyard. He raised his eyebrow at the destination.

"We're not staying in the house?" he asked.

Lisa's voice reverberated through the structure, the tone remarkably similar to Kate's. The sound made him smile and he followed her into the darkened yard. Unlike the front yard, which was mostly rocks and a few cacti, the backyard had patches of yellow grass and a towering tree in the corner. A platform of boards lay nestled in the branches, the wood faded and worn.

"Come on," she said. "We might as well watch the sunrise while I get you cleaned up."

He climbed the rickety ladder and took a seat on the platform, his legs dangling over the edge. Kate took a seat next to him and gingerly wiped at the dried blood that lined his lip and neck.

The sun had yet to appear, but the region glowed with predawn light. The air was cold but not overly so, the crisp breeze brushing across Reed's lip to elicit a wince. With daylight just touching the horizon, the city of Phoenix was just beginning to rise.

"Your city is beautiful," he said.

She reached up and brushed the towel across his lip. "I'm sorry about my brothers."

He realized her hand was trembling and reached up to take it. She swallowed and looked down at the towel, which she twisted and retwisted with her free hand. Realizing just how afraid she'd been, he leaned over and kissed her on the cheek.

"I'm fine," he said softly.

"I can't believe Baker almost got you killed."

"That's a bit of a stretch," he said. "They put me in danger, but they also got me out."

He took the towel from her and began the story. Starting with waking to Baker's painted features, he detailed their silent departure and the ride to the mysterious destination. Then he described seeing Tim for the first time in four years.

"I can't imagine what that was like," she said.

"I didn't think I'd ever see him again," he said. "And when I did . . ."

He shook his head, unable to voice the sheer volume of anger that had pooled in his stomach. It was shocking and terrifying, yet oddly empowering. It had stripped away his reserve and left a haunting power.

"I wanted to kill him," he said quietly.

"I can't imagine you being so upset," she said. "I've hardly heard you raise your voice."

"He talked about Aura like she was a conquest, like killing her was something to be praised. But I felt I could see his guilt. He may have caged it with a bottle, but it was still there, and I just couldn't stand still."

"But you didn't hit him?"

"I probably would have," Reed said, "but when I stood in front of him I just wanted him to feel the pain of what he'd caused, and breaking his jaw just didn't seem enough."

133

"You could have broken your hand," she said. "It's what happens if you don't know how to throw a punch."

"Maybe that's something your brothers will teach me," he said with a smile.

She smiled faintly. "What exactly happened after you made a grown man cry?"

"He was surrounded by his group of friends," he said. "They were brutes, probably kings of high school that tumbled from their thrones the moment they graduated. And they didn't like that I toppled Tim, so they came after me. Bake intervened."

"To protect you," she said.

"I was surprised too," he said. "At first I thought he did it out of duty, but I think your brothers liked my reckless charge."

"They still shouldn't have taken you out there," she said, pursing her lips.

"I wasn't the only one to discover rage tonight," he said.

She grimaced. "I'm sorry," she said. "When I heard what they'd done . . ." she looked away. "I've never been so afraid."

"Neither have I," he replied.

She leaned over and put her head on his shoulder, and for a moment they sat in silence. The sun was just peeking over the horizon, bathing the city in light as it continued to rise. Reed leaned against her.

"I'm proud of you," she eventually said.

"For what?"

"For standing up to my brothers." She shifted to look at him. "You've impressed them, and that's not an easy thing to do."

"They are rather intimidating," Reed said.

134

"I know," she replied. "I always knew that my boyfriends wouldn't have to get my father's approval, they'd have to gain my brothers'. And I think you've done that."

"It only cost me a few drops of blood," he said.

She smiled and leaned up to kiss him. When they parted she remained close. "What did I do to deserve you?"

"I have the honor," he murmured, and kissed her again.

The creak of a door drew their attention and Reed looked to the back door. Orin strode into view and looked up at them, squinting as the early morning light fell on his face. He'd changed into jeans and a shirt, and the paint was gone from his face.

"Reed," he called. "We're going to play some Halo, want to join?"

Reed exchanged a look with Kate and then looked back to Orin. "You play Halo?"

"We like the classics," he said with a shrug, and tossed a controller up to him. "Come on. We've already got your character set up for you."

"Is it pink?"

"Maybe," he replied, flashing a smile as he entered the house.

Reed looked to Kate and she smiled. "Go."

"You sure?"

"It's the first time I've seen them invite one of my boyfriends to play with them."

"Really?" he paused in reaching for the ladder. "Not even Jason?"

"He didn't stand up to his test very well," she said ruefully. He raised an eyebrow but she merely smiled. "Go. Have fun. I'll tell you about his test later."

"What are you going to do?"

"Watch the sunrise and ponder the ramifications of how much my family likes my boyfriend."

He grinned and kissed her again, grateful the sting of his split lip had begun to fade. He climbed down from the tree and entered the house, but paused in the bathroom to wash off the stripes of paint. Then he changed into regular clothes and entered the living room, where Kate's brothers were sprawled across the couches and chairs. The smell of waffles and coffee came from the kitchen, as did Lisa's voice, singing softly as she cooked.

Reed sat down and powered on the controller, grateful that Jackson had forced him to play in their first year as roommates. Jackson had always said that friendship was forged in the heat of cooperative video games.

He talked with Kate's brothers as he played his bright pink and purple character. After playing so much with Jackson he managed to hold his own, but they teased him endlessly each time he died. Rather than being offended, he found an entirely different emotion welling within his chest.

He'd never had a brother, but in that living room he found the companionship unique to a brotherhood. It was not obvious, but in the laughter after a grenade sent Baker soaring into the sky, Reed realized they'd accepted him, that he wasn't just Kate's boyfriend. He was their family as well.

And it felt like home.

Volume 23: The Christmas Date

Chapter 1

"Do you know anything?"

Kate looked up at Ember as she rolled her suitcase into the living room and placed it with the others. The semester had ended with all its customary relief, and yesterday Kate had watched Reed graduate. Now they were all separating for Christmas break.

"I really don't know," Kate said.

"But you are going to Tennessee," she said.

"Illinois, actually," Kate said.

"Will you leave her alone?" Marta said. "All we know is that she's leaving tomorrow."

With most of her family in Boulder, Marta was the only one not leaving, and she'd sworn to wear pajamas for the entire week. Her hair in disarray, she wore flannels and a comfy shirt, and, if Kate wasn't going on a trip with Reed, she would have been envious.

"What's wrong with wanting to know how your roommate is getting to her Christmas?" Ember demanded.

Kate grinned. "I really don't care."

"You're traveling a thousand miles and you don't care how?" Brittney asked, shouldering into her coat.

"I don't," Kate said, a thread of excitement seeping into her voice.

Two days after their return from Phoenix she'd found a letter in the mailbox from Reed. Although he only lived a few streets away, Reed had mailed the invitation, and the contents contained a pair of tickets, the tops torn off so they only showed the time of the departure, not the method of travel.

"I assume it's a plane," Ember said.

"Or a bus," Brittney countered.

"Or car," Jackson called, rolling his suitcase to the door. He smirked at Brittney's frown. "Reed does like to throw a twist into things."

"Do you know?" Ember asked Shelby.

She shook her head and carried her plate to the sink. "I would have told you if I knew," she said. "And trust me, I tried to get it out of Jackson."

"I am resistant to your charms," Jackson said, pouring the last of Brittney's blueberry syrup on his waffles. "Brit, these are amazing."

"You've said that," Brittney said with a smile.

"I really don't know how we're meeting his family," Kate said. "I haven't seen Reed much the last few days because of finals and everything."

Finals had ended two days ago, but Reed had extra work grading papers for Dr. Caldin. She'd even gone a full day without seeing him, a gap she hadn't experienced in months. They'd all gathered for breakfast at Kate's house, a final farewell before they parted. Reed had left to get his bag from his house.

A car door echoed and she stepped to the window, spotting Reed. Even bundled up in a coat, he looked stunning, the black beanie highlighting the blue of his eyes. He caught her looking and smiled.

"Careful," Brittney whispered. "You're melting."

Kate grinned and threw her friend a resigned look. Brittney grinned in return. Then Kate swung the door open. Reed stood in a snug jacket. Had he always had such nice shoulders?

"It's about time," she said.

"Sorry," he said, reaching for her bag. "I had to finish a few things. You ready?"

"Just need to say goodbye," she said.

He waved to all of them and then carried her bag to the car. Kate embraced her roommates, Jackson, Shelby, and Tanner, savoring the sense of family that now permeated her home. She hoped she would find it with Reed's family.

"Good luck with his family," Brittney said.

"Remember," Ember said, lowering her tone. "It's his sister that matters the most. Get her to love you and it will be smooth sailing from there."

"How is it possible you've talked to Natalie more than Kate has?" Marta asked.

Ember shrugged. "Some people appreciate my fire."

"We *all* appreciate your fire," Kate said with a smile, hugging the redhead.

"And send us a pic when you know how you're getting there," Brittany said. "We're dying to know how you're getting there."

"I still say it's just a plane," Ember said.

"I'll find out soon enough," Kate replied, swinging open the door.

She paused in the doorway and her eyes swept the room. The house had been her home for years, and the last year had cemented her friendship with her roommates. She sensed a change coming with Reed's departure, but she hoped it would be a new beginning.

"Excited?" he asked, sliding into the driver's seat.

He'd kept the engine running and the air was warm. "Of course," she said. "But my roommates are dying to know what the ticket is for."

"You'll find out soon enough," he said.

He flashed a mischievous smile and leaned over to kiss her. Then he shifted into reverse and eased onto the snowy street, where he turned toward the freeway. They talked about the graduation ceremony as he got on the on-ramp that would take them south. She motioned south, towards Denver.

"Ember thinks the ticket is for a plane."

"And the others?" Reed asked, flashing his easy smile.

"Marta liked the idea of a bus," she said. "She thought it would be fun to just ride across the country."

"And Brittney?"

"She thought it was for a motor home," Kate said.

Reed laughed. "I like their guesses."

"Are any of them right?"

"Maybe," Reed said. "Maybe not."

She shook her head and gestured to the road. "I did think it was just a ruse, and you planned on driving the whole way."

"Sadly, I don't think my car would survive," he said.

"So what is it?" she asked, her curiosity getting the best of her.

"You'll find out in . . . just over an hour." He smiled. "But I think you're going to like it."

She smiled and took his hand, intertwining their fingers. "I get to spend the next week with you. That's all I want."

141

"Are you happy the semester is over?" he asked.

"Very," she said fervently.

He laughed, and for the next hour they talked about their classes and finals. She noticed they both avoided conversation about his upcoming departure, which was just a month away. It was frightening to realize that this was his last time taking her on a challenge date. Then it would be her turn to be in charge before he was gone.

"I'm sorry your family couldn't come," she said.

"You said that last night at dinner," he said.

"It's still true," she said.

"I had you," he said, squeezing her hand.

After the ceremony they had all gone out to dinner, and enjoying a final outing before the holiday. Kate had relished the conversation and laughter, but her thoughts continued to dwell on Christmas, where she would be meeting Reed's family. She hoped a knife fight would not be involved.

They got off the freeway outside of Denver and he drove into town. As they threaded their way through the snowy streets she perked up and attempted to figure out their destination. Her suggestions became more absurd he reached downtown. She looked to him but he merely smiled.

"We're here," he said, and pulled into a parking lot.

Her eyes widened as she saw the long, squat building, the tracks running on the other side, and the gleaming white and blue machine waiting for them. She turned to Reed in shock.

"Please tell me this is real."

"Care to ride a train?" he asked.

"Is that even a question?" she asked fervently.

142

He grinned and they got out of the car. Then he opened the trunk and grabbed their bags and they made their way to the entrance of Union Station. All the while she bombarded him with questions regarding their trip.

"How long is it going to take? What about meals? What are the seats going to be like?"

He smiled and waited until she was done. "We'll be on the train for two days until we get to Chicago. The cabin my mom rented is about an hour outside the city."

"So we're going to sleep in our seats?" she asked, picturing the uncomfortable seats on an airplane.

"We have a private room, of sorts," he said. "It's got two chairs and a small table. They fold down and a top bunk drops down, too."

"We're going to sleep in the same room?" she asked, smiling at the mental image.

"Don't get any ideas," he said. "Besides, the beds are tiny."

"You've done this before?"

"Once," he said. "But the ride was only a couple of hours and I always wanted to take a longer trip. Can you grab the spare bag while I get our tickets?"

"What's in it?" she asked, hefting the weight. "Is this our meals?"

He shook his head. "All our meals are included. We just go to the dining car to eat. That bag is the entertainment. Feel free to take a peek."

He smiled and stepped to the counter. As he spoke to the lady behind the glass, Kate unzipped the bag and found it full of board games. She recognized a few of the games like Monopoly and chess, but others were foreign to her, including Agricola, Clank, and Ticket to Ride.

"What are these?" she asked when he returned.

"We aren't just riding a train," he said. "We're also playing games."

She gathered her bag and the game bag and followed Reed out onto the platform. They'd arrived shortly before boarding, so she only had to fidget half an hour before they were permitted to board the train. While they waited she took pictures of the train and them and sent them to her roommates, who responded with the appropriate amount of jealousy.

The conductor led them down a narrow corridor and gestured to a small room. Tiny was an understatement, but she ducked inside and took a seat, her gaze drawn to the people still on the platform. Reed dropped his bag next to his chair and took a seat across from her, smiling at her attention.

"The seats fold down into the bottom bed," the conductor said, and then reached up to a lever above, "and the second bed drops down from here. Let me know if you have any questions."

"How soon do we leave?" Kate asked.

The man smiled at her excitement. "Ten minutes. Enjoy the ride."

When he departed, Kate could hardly sit still. She explored the seats, the table that folded out, and worked the top bunk, which she promptly claimed. He watched her examine everything with an amused expression on his face.

"I've always wanted to do this," she exclaimed when the whistle blew.

"Most people do," he replied. "But like I said, I've never done a train ride for so long. I'm as excited as you are."

She swallowed the surge of elation and took her seat as a distant clanking sounded, and then the car lurched forward. A tingle of excitement passed across her flesh. The car gradually picked up speed, rocking back and forth and passing beyond the station. Kate watched the city glide by, her face all but plastered to the window.

"One day I want to go to Europe and do this," she said.

"Perhaps another date," he replied.

She shot him a surprised look. "Are you serious?"

"Why not?" he asked, his eyes sparkling with amusement. "Who says our dates can't go international?"

She stabbed a finger at him. "Don't suggest it if you aren't serious."

"I am," he said with a coy smile. "But let's see how we enjoy this ride first, shall we?"

They'd slept in adjacent rooms and tents, but never in the same space. Although they had separate beds, the knowledge that they would be sleeping just inches from each other was intoxicating. She contained her desire with difficulty and leaned back.

"So you like your surprise?" he asked.

"I'm riding a train," she said, and sank into her seat with a sigh. "I couldn't be happier."

"Then the only question is, what game are we going to play first?"

Chapter 2

They played board games all morning, the privacy of the tiny room and the rolling landscape inspiring a sense of solitude and companionship. Time bled away but the train was slower than she'd expected, giving the day a lethargic feel.

They took a break for lunch and headed to the dining car, where the wide windows permitted an even better view. They sat in a booth that looked like it had come out of a fifties' diner and had milkshakes after their burgers. Then they took a picture that framed the dining car in the background, the server standing behind Reed's shoulder, talking to a family of eight. One of the little girls had turned just when the picture was taken, and her smiling face and pigtails were visible at the side of the frame.

With the exception of the large family and six rambunctious kids, the dining car was largely empty. At the suggestion of the server, Kate and Reed took a detour to the observation car, which boasted walls and ceilings made of glass, allowing for a stunning view of the sliding vista.

Snow blanketed trees and clearings, filling crags and topping cliffs. A waterfall appeared on a nearby cliff, its current frozen from the deep winter freeze. Sunlight glistened across the afternoon, causing the unbroken snow to sparkle.

Kate took pictures and sent them to her roommates, adding more photos she'd taken outside the train. With the two of them smiling and the gleaming train in the background, she liked how they looked together.

The train wound its way through the mountains of eastern Colorado until it descended onto the Great Plains. Carpets of white gave way to patches of hardy grass and the occasional tree. When the observation car became crowded they returned to their refuge and started another game. More complicated than the first, it seemed to go on for hours, but she didn't care. With the sun setting and nothing but time and empty tracks, she hoped it would never end.

Their conversation ranged from school to stories of Kate's brothers when they were little. At Kate's request, Reed talked about his sister, Natalie. She was younger than Reed and in her sophomore year at Florida State.

"What's she studying?" Kate asked.

"Biology," Reed said, "she wants to be a doctor."

"How did she handle your parents' divorce?" she asked.

"Not very well," Reed said. "She went through a period where her grades declined and she quit her lacrosse team."

"She played lacrosse?" Kate asked. She'd imagined Natalie as a smaller version of Reed.

"She got into sports in high school," Reed said. "Got really good too, and managed to snag a partial scholarship to FSU."

"What else can you tell me about her?"

Reed showed her a recent picture of Natalie at the beach in Florida. The girl was tanned and fit, her hair black like Reed's, her eyes also blue. She was shorter than the other girls in the picture, but there was something about her gaze that seemed intimidating. Reed talked about how she refused to quit, even when her team was down she would fight to the last second. It had also led to several ejections from the game.

"No wonder Ember likes her," Kate said, and told him about how often Ember talked to her.

"They certainly have a similar passion," Reed said. "But Natalie is more powered by will than anger."

147

The conversation shifted to Ember and Tanner, who were still together despite a rocky couple of weeks. Finals had forced them both to study and the time apart had made Ember cranky. Tanner had been up late studying and had actually responded with irritation when Ember snapped at him, causing a brief breakup.

"Are they back together?" Reed asked in alarm.

"They are now," Kate said. "But it was touch and go for a few days."

"He agreed to take my spot when I move to New York," Reed said. "So I hope he and Ember manage to stay nice, or Jackson and Shelby will stop hanging out with your roommates."

"Tanner's moving in with Jackson?" she asked.

Reed nodded and began cleaning up their latest game of Ticket to Ride. "I thought I told you. His lease was up and he wanted to get out of the apartments, so I offered him my room."

Kate looked out the window, considering how that changed things. Reed and Jackson had been friends since Kate had known him, and for the first time she realized that he was leaving more than her.

"What are you doing with your car?" she asked.

"Roman, Marta's cousin, agreed to buy it."

She frowned. "You aren't taking it with you?"

He paused in putting the box into the bag. "I thought you hated my car."

"I don't hate it," she said. "I think it's a pile of junk."

"Fair point," he said. "But I can't very well take it with me. New York City would eat it for breakfast."

"True," she said, and looked out the window. It felt like Reed was leaving everything behind, shedding even his car, which he'd had for a decade.

"Are you getting tired yet?" he asked.

It had grown dark in the last hour, the sun gradually sinking below the horizon as the train rattled on. She shook her head but a yawn betrayed her. He smiled and stood, motioning to the seats.

"I know you had to get up early to pack so I'm okay if you want to sleep. We've got all day on the train tomorrow, so it's not about to end."

"I want to stay up," she said, but yawned again.

He laughed and motioned her out of the room, and together they worked the mechanism until the seats had turned into skinny beds. Reed lowered his and then ducked out so she could change into pajamas. Then they brushed their teeth in the bathroom, bracing themselves against the wall as the train slowed for a crossing.

They returned to their makeshift bedroom but the train lurched again. Unprepared, she fell into him, pressing her body against his. She swallowed the surge of desire and clung to him until the train car resumed its speed. Then she leaned up on her toes and kissed him, her lips gently touching his.

"Let's go to bed," she said, her tone teasing.

He grinned and climbed into the bottom bunk, allowing Kate to ascend to the top bunk. She wiggled herself into the semi-comfortable bed and then pulled the covers up over her shoulder. Yawning, she leaned over the edge of the bed and watched him shut the curtains and the door, plunging them into shadow.

"This is one of my favorite dates," she said.

"But we're only one day into the trip," he replied.

"It's still one of my favorites," she said.

149

"Why?"

She considered her answer and then smiled. "Because it's the first time we've really been alone overnight."

He pulled the covers up over his chest, his expression turning to alarm. "What do you plan to do to me?"

"To kiss you," she said. "A lot."

He laughed and lay down, his posture allowing him to meet her gaze. "I love you."

"I love you, too," she said.

She rolled out of view and stared at the ceiling. Now that she was in bed she was loath to let such a wonderful day end, so she asked Reed about Christmas. They'd agreed to buy a single gift for each other, but it had to cost less than $50. Her gift for him was tucked into the interior of her bag, while she hadn't seen any sign of his gift to her.

Reed talked about the few days where they'd spend Christmas with his family, of traditions he'd grown up with and loved, but he avoided talk of Christmas Eve, claiming there were a few surprises in store for that night. The train would be arriving Christmas Eve morning, so whatever he planned would be the first thing they would do.

As he talked she struggled to stifle her mounting desire. She lay so close to him it would be so easy to climb out and descend to his bunk, to hold his gaze as she began to remove her . . .

She swallowed and fought the impulse, afraid that he and his irritating walls would leave her hurt. Instead of acting out the image, she played it out in her mind before forcing herself to pay attention to Reed's words. Her responses gradually grew more muted as the rocking of the train lulled her to sleep. When it finally claimed her, she fell asleep with a smile.

Chapter 3

The second day passed in a blur of games, food, and laughter. Reed surprised her with some of her favorite treats, including Twizzlers, dried apricots, and Swedish Fish. She wished the ride could go on forever, but all too quickly sleep beckoned her and she relaxed to the sounds of the train clattering through crossings.

The next morning they packed their things. Snow had begun to fall overnight and she watched it blow about, disturbed by the train's passage. They ate a final meal in the dining car and then gathered their things. Before she knew it they were pulling into the final station.

"Don't look so sad," Reed said as they stepped off the train. "We still have the ride back, you know."

"I know," she said, her tone regretful.

He smiled and leaned down to kiss her. "I promise there are more trains in our future."

She perked up at that and they went outside the Chicago station, where they hailed a cab that took them to a car rental place. Snow continued to descend, adding to the growing drifts as they loaded into the car and headed south toward the cabin, following the directions on Kate's phone.

The roads were jammed with traffic and the drifting snow made it even slower. By the time they exited the city, there was an inch on the roads and slush ground under their wheels. Their conversation faded as Reed gripped the steering wheel tighter, controlling the frequent skidding. The wind picked up, driving the snow into a blizzard.

"At least we're used to driving in the snow," she said.

He smiled faintly but didn't respond, and she caught herself holding her breath. Several cars skidded, narrowly missing their bumper. She braced for an impact but it did not come, instead happening two cars away when someone went too fast and collided with the back of a truck.

Both jumped as the small accident happened just feet from them. "That's going to slow it down more," Reed said, craning to look. "But it looks like they're okay."

"We should get off the freeway," Kate said. "I'd hate to get stuck out here."

Reed nodded and turned off the freeway. They headed straight for the cabin, their car climbing through trees and hills outside the city until they reached their destination.

Two cars were already present and Reed eased his into the driveway. The wheels slid down the incline but Reed managed to bring it to a stop, avoiding striking his sister's car. He breathed a sigh of relief and cast Kate a smile.

"Well that was stressful."

"Thanks for getting us here safe," she said.

"I think my car would have quit on us," he said ruefully.

"I think it runs on loyalty," she agreed with a smile.

She stepped out and shivered in the blast of freezing wind. Her feet crunched in the fresh snow as she went to the trunk and gathered her suitcase. Then they picked their way up the path to the front door.

The trees were blanketed in white, and her footsteps crunched across the newly fallen snow. She paused on the doorstep and looked to the trees, spotting several other cabins visible by their porch lights. Although it was only mid afternoon, it felt like night, and she breathed in the cool air, grateful they'd made it safely.

The door swung open to reveal a woman dressed in jeans and a bright red sweater. She caught sight of Reed but brushed past him to engulf Kate, clenching her so tightly that she struggled to breathe.

"Mrs. Thompson," she said when she managed to extricate herself.

"Cindy, please," she said, turning to her son.

"I get the *second* hug?" Reed asked with a smile, leaning down to hug his mother.

"As long as you are dating Kate, you get the second hug," she replied with a warm laugh. "Come in, you must be cold." She ushered them inside and shut the door.

"The storm's getting pretty bad," he said, brushing snow off his shoulders.

"I'm glad you made it at all," she said. "The news says they're starting to close roads. We may be stuck here for a few days."

The entranceway lead into a large living room with a staircase to the second floor. The upper rooms looked down on the living room, which boasted enormous windows with a view of the slope. With no walls to block the space, the living room extended into a dining area and the breakfast bar at the edge of the kitchen.

A large fireplace sat on one side of the living room, a flat screen resting on the mantle. A Christmas tree stood in the corner with a small pile of presents beneath. The tree's lights twinkled and faded, the lights dancing off the windows and the snow beyond.

"Where's dad?" Reed asked, hanging his coat on the hook next to them.

"Not coming," she said with a dismissive wave. "He called this morning to say he has to work. Looks like it will just be us five."

"Five?" Kate asked. "Did Natalie bring someone?"

"Actually . . . I did," Cindy said, a slight blush lighting her skin.

153

At that moment a man poked his head into view from the kitchen. "I'm Joseph," he said. "Hope you don't mind me joining you."

At an inch taller than Cindy, Joseph was not overly tall. He had a bald head and a hairy chin, the color a deep red. He too was wearing jeans and a festive sweater, this time green, most of it hidden behind an apron that read, *Redheads Have the Most Fun.*

"I didn't know you were dating someone," Reed said, glancing between them.

"For a few months now," she said.

"It's good to finally meet you," Joseph said, shaking Reed's hand. "I've heard a lot about you." He leaned over and slapped Cindy on the rump before returning to the kitchen. "I'll have dinner ready soon."

Joseph glanced at Kate as he disappeared. He didn't speak to her, but something about his eyes set her on edge, and she took an immediate dislike. She tried to figure out what had sparked the animosity but could only assume it was his leer toward Cindy.

"He's cooking my dinner?" Reed asked, a touch of irritation in his voice.

"He's just trying to help," Cindy said.

"*Your* dinner?" Kate asked.

"After our divorce, Reed insisted on cooking Christmas dinner," Cindy said. "It's sweet, but Joseph is great in the kitchen too."

"Is that Reed I hear?"

A girl descended the stairs and smiled as she approached Reed. She looked exactly as she had in the picture. Her black hair lay straight down her back, while her blue eyes were a striking contrast that made her seem untouchable. She smiled and embraced her brother before retreating a step to regard Kate.

"You must be Kate," she said.

154

"Natalie," Reed said, leaning over to peer into the kitchen. "Be nice."

"I am being nice," Natalie said, and stepped in to give Kate a stiff hug. "It's good to have you here."

"I'm glad to be here," she said.

"He's going to burn the bacon," Reed said with a frown, and then glanced to Kate. "Why don't you find your room and I'll jump into the kitchen."

Kate would have preferred to stay with Reed but Natalie put her arm around her and guided her toward the stairs. "Let the boys cook. I'll show you to our room."

"*Our* room?" Kate asked.

"I know all about Reed's fear of intimacy," she said.

"It's not a fear!" Reed called, causing her to grin.

"My room has two queen beds," she said. "So we get to share. You don't mind, do you?"

Uncertain how to respond, Kate nodded and followed her to the second floor, which proved to contain a short hallway, a bathroom, and two bedrooms. She led Kate to the one attached to the bathroom and motioned to the other bedroom.

"Reed gets the kids room," she said, opening the door for her. "We get the big one."

Kate stepped inside and found the room spacious, with two large beds and a nightstand between them. Walls of stained wood gave the room a warm feel, while the two pictures of mountains added to the atmosphere.

Kate put her suitcase on the bed while Natalie flopped onto hers, watching as Kate unpacked. Kate glanced her way but she seemed content to wait until Kate had unloaded her things.

155

Ember's words came to mind and Kate realized that she was right. Cindy was distracted by Joseph. Her hug had been effusive and warm, indicating she'd already accepted Kate into the fold. After all their talks the last few months, Cindy's welcome was expected, but Natalie was a different beast altogether.

"Have you slept with Reed?"

Startled by the question, Kate set her bathroom bag down and met Natalie's gaze. "You want to know if I've had sex with your brother?"

"Reed isn't like most guys," Natalie said, coming to her feet and folding her arms. "And he deserves someone as good as he is."

"And I'm not?" Kate asked, her voice gaining an edge.

"I don't know," she said. "Reed's always been good at keeping the trash at a distance, and you're the first he's let in."

"Now I'm the trash?" Kate asked, her anger rising.

"We'll find out," Natalie said, and strode to the door.

Alone, Kate seethed in silence. Natalie's blunt questioning had made her feel even more unsettled and she ground her teeth together. It rankled that Natalie was taller, and just as intimidating as Baker. But Kate would not be cowed, and she slammed her bag down on the floor and stepped to the door. She clenched a fist and then released a breath before exiting and descending the stairs.

"You girls all settled?" Cindy asked from the couch.

"We're good," Natalie said with a smile.

Kate strode into the kitchen and wrapped an arm around Reed. Then she went up on her toes and kissed him in full view of Natalie. When Kate stepped back his expression was curious but she merely smiled sweetly and turned to Cindy.

"I'm good," she said.

156

Reed, his eyes on Kate, shook his head. "Looks like it's going to be an interesting Christmas . . ."

Chapter 4

Kate expected a traditional Christmas dinner, but Reed's meal turned out to be different. Waffles. Complete with several toppings, various juices to drink, and multiple sides, the dinner had been dubbed Death by Waffles, and it looked delicious.

"Why waffles?" she murmured to Cindy.

"He couldn't cook anything else," Natalie said, overhearing the comment as she added silverware to the large table. "But he refused to use a mix so he found a recipe and made it from scratch."

"You should have seen him in his little apron," Cindy said with a smile. "It was the first Christmas after my divorce, and because of him I didn't cry." Moisture dotted her eyes and Kate impulsively put her arm around her.

"He never ceases to amaze," Kate said.

Her eyes flicked to Natalie, all but daring her to respond, but her expression was inscrutable. Cindy put her arm around Kate's waist and lay her head on her shoulder. Reed chose that moment to enter the room wearing an apron several sizes too small for him. Kate burst into a laugh.

"Is that the same apron?" she asked.

"What if it is?" he asked.

"You really need to retire the apron," Natalie said critically. "It looks strange for a grown man to wear an apron with a choo-choo train."

"Did Michael Jordan retire his jersey?" he asked, indignant as he put the plate down.

"Actually he did," Joseph said, entering with a tray of bacon.

"Thanks, Joseph," Reed said sourly. "Your timing is not appreciated."

"Sorry," Joseph said. "We ready to eat? I'm *really* excited for these waffles."

"They're delicious," Cindy said, motioning him to the seat at the head of the table.

Joseph reached for the chair and then hesitated, his eyes flicking to Reed, who was conspicuously focused on the waffles. Then Joseph smiled and claimed the seat. As he settled into the chair he pointed to Reed.

"You don't mind sitting in another chair, do you?"

"Of course not," Reed said, taking the seat at the opposite end.

The sudden tension again set Kate on edge, but this time she noticed Natalie's expression. Her eyes were narrowed and she all but glared at Joseph. Reed showed no outward sign at Joseph taking what had likely been his chair since his parents' divorce, but his smile was not so easy.

From the tail end of the table, Reed looked to the group. His gaze swept across those present and he reached out for Kate's hand. She squeezed his fingers and tried to ignore Natalie's annoyed exhale.

"Our family has added a few new faces," he said. "But we're still family. Merry Christmas."

"Merry Christmas," they called, and raised their various glasses containing orange juice, eggnog, milk, or wine.

Kate took a waffle and poured on the hot raspberry sauce, and then topped it with freshly made whipped cream. She'd made it while he'd made the waffles, using the focus to distract her from the tension in the kitchen. Cindy alone seemed not to notice the simmering conflict, and only had eyes for Joseph. Then Kate took a bite and her worries evaporated.

"This is incredible," she breathed.

Reed smiled. "It wouldn't be Death by Waffles if it wasn't to die for."

She laughed and took another bite. The waffle was crunchy and light enough it could float off the plate, while the tartness of the raspberries balanced the sweet taste in the whipped cream. She savored the next bite, and then the next.

"Why didn't you tell me you could cook like this?"

"Because I can't," Reed said.

"He has a handful of exceptional meals," Natalie said in an aside, "beyond that . . .?" she smiled and added cinnamon buttermilk syrup as well as fresh strawberries.

Kate risked leaning over and asking, "What was the first year like?"

"Not this good," Natalie said, a small smile appearing on her face.

Grateful for the tenuous bridge, Kate withdrew and looked to Reed, who was offering her the bacon. Some was burned and she suspected Joseph had played a hand in that, but Reed didn't point a finger.

The dinner was delicious and full of tales from Natalie's and Reed's childhood. Both tried to stop Cindy, but she gushed about the mischief they'd gotten into as kids, the stories ranging from The Great Nesquik Caper to the Flour Party. Natalie made no reference to their tense conversation upstairs, but Kate caught her lingering looks and knew Natalie's feelings hadn't changed.

At Cindy's request, Joseph shared stories of his own family. He too was divorced, his two daughters also in college. He'd grown up in

160

Miami and joked about how much sunscreen he had to put on his bald head.

He drank frequently, and as the meal progressed his speech became louder, like a barking dog. He used his hands to gesture emphatically and several times showed a burst of anger. Kate was suddenly grateful she sat at the other end of the table with Reed.

"Where did you two meet?" Reed asked, his tone diplomatic.

"I was in Tallahassee for work," he said, "and stopped at a diner to eat. Then I saw her and knew we just had to meet." He smirked. "She had a body that—"

"He's a truck driver," Cindy said, flushing.

"I drive from Miami to Tallahassee and back," he said. "Been doing it for fifteen years now."

Kate noticed Reed changed the subject again and asked Natalie about her grades and classes. She was studying for her MCATs and would be taking them in the summer. Kate had no doubt she would nail them.

The snow continued to fall outside while the fireplace crackled in the hearth. Reed had dimmed the lights, adding a sense of warmth and comfort to the cabin that eased the sparks from the dinner. The Christmas tree illuminated the corner of the room, the lights twinkling off the windows. The shifting lights sparkled in Reed's eyes, his smile soft, as was his touch when their hands intertwined.

When the conversation and food had cooled, Joseph slapped his stomach. "I'm morally opposed to leaving good food on the table, but my belly has gone on strike. I'm sure you girls don't mind doing the cleanup."

Natalie bristled, but Kate nodded. "The boys cooked, so I'll do the dishes."

"I'll help," Reed said, rising to his feet.

161

"*I'll* help," Natalie said, pointing to the living room. "You can set up the movie."

Reed glanced to Kate but she managed a nod. "We'll be done soon enough."

"I guess I'm on the activity setup," Reed said.

"Joseph can help," Cindy said.

Reed's smile faded but he nodded. "Did you bring the boxes?"

"Why do we need boxes for a movie?" Kate asked.

"You'll find out soon enough," he said with a smile, leaning over to kiss her on the cheek. "And no peeking."

They cleaned up the table and then Kate claimed the sink. Natalie put food away while Kate began washing, and for several moments there were only the sounds of running water and Reed talking to Joseph. Cindy appeared and snagged a bottle of wine and two glasses from the fridge before disappearing back into the living room.

The dinner had been wonderful, but marred by Joseph's presence, and Kate wondered why she disliked him so much. There was just something about his eyes that seemed . . . dark. Still, she recognized the opportunity to talk to Natalie and cast about for a subject.

"Did Reed tell you what he had to do for my brothers to accept him?" Kate finally asked.

"No," Natalie said. "But I'm not surprised. Since he's been dating you, we haven't talked much."

Kate controlled her irritation by scrubbing the plate harder. "They took him to a parking lot outside a strip club, where they got into a knife fight."

Natalie stopped and stared at her. "Really?"

The shock on her face drew a smile from Kate's lips. "Really."

"Did he get hurt?" Natalie asked sharply.

The sudden fear on Natalie's face caused Kate's perspective to shift. Natalie was Reed's younger sister, but she'd protected him as much as he had protected her. She viewed Kate as a foreign influence, an incursion that needed to be repelled.

"Reed split his lip," she said, "but that was all."

"And your brothers?" she asked.

"My mom ripped them apart," she said, and then grinned. "After I did, of course."

Natalie gave a wry laugh and reached for another plate. "I never thought of Reed as a fighter."

Kate lowered her voice. "My brothers took Reed to see Tim."

She frowned, and then her features contorted with anger. "*Aura's* Tim?"

Kate nodded and told the whole story. Natalie's expression revealed a range of emotions from fear, worry, and finally amusement. By the time Kate was done, she was wiping out the sink and the dishes were done.

"Why'd you tell me all that?" Natalie asked.

Kate turned to face her as she dried her hands. "I've never had a sister. I just hope it doesn't require a knife fight to get one." She dropped the towel before walking into the living room. Natalie's comment made her turn.

"Just how serious is your relationship with Reed?"

For the first time she realized how she'd instinctively thought of herself as part of Reed's family, not as an appendage, not as a girlfriend, but as a full part of his family. She smiled, and repeated Natalie's own words back to her.

163

"I guess we'll find out," she said, and slipped away.

Chapter 5

Kate stepped into the living room to find it full of boxes and piles of tape. Confused, she threaded her way to Reed, who stood, beaming, where the couch had been. She gestured to the pile and shook her head.

"What's all this for?" she asked. "I thought we were going to watch a movie."

"We are," he said. "We're doing a drive-in movie tonight."

"Without cars?"

He grinned. "We have to make them," he said, pointing to the boxes.

Kate smiled as she realized his intent and accepted a pair of scissors. "I think my car will fit two."

"Then it had better have two builders," he said.

They set to work building a car, using long stretches of cardboard to craft the sides. With Christmas music playing in the background, Joseph jumped into the mix and insisted the holiday needed a truck. Kate expected Natalie to be too aloof to get into the piles of boxes but she waded in and began building a sleek sports car. Cindy remained on the couch with a glass of wine and waved at them to start without her.

Laughter and a crumbling car slowed the process, but an hour after dinner Kate and Reed stood before a wide jeep. Kate used markers to draw wheels on the side while Reed used tape to hold the boxes together.

"Good enough for an engineer?" Reed asked.

"No," she said. "But it will have to do."

"Who would trust a girl to be an engineer?" Joseph asked, squeezing into his big semi truck with an obnoxious laugh.

Cindy gave Kate an apologetic look. "I think you've had enough to drink, Joe."

"Don't tell me how much to drink," he said, and then winked to Reed. "We can drink us much as we like."

"I don't drink," Reed said flatly.

"Me either," Natalie said.

Joseph looked between them, blinking as if the surprise took time to register through his stupor. "Ya'll got problems," he said, laughing again.

Kate hid a smile as the portly man struggled to fit into his big rig that was not so big. Then Kate climbed into the jeep and sat on the couch pillow Reed had grabbed for her. As Natalie dimmed the lights, Cindy used the remote to turn on the TV. In all the haste of building, she'd completely forgotten they were watching a movie.

"What are we watching?" she asked.

"*October Sky*," Reed said.

"The movie about the rockets?" Kate asked in surprise. "On Christmas?"

"Reed got to choose the dinner when dad left. I get to choose the movie," Natalie said.

"You change the movie every time," Reed protested. "I keep the dinner the same."

"You can change the dinner if you want," Natalie said with a teasing smile.

166

"Please don't," Kate said in alarm.

"Have no fear," he murmured.

They settled in for the movie and she leaned against Reed, grateful that Joseph was momentarily quiet. The back of their jeep abutted the couch and they had a pile of pillows as seats. With her shoulder on his and his arm around her back, she found herself surprisingly comfortable, except for the fact that Joseph was a few feet away. Natalie, too, seemed more annoyed with Joseph than with Kate, and she'd placed her car next to Kate rather than stay by Joseph's truck. Still, Kate leaned back and enjoyed the strange choice for a Christmas movie.

She hadn't seen the movie in years and enjoyed it, even if it was an odd choice for the holiday. Although it was late she did not fall asleep, and enjoyed the warmth of Reed's chest, privately deciding she liked the cold because of how he looked in a sweater.

When the credits rolled she sat up and yawned, and found Cindy asleep. Joseph held a bottle of rum in his hand, sipping it like it was a soda. His face had gained a reddish hue. Kate gestured to the movie and praised the choice, but Natalie wiped at her eyes before standing and turning off the TV.

"It's always been my favorite," she said, and then noticed Cindy. She grinned and raised her voice. "Mom, time for bed."

"What?" she asked, and then noticed the dark TV. Releasing a wide yawn, she stood and nudged Joseph. "Ready to sleep?"

"I'm not going to sleep," he said, leering at her.

"Joe," she said, glancing to Reed and Natalie in embarrassment. "How much did you drink?"

He held up the nearly empty bottle. "Only one bottle," he said, laughing again. "Now let's get to bed, woman."

"I think that's enough," Reed said, rising to his feet.

167

"I got it, Reed," Cindy said. "Joe, you need to—"

Joseph grabbed her outstretched hand, and squeezed, causing Cindy to wince. When Joseph spoke his voice was hard. "I said don't tell me what to do."

"I'm sorry," Cindy said.

Kate was on her feet, the tension in the room sharp and bitter. She looked between Reed and Natalie, both of whom stood rigid. Cindy tried to laugh and pass off Joseph's actions as the drink, but the way she massaged her hand made it clear it had hurt.

"That's enough," Reed said quietly.

Joseph managed to get to his feet. "What are you going to do, *boy?*"

Joseph swayed on his feet but his hands were balled up, his shoulders bunched like he wanted to throw a punch. Reed stood his ground and Natalie drifted closer, her features set in a grim line, like a bouncer about to throw out a rowdy guest. Cindy's protestations went unheard.

"I think you should leave," Reed said. "Natalie, do you want to call him a cab?"

"Of course," she said. "But I'm not sure if they do garbage pickup this far out."

The tension in the room did not lend itself to amusement, but Natalie's comment drew a smile to Kate's lips. Joseph noticed her expression and sneered at her. He took a step in her direction.

"You find something funny, girl?"

"Joe," Cindy said, her voice stricken. She was also on her feet. "You need to sleep it off."

"Don't tell me what to do," he snapped, and swung his hand at Cindy.

Cindy flinched, leaning back to avoid the blow. Joseph's hand passed inches from her nose, the miss causing him to stumble. Reed caught his shoulder and "helped" him keep his feet, moving him away from his mother.

"When the cab arrives," Reed said, his voice harder than Kate had ever heard. "I suggest you do not come back."

Joseph began to laugh, the sound filled with amusement and scorn. "And who's going to stop me? You? You don't have the stones. I have half a mind to teach your little hottie what a real man is like."

He reached around Reed . . . and slapped Kate's butt.

Everyone froze, the shock of the assault too much to absorb. But Kate was already in motion. She caught Joseph's hand and yanked. His leer turned to surprise as he was pulled off balance. Kate twisted his arm, using a grip Baker had taught to force Joseph's hand up his spine.

He cried out in pain, the sound cutting off as Kate slammed him into the wall. His alcohol induced brain registered what Kate was doing and he struggled, but she twisted his hand further, stretching the tendons to the breaking point.

"Touch me again and I'll break your arm," she said coldly.

"I don't think he meant to do that," Cindy was saying, but Reed shot her a look, and she fell silent.

Joseph snarled. *"You think you can talk to me like that you—"*

He tried to swing his free arm at her but she swatted it aside and put her arm against the back of his neck. She used both grips to pull him back and smash him into the wall again. Then she leaned in.

"Touch *Cindy* again, and I'll break the stones you seem to be so proud of."

He tried to speak but she clenched her hand, causing him to wince again. The pain seemed to finally breach the drunken stupor and he

169

began to whimper, tears forming in his eyes. She relinquished her grip and pushed him toward the kitchen table, where he righted himself and turned. He tried to look tall but he was rubbing his arm.

"What's the matter with you?" he demanded. "I was just playing around."

"No you weren't," Reed said, and stabbed a finger to the door. "And I think you should wait outside."

Joseph licked his lips, but his sneer was too filled with fear to be condescending. He shifted his feet, his eyes flicking between Reed and Kate, who stood shoulder to shoulder. Kate privately realized she stood at eye level to Joseph, and he was the one to cower.

"Cindy," he said, turning to her. "You're really going to let them throw me out?"

She glanced between Kate, Reed, and Natalie, who nodded emphatically. Then she straightened and nodded.

"Yes, I am."

Joseph scowled, his anger returning. "You won't get lucky a second time," he said to Kate.

Reed burst into a laugh, the mocking sound causing Joseph to flush. "She was trained by a *Marine*," he said. "*You* won't be lucky a second time."

Joseph sneered and his eyes flicked to Kate, who offered a broad smile. She hadn't sparred with her brothers in years, but the moment his hand had touched her, she'd reacted. Tense and ready, she would put him down if he tried to retaliate. But fear gradually replaced the arrogance and he spun about.

Stomping to his room, he returned a moment later with his bag. He threw a final curse at Cindy and then left, slamming the door as he departed. Natalie stepped to the door and locked it, sealing Joseph

170

outside. Silence persisted for several moments and Cindy refused to look at anyone. Then Natalie turned and motioned to the kitchen.

"Now that the Grinch is gone, who wants pie?"

Her question drew a round of laughter, even from the distraught Cindy. Natalie served the pie, placing a generous portion on Kate's plate. Their eyes met. Natalie offered a nod of respect, which Kate returned.

"No blood needed," Natalie said.

"Except from Joseph," Kate said.

Natalie laughed and set the plate down. A moment later she added a cup of milk, and Kate recognized the offerings for what they were.

An apology.

Chapter 6

In the wake of Joseph's departure the atmosphere of the cabin lightened considerably. Christmas music was played and they decided a second movie was in order. Kate half expected Joseph to attempt a return, but the faint honk of a cab was the only sound to indicate his departure.

Reed turned to Cindy. "Mom? You okay?"

Cindy stared out the window, the glass of eggnog forgotten in her hand. "He was nice, in the beginning."

"They all are," Natalie said.

"That's the truth," Kate said.

Cindy smiled sadly and patted Reed on the knee. "I just wish I didn't need my children to protect me." Her eyes settled on Kate. "Or my son's girlfriend."

"We've all been treated that way," Kate said. "Doesn't mean we have to take it."

Cindy's tone became one of admiration. "Wherever did you learn to do that?" she motioned to where Kate had subdued Joseph.

"My dad and brothers are military," Kate admitted. "I knew how to defend myself in the second grade."

"Second graders," Natalie lamented. "They always try to steal your milk."

Reed grunted. "You should see her brothers."

Kate leaned over and kissed him on the cheek. "They like you now."

"I hope so!" Reed said with a laugh.

Cindy joined in the amusement and then collected the blanket. "I think I'm going to bed," she said.

They tried to console her but she insisted, and embraced each of them, Kate most of all. Kate had thought she would be angrier, but instead there were tears in her eyes when they parted. Cindy smiled and nodded before retreating to her room.

"I'm going to bed too," Natalie said with a yawn "Since you cooked dinner, I'll handle breakfast."

"Cold cereal?" Reed asked.

"You know it," Natalie said.

Reed looked to Kate. "Care to step outside for a moment?"

Kate looked to the window to find the wind had died but it was still snowing, the flakes drifting past the window in sparkles of white. She reached for the blanket and wrapped it around her shoulders.

"Sure."

Natalie stepped in and hugged Reed. "See you in the morning." Then she stepped through the cardboard cars and disappeared into the kitchen.

Reed opened the door and they stepped onto the back porch. The cabin was high on the slope, providing a view of the snow blanketing the trees and lower cabins. She shivered and leaned against Reed.

"Thanks for what you did," Reed said.

"You would have done it," she said. "I just beat you to it."

173

He chuckled, the sound muffled by the snow. "I'm afraid if I'd tried what you did, it would have been much messier."

"I'll have to teach you," she said, and then smiled. "Just remember that in sparring, someone usually ends up on their back."

"I look forward to it," he said. Then his voice hardened. "I still can't believe he did that to you."

"It's happened before," Kate said, staring into the snowstorm and seeing the few guys that had thought it was okay to touch. "I'm just glad your mom isn't mad at me."

He sighed and looked out over the snow. "Unfortunately, she's had too much experience with guys like that."

They sat quietly, and Kate pondered what he meant. Reed rarely spoke of his parents' divorce, but when he did, he made it clear that he did not care for his father. She wondered if there had been more than drinking that had torn them apart.

Abruptly he laughed. "Two visits with family, both ending in a fight. I hope this isn't starting a trend."

"Me too," she replied, and then motioned to the vista. "Joseph aside, this is beautiful."

"I hope it keeps snowing," he said. "I would love for it to snow on Christmas Day."

"I like your family," she said.

"What about Natalie?" he asked, glancing her way. "Are you two okay?"

Kate looked back through the window and spotted Natalie in the kitchen getting a glass of water. Their eyes met. Instead of animosity, there was a slight smile on her face before she turned away. Kate doubted Natalie had fully embraced her, but a softening was enough for now.

"I think we will be," she said, turning back. "But with everything tonight, I'm glad your dad didn't come."

"I wanted you to meet him," Reed said softly. "But he never comes."

"But I thought you said he was coming . . .,"

"He promised," Reed said. "And I actually thought he would show up this time because of you."

"I'm sorry," Kate said.

"Me too," Reed said. "But if he won't come to meet you, then he doesn't deserve to know you."

"You still have me," she said, nudging him with her shoulder.

He smiled and met her gaze. "What did I do to deserve you?"

"Nothing," she said, her smile mischievous. "I'm the one who won the challenge."

He laughed lightly, the sound muffled by the falling snow. "How can I ever be sad when I have you at my side?"

She leaned closer to him and put her head on his shoulder. "You make me happy too, you know."

He reached around her back and pulled her into a kiss. With snow falling into her hair and swirling around her, the wind seemed to hold its breath at the magic of the moment, dispelling the vestiges of animosity Joseph had left behind. Then someone turned up the music, causing her to look at the window. Natalie pointed to the iPod connected to the speaker and smiled as if to say, *have fun*. Then she set it down and turned off the lights before ascending the steps to their room.

"I think Natalie likes you," Reed murmured.

"I hope so," she said. "Because she wasn't very nice earlier."

"What did she say?" Reed asked, leaning back and looking into her eyes.

"She asked if we'd slept together."

Reed snorted. "Why?"

"She doesn't want me to corrupt you."

Reed laughed and shook his head. "Sometimes my sister can be overprotective—a trait you two seem to share."

"Perhaps," Kate said ruefully.

He regarded her for a moment but didn't press the issue. "Can I give you your gift early?"

"Christmas isn't until tomorrow."

"True," he said, "but I think I want to give it to you now."

She considered refusing, but with the soft light glittering off his jacket he seemed to glow, and she couldn't resist his soft smile.

"Okay," she said.

Instead of going inside he reached into his pocket and directed her to close her eyes. When she had, he said, "I knew when I saw this that it belonged on your neck, so I borrowed some money from my mom to buy it."

"Just how much did it cost you?" she asked.

"More than I could afford," he said. "It's actually part of the reason our marathon date was so cheap."

"You bought it in October?" she asked, and her breath caught when she heard a jewelry box snap shut. Then he reached up and his hands wrapped around her neck, his fingers brushing her skin and sending a shiver into her flesh. He worked the clasp and then withdrew, allowing the cold chain to fall down her throat.

176

"Open," he said softly.

She opened her eyes and looked down, and found herself staring at a large emerald bracketed by a trio of small diamonds. Silver curved around the gemstones into a heart, with the teardrop green at the center.

"It's beautiful," she breathed.

"Last February you opened the door and I saw your eyes for the first time," he murmured. "It changed me. I didn't recognize it at the time, but now I know. The way you look at me makes me feel wanted. You made me feel whole."

"All that with my eyes?" she asked, stunned by the gift and his words.

"It's true," he said with a smile. "And your beauty—inside and out—is incredible. Merry Christmas, Kate."

Her heart burned in her chest and she clung to the moment, to the cold, to the thrill, to the proximity to the man she loved. Deep down she sensed the inexorable pull of the clock, that just weeks away from now they would be parting. But for now they were together, and even time would have to wait.

Volume 24: The Memory Lane Date

Chapter 1

Reed sank into his chair and stared at the last remaining object on the wall. The calendar. For four years it had marked his life, catalogued every date with hundreds of girls until Kate's sudden arrival last February. It depicted the gradual decline of other dates until only the dating challenge remained. Until only Kate remained.

His possessions were largely packed. Stacked against the walls were boxes containing clothes, books, and other school supplies. The pile represented the sum of his college life yet was smaller than he expected.

He looked around the room, at the desk where he'd done his homework, his bed where he'd crashed after late night cram sessions, and the floor where he'd paced, first to figure out what to do with Kate, and now as he agonized over how to leave.

Jackson appeared in the doorway as he always had. It was dinner time but his bowl of cereal was absent, his hand stuffed into his pockets instead. Bereft of his evening ritual, he seemed forlorn, prompting Reed to stand and gesture to the room.

"Tanner will be a good roommate," Reed said, "and because he's dating Ember, you'll get to see the blondes."

"I know," Jackson said.

"And I'll be back for your wedding."

"I know."

"And I'll eat a bowl of cereal for dinner once a week, just for you."

Jackson finally cracked a smile. "Promise?"

"Promise."

Jackson nodded but his smile faded. "It never feels like it's going to end."

"Just because I'm moving away doesn't mean our friendship has ended."

"It better not," he said.

It was said with a joking smile but Reed heard the worry in his voice. Jackson had never been good at expressing real emotions, but they had been roommates for years, and Reed saw the concern in his eyes.

"You know, I never had a brother," Reed said.

Jackson finally smiled for real. "You do now."

Reed closed the gap and embraced his friend. Four years of friendship, of brotherhood, a lasting impact. Reed retreated before tears would betray him and Jackson slapped him on the shoulder, coughing as he pointed to the boxes.

"I'll ship them to you once you have an address."

"When does Tanner move in?" Reed asked.

"Sunday," Jackson said. "You all packed for your flight?"

Reed motioned to the luggage next to the empty closet. Part of his contract included an apartment the institute provided, one that he would share with three other interns. He'd gotten a friend request from one of them but hadn't had a chance to reach out. He doubted any could reach the bar Jackson had set.

"Are you ready for your cushy internship?" Jackson asked.

"It's not cushy," Reed protested.

"They're putting you up in a place in Manhattan," he said. "That's cushy."

"When you put it that way," he said with a smile.

In reality it was cushy. The institute accepted only the best applicants and sought to demonstrate the superiority of their program at every turn. Many interns later returned to work at the institute, including Dr. Dickson, who'd been an intern before getting his doctorate.

"Are you sure you're doing the long-distance thing?" he asked.

"It's the best we can do," Reed said. "It's too late to apply to anything else, and I can't take a year off."

"A gap year doesn't look well on scholarships," Jackson said with a nod.

"So this is my best and only shot," he said. He checked his phone and reached for his shoes. "Kate will be here soon. Do you know what she has planned?"

"Of course," Jackson said with a smirk. "It's kind of your last date."

They were walking into the living room but Reed came to a halt. In all the planning of their departure he hadn't thought about what a long distance relationship would mean for the dating challenge. His flight was just ten days away, meaning today marked the final date of the challenge.

He sighed and sank onto the couch, the shoes in his hand forgotten. "Am I making the right choice?" he asked.

"I don't really see another option for you," Jackson said. He disappeared into the kitchen and returned with a bowl of cereal. "But it doesn't make it suck any less."

"You think we can survive a long-distance relationship?"

"You love her, don't you?"

"You know I do."

"Then you'll be fine," Jackson said, taking a bite and munching blissfully. "She loves you too," he said, his words distorted by Captain Crunch.

"I guess," he said, "But I feel like I'm tearing in half."

"Me too," Jackson lamented. "I mean, Tanner is fine, but he doesn't even play basketball—or snowboard."

"Then you get to teach him," Reed pointed out.

"A protégé?" Jackson grinned. "I like the sound of that."

Reed laughed at the mental image of Jackson teaching Tanner how to be a good roommate. Tanner was a sophomore, but in many ways he was more mature than Jackson. Reed hoped they would be able to learn from each other.

"You sure you don't mind me crashing on your couch after he moves in?" Reed asked.

Jackson threw him a look like he was stupid. "Do you need to ask?"

Reed thanked him just as the doorbell rang. Hurriedly lacing his shoes, he stood and swung the door open to reveal Kate bundled up in a thick coat. A blast of frigid air ushered her in and she shivered.

"I love Boulder but the winters are brutal," she said, leaning up to kiss him.

"That's one thing I won't miss," he said.

"Yes you will," Kate said. "And today will remind you of that."

"Oh?" he asked. "A clue as to what we're doing?"

"The only one you're going to get," she said. "Are you ready?"

182

"All packed up," he said, pointing to his room. Through the open door the bare desk and walls were visible.

"Then let's go," she said. "We have a lot to do today."

He grabbed his coat and pulled on a beanie before stepping outside. The heat in the car had already perished and had to be revived. Fortunately the engine was still warm and it didn't take long for heat to fill the interior of the car.

"Are you going to explain why it's a morning date?" he asked, and gestured to the clock on the dash. "It's only eight."

She dodged the question. "Did you eat?"

"You said to come hungry," he said. "I must admit you've piqued my curiosity. You've been very specific about this date, even telling me what to wear." He gestured to his pants.

"We've got a busy day," she said, "and it's going to be long. I didn't want you getting cold."

He smiled and reached out to take her hand. "How thoughtful."

They drove toward campus and climbed a hill, the tires slipping on the snow. The last few days had seen an enormous snowfall and the plows were still trying to clear the roads. Today would have been perfect to go snowboarding but his gear was already packed and stored in Jackson's room. He also wouldn't miss this date for anything, even fresh powder.

"Jackson made me realize this is the last date of our challenge," he said.

"We can do long-distance dates," she said.

"We should," he replied. "But I don't think it will be the same if I can't kiss you at the end."

She laughed lightly. "It took you six months to kiss me, and now you can't go a day without?"

183

"What can I say? I'm addicted."

She smiled. "You aren't the only one. But I thought we weren't going to talk about you leaving."

"Sorry," he said. "Jackson got all sad on me this morning like he was saying goodbye."

"You don't leave for ten days," she said.

"I know," he replied. "But Jackson is really feeling it." Reed didn't add how much he was feeling the impending departure.

"Guys," she said with a snort. "They hoard their emotions like a pirate."

Reed raised an approving eyebrow. "That was very insightful," he said.

"Perhaps for an engineer," she finished. "But no more talk of you leaving."

He heard the tremor in her voice and realized she didn't want her emotions to surface, not now, not yet. No comfort could be offered so he nodded and squeezed her hand, drawing her gaze to him.

"No more today," he agreed.

"Good," she said. "Because it's time for a trip down memory lane. And we're at our first stop."

They pulled into the parking lot and came to a stop near the entrance of a building. He smiled as he got out and lifted his gaze to the distinct dome-topped structure. Kate had brought him to the observatory, the location of their first date.

Chapter 2

"It's not quite as warm as I remember," he said as she parked near the front door.

"Last winter was lighter," she said. "And we did go downhill boating."

He smiled at the memory. "It was certainly a fun first date."

"I don't have the key you did," she said, "but I do have raspberry and white chocolate hot chocolate. There's also some breakfast supplies to go with it."

She pulled out a thermos and two cups. As they sipped the steaming liquid they talked about the first date, with each sharing insights that they'd previously not spoken of. Then Kate mentioned the moment where she'd leaned in for a kiss.

"I'd forgotten about that," Reed said.

"You almost kissed me," she said. "I saw it in your eyes."

"I wanted to," Reed recalled. "But my habits were too strong."

"I had to wear down your walls," she said. "Before we leave, care to try again? We're parked in the same spot."

"Really?" he looked around and realized it was true. "Then by all means. Let's finish what we didn't get to do then."

They braved the frigid temperatures and she stood by the passenger door, tilting her head upward, her smile turning coy. He grinned and leaned in, kissing her soundly, the heat from the contact spreading through his body like the hot chocolate. When they parted her smile was smug.

"Worth the wait."

He laughed and they got back into the car. Then she backed out and headed to their next stop, the park where they'd had the color war. Covered in snow and ice, with trees bereft of leaves, the park looked very little like he remembered. But he remembered how she looked covered in paint.

"My car still has a spot of paint on the seat," he said.

"You didn't clean it off?"

"It reminds me of our early dating," he replied. "And I can't bring myself to clean it."

They got out and stood where the fire truck had hosed them off, pushing through the snow to get there. Shivering and laughing, they climbed back into the car and she backed out, already headed to the next location.

"We aren't doing them in order?"

"Not enough time," she said. "They're all over the place."

"Are we going to hit the Denver ones?" he asked.

"Some stops are meant to represent the distant locations, but we do have one stop further out that I couldn't resist."

"Are you trying to make me remember how much I love you before I go?"

Her smile turned mischievous. "Yes."

"It's working," he said, taking her hand. "But I find myself wondering why it took six months for us to get together. I *really* liked you."

186

"I'm glad we waited," she said.

That caught him by surprise. "Why?"

"We both had some things hanging over us," she said. "Dating the way we did gave us a chance to work through them and choose to be together without doubts."

"So you're saying you chose me?"

"I did," she said, her lips twitching with amusement. "But you didn't give me much choice. Every date just made me fall for you a little more."

"Then I'll just have to keep dating you," he said.

From stop to stop they worked their way around town, visiting every place of the challenge. For those that were too far away, she'd chosen clever replacements. They stopped at a large swing in a children's park and took pictures with both attempting to swing. Shortly after they stopped at the park where he'd broken her heart on July 4th. They shared a kiss on the spot where he'd refused to kiss her last time, repairing the event in their memories. Reed stood in the snow in the empty field, grateful that the moment had not broken them for good.

She kept checking the time and frequently spoke of them being late, but they were burning through the locations at such a pace he guessed they'd be done by lunch. What did she have planned for the afternoon?

He asked, but she refused his invitation with a cryptic, "Something old, something new."

"Isn't that what you give a bride?"

"Yes," she said, a touch of pink appearing in her cheeks. "But it's true."

He wondered at her response as they worked through the list until only one remained—the date his car had broken down. Instead of stopping at any location, she drove them out of town on the same road, headed west.

"Are we really going to kiss in the same spot where my car broke down?" he asked. "It's way outside of town."

"True," she said. "But we've made up some time so we should be okay."

"I love the dates you plan," he said. "I never know what's happening but I've come to trust that whatever it's going to be, it will be stunning."

"You really have such faith in me?"

"How could I not?" he asked. "Just look at what you've done today."

She smiled as they came down the hill where his car had died and pulled onto the thin space between the road and the snow. He looked out over the white landscape and imagined the rainy day when she'd given him an ultimatum.

"You threw down quite a gauntlet that day," he said.

"That's not exactly how I remember it." She parked the car and looked to him, her eyes sparkling.

"That's what you said," he accused. "And as I recall, I did provide lunch."

"You did," she said. "But I suspect mine will be better."

She started the car and advanced a short distance to the nearest driveway. Then she turned in and headed for the house. He raised an eyebrow but she merely smiled. Large and boasting a wraparound porch, the house belonged to Harold and Pepper, the couple that had helped them when they'd been stranded.

"Is this a surprise visit?" he asked.

"If it was, Pepper wouldn't have made hot bread," she said, her eyes bright with anticipation.

"They know we're coming?" he asked, raising an eyebrow.

"I didn't have their phone number so I came out here a few days ago to ask if we could stop in. Pepper was very kind, and promised to provide lunch of hot bread, just like last time. She also insisted on adding to the meal."

They got out and walked to the door, and Pepper opened on the second knock. The short, white haired woman regarded them with a knowing smile, and then motioned them inside with a flourish.

"Took you long enough to get here."

"Sorry, Pepper," Kate said, stepping in to hug her. "We took a little longer at our stops."

"Harold!" she roared. "Lunch is ready!"

"Yes dear," came from the living room.

Kate and Reed divested themselves of their coats and then settled in at the table, which had much more than just bread. Homemade soup sat next to a salad and a bowl of fruit. She filled glasses with milk as Harold lumbered into the dining area and took a seat.

"Thank you for letting us visit," Reed said.

"Nonsense," Pepper said. "You're welcome anytime."

"You overpaid for the bread," Harold said.

Reed threw him a sharp look. On the last visit Harold had replaced Reed's fuel pump but Pepper had refused payment. So Reed had sent money with a note saying it was for the bread. Harold's lips twitched beneath his red beard, causing Reed to level a finger at him.

"You have a sense of humor," Reed accused.

189

"No one said that," he rumbled.

Reed and Kate exchanged a look and then laughed. Pepper returned with a loaf of hot bread and deftly sliced it for each of them. Before they ate, Harold rumbled a prayer and they all dug in. The food was delicious and hot, a perfect break from the freezing visits of the morning. Harold didn't talk much, but when he did his sense of humor came through in a dry wit. Pepper admitted she'd been following them on Ember's blog and knew all about the dating challenge. When she disappeared into the kitchen for more jam Harold leaned in.

"I don't appreciate the example," he said.

Reed couldn't tell if he was serious. "Why?"

"Because now she wants a *real* date," Harold said. Then his lips twitched beneath his beard. "She wants me to work for it."

The dismay in his voice left Reed laughing into his soup, nearly spilling it on the table. Kate too struggled to keep her amusement in check but Harold remained stoic. Only his twitching beard and the sparkle in his eyes indicated amusement.

The warm meal ended with large slices of brownie and fudge, leaving Reed stuffed to the gills. Reed and Kate insisted on helping with the dishes and gave Pepper hugs before they left, calling out a farewell to Harold, who'd already retired to the living room.

"Until next time," Pepper said.

"When's next time?" Reed asked, glancing to Kate.

"Oh, honey," Pepper said. "You've been adopted now. It's too late to escape." Laughing to herself, she shut the door, leaving them on the porch.

Chapter 3

When they were out of earshot Reed gestured to the house. "It appears I have new grandparents."

"They're sweet," Kate said. "When I talked to them last week I learned their kids don't visit often. They live several states away, so work keeps them from traveling."

"You've reminded me of my family and friends," he said wryly. "If you wanted to make me regret my departure, you've certainly succeeded."

"Oh, but I'm not finished," she said. "There's one more thing left to do."

"And what's that?"

"You should never have given me a taste for surprise," Kate responded with a smile. "Now I crave it."

They braved the blast of wind to reach her car. Once back on the road, she turned west, heading away from Boulder. Reed cocked his head in surprise and glanced to Kate, but she sat content, a small smile on her face. They'd never traveled so far west on a date, so whatever they were doing was not reminiscent of a shared event—it would be something new.

"Have you figured it out yet?" she asked.

"No," he admitted.

Clearly pleased she'd managed to leave him puzzled, she drove them west and south before pulling into a market in a small town.

Instead of parking close to the building, she parked at the back, were two other vehicles waited, Ember's jeep and Jackson's truck.

"What are they doing here?" he asked.

"They're coming with us," she replied.

Upon seeing their arrival, the blondes, Jackson, and Shelby all exited their cars. As they approached, Reed noticed they were wearing heavy winter gear, and he recognized Jackson's favorite beanie, a bright blue batman hat that looked like a comical version of the Dark Knight when pulled down over the eyes. He only used the hat for one thing.

Snowboarding.

Reed began to laugh. "Please tell me we're doing what I think we're doing."

"Eldora Ski Resort," Jackson confirmed, hitting him on the shoulder. "And Kate let us come along."

"My board?" Reed asked.

"In the back," Shelby said. "We loaded it up after you left this morning."

Reed turned and snaked his arms around Kate, whose expression was positively devilish. "I can't believe you're doing this to me," he said.

"Taking you snowboarding?" she asked sweetly. "Can't a girl let her boyfriend do something that he loves?"

Ember sniffed. "You'd think he would say thank you."

Reed's gaze swept the group and he nodded. "Thank you," he said.

Emotion clogged his throat as he looked to his friends. Brittney and Marta were both smiling, while Ember seemed a trifle annoyed. Jackson and Shelby stood together, her diamond ring reflecting the light.

They were his friends, his companions, his family for the last year. A glance at Kate revealed her true intention. Showing him places had been merely a teaser of what he would truly miss. Those who stood around him were the real loss.

He would be gone a year, and in that time Marta was set to graduate, as were Jackson and Shelby. By the end of the year most, if not all, could be gone. With the cold certainty of autumn's end, he sensed today would be the last time they would be able to spend time together. And this was the gift Kate had given on their final date.

"Thank you," he repeated, his voice tight with regret.

"Now don't start that," Marta said, wiping at her eyes. "You'll ruin the moment."

Ember blew out her breath. "Are we going or what?" she asked. "I want to get to the slopes before the snow melts."

"I'll miss you too, Ember."

Ember scowled at him but moisture gathered in her eyes. Then abruptly she whirled and climbed into the driver's seat, the closing of her door echoing with a note of sadness. Jackson shook his head.

"You really know how to bring the sadness," he said.

Jackson's dry humor brought smiles to them all. Reed and Kate took the back seat of the jeep while Marta rode with Jackson and Shelby. Brittney claimed the passenger side of the jeep and they pulled out of the driveway.

Leaving Kate's car behind, they climbed into the mountains, the jeep and truck struggling despite the four-wheel drive. It had snowed the last two days but it had cleared that morning, and Reed felt a familiar thrill, anticipating hitting the fresh snow on his board.

As they ascended into the mountains they talked snowboarding. Marta was a skier, while Ember and Brittney had never been. Kate, too,

193

would be new to the slopes, a fact Reed had known but, oddly, he had never thought to take her up the mountain.

"I figured you wouldn't mind being my instructor," she said.

"You really never learned?" Reed asked.

"A friend tried to teach me once," Kate said, "which translates to following me down the hill once before ditching me to hang out with his other friends. I retreated to the lodge and questioned my choice in friends."

"I'd be happy to teach you," Reed said.

"I'm excited to learn," Brittney said. "I've wanted to go for a while because I'd heard it was like skateboarding."

"You skateboard?" Ember asked in surprise, swiveling to glance at Brittney.

Brittney allowed a small smile. "All the way through junior high. Then I broke my arm on a trick and my parents forbade me from ever skateboarding again."

"How did we not know this?" Kate asked.

"It never came up," Brittney said with a shrug. "I wasn't really into traditional sports—the nontraditional ones were more my style."

"Is there a picture of you in skater clothes?" Reed asked.

"Not one I'd show you," she said with a laugh.

"If I'd known you were a skater I would have set you up with a friend," Reed said. "He was a lot like you. He grew up skateboarding until he snapped his wrist for the fourth time. Then he took up snowboarding."

"Is he cute?" Brittney asked.

"I'm not the best judge of that, but I think so," Reed said. "And he loves cooking."

"How do you know him?" Kate asked.

"Caleb is a friend in my program," Reed said. "We've had a lot of classes together and he's a good guy."

Brittney's smile was radiant. "I'd like to meet him."

"And he's still single?" Ember asked.

Reed smiled. "He liked my creative dating and started his own trend."

"Oh?" Brittney's eyes sparkled with interest and she glanced at Ember.

"If he's so available, why didn't you mention him before?" Ember asked.

"He was dating someone until November," Reed said, raising a hand to placate her. "But he's single now."

"Set me up," Brittney said.

Ember cursed as the jeep slid, causing Reed's gut to clench. But Ember masterfully steered through the slick snow and ice to keep them on the road. Kate and Brittney laughed nervously at the near hit on the guardrail, and the topic shifted. After several minutes Kate leaned over and lowered her voice.

"You just made her day." She motioned to Brittney.

"She deserves it," Reed whispered back.

"She's the best of us," Kate said.

Reed recalled the many times Brittney had selflessly helped her friends, including Reed. She'd cooked and prepared decorations for invites and dates, and helped Ember and Marta whenever they needed

195

assistance with homework. He couldn't recall her ever complaining or even being upset as she quietly took care of her friends.

Reed realized how often he'd taken Brittney for granted and determined he would set Caleb up with her. He sensed a good match in the making and hoped it would work out for the two of them, if only to see Brittney happy.

The jeep topped the last curve and descended into the parking lot. Eldora was not a widely known ski resort but it was popular with Boulderites and locals. It also happened to be the first place Reed had snowboarded, and his favorite.

They piled out of the two vehicles and layered up. The weather was in the high twenties with a touch of wind, perfect for hitting the slopes. Jackson, Shelby, and Marta were quick to say goodbye after they made plans to eat dinner in the lodge. Much to Ember's delight, Tanner was waiting for them inside.

"When did you get here?" Ember asked, leaning up to kiss him.

"Jackson invited me," he said. "I hope you don't mind." His eyes flicked to Kate and Reed.

"Not at all," they said in unison, and then shared a grin.

Reed picked up lift tickets while Tanner and the girls rented boards, and shortly after they were riding the Little Hawk Lift to the beginner area. Sitting with Kate, Reed smiled to her and described how to get off the lift on a snowboard. When he was finished he pointed to the rapidly approaching exit.

"Are you ready?" he asked.

"I think so," she said, her voice nervous. She braced herself and stood when they reached the end.

And fell on her face.

Chapter 4

She hit the ground and flipped awkwardly over her board. Snow went flying and she skidded to a halt, a laugh bursting from her lips. She'd lost her hat and goggles from the impact and Reed smoothly glided to a stop at her side.

"You okay?"

"Is it always that hard to get off the lift?"

"On a board?" he asked. "Yes."

The two skiers from the chair stood and glided by and Kate's expression turned envious. "Sure we can't ski?"

"Trust me," Reed said, helping her to her feet. "You'll see in a few hours."

"So what happens for the next few hours?"

"You fall a lot," he admitted, and then smiled. "But I'll be with you every step of the way.

Tanner and Ember came off next and she skidded for ten feet before both disappeared into a snowdrift. Reed and Kate laughed as Tanner sought to dislodge her. Ember's face was so red he wondered if the snow would just melt.

Alone, Brittney's chair came next and she kept her legs bent, her arms out. She glided straight until friction gradually brought her to a stop, still on her feet. She cried out in excitement and raised her hands in victory, and promptly fell on her back.

Reed hopped over to her and helped her up. "You did good," he said.

"That was *awesome*!" she replied.

"You haven't even boarded yet."

"Then let's go!"

Reed grinned at her enthusiasm. Then he slid back to Kate and knelt to buckle her second boot. As he prepped the girls for the descent, he described how to stand and slide the board to learn how to balance. Twenty feet away, Tanner and Ember scooted closer to listen.

Reed stood and demonstrated what to do and then sat, allowing Kate and Brittney a chance to try. Kate managed to get to her feet and glided a short distance before falling on her butt. Brittney struggled to rise and failed, repeatedly.

For the next hour Reed shifted between his students. Tanner and Ember gradually drifted away and Reed didn't want Brittney to feel alone, so he made an effort to help her. At first Kate excelled, standing up and gliding further each time. Then Brittney figured out how to get on her feet and soared down the mountain.

"I did it!" she cried.

Sitting next to Kate, Reed shouted to her and then looked to Kate. "See?"

"Is it bad that I'm jealous?"

"It's hard for everyone the first day," Reed replied.

Brittney took to the board like she was born to it, and within another hour was carving her way down the slope, shouting for joy. Kate was obviously frustrated, but soon after it clicked for her, and she boarded across the breadth of the slope without falling. Reed shouted and rushed to catch up, braking to a stop at her side. In his haste he landed on his back.

198

"How was it?"

"*Awesome*," she breathed.

"Ready for more?"

"Yes!"

She lifted herself up with practiced ease and went again, going even further. As Reed followed Kate through her stumbles and triumphs he discovered a profound sense of closeness. She'd trusted him to be her teacher, and done so without reservation. Although he'd taught dozens of others how to snowboard, he'd never felt such a desire for one to succeed. Each new success by Kate felt like he was part of the victory. They fell together. And they rose together.

It was as if their lives had intertwined, like their relationship had moved past the point of being separate individuals and they'd become parts of a single whole. He'd never felt closer to anyone, and wondered if it was merely a fleeting moment, or a lasting mark.

As darkness began to fall they moved off the bunny slopes and tried a steeper hill, and Reed followed her as she carved her way back and forth. He marveled at how her accomplishment could feel like his own.

She whooped as she soared around a curve and squeaked when a bump nearly sent her tumbling. When she righted herself Reed's heart soared like it was him on his first day. He boarded up close to her and braked so he wouldn't cut her off.

"How are you doing?"

"This is incredible," she cried.

Brittney flew by, her voice rising and falling. "It's like flying . . .!"

"Why is she so good?" Kate asked. She stopped and sucked in her breath.

"Skateboarding requires the same type of balance," he said, scooting to sit next to her. "So it was easier for her."

199

Her laugh was quiet and self-deprecating. "I'm at a loss for words."

"You didn't think she'd be doing better than you," he guessed.

"I should be glad she's enjoying herself," she said.

"If it helps at all, you're still doing better than average." He pointed to Brittney, who was curving around the base of a hill. "She's just doing *much* better than average."

"So I'm not a bad friend?"

"Of course not," he said, and leaned over to kiss her. "You're doing great."

"My pride aside, this is stunning," she gestured to the slope, which had emptied in the last half hour.

They were sitting on the side of a run. The sun was dipping below the mountain and the air froze the hair on his chin. Their breath came in white puffs that condensed on their goggles, obscuring their vision.

Trees draped in snow towered over the run, large drifts leaning against their trunks. Small icicles and frost covered the bark and branches, the forest beautiful in its stark emptiness. Wind kicked up snow into swirls of white that floated across the run.

"It's one of my favorite parts of snowboarding," he said. "The solitude, the scrape of my board on the snow, the sensation of flying down the mountain. It's indescribable."

She picked up a handful of snow and let it fall through the fingers of her glove. "I wish we would have come sooner. I had no idea it would be like this."

"Great things come to those who wait," he said. "And now that you know how, we'll have to come again."

"People say that," she said, lifting her goggles to look at him. "But it never works out that way."

He swept his gloved hands to the resort. "I wait all year to do this. A year is not so long."

"A year is always long," she said.

"Then the question is, how much do you love to snowboard?"

"A lot," she said with a smile. "But a year is still a long time."

"It's worth the wait."

"So is this what we're going to do when you get back?" she asked.

He reached out and grasped her hand. "I know you're worried, but my feelings for you aren't going to change."

"How do you know that?" she asked.

"Because I love you," he said. "And I don't use that word lightly."

She sighed and gazed down the mountain. "I'm afraid, Reed. I'm afraid you'll go away and we'll start to talk less, that our schedules won't line up and we'll start to drift apart. I'll leave messages you won't return, and soon after, you will tell me you've met someone else. That it's over."

He scooted as close as he could and reached out to her. "That's not going to happen."

"I planned this day to remind you of what you would miss," she said, her features tight with emotion. "But it's reminded me of what I'll be missing."

"I'm sorry," he said.

"I'm just hoping this isn't the end," she said.

Abruptly she wiped at her face with her glove and then put her goggles down. Shoving herself upward, she pointed herself downhill and snowboarded away. He remained in place, the cold seeping through his clothes. She was right. He was about to leave and all the promises in the world could not stop time. The wind gusted again and he shivered, finally cold.

Chapter 5

When they reached the bottom, they found Brittney flushed with excitement, waiting to go up the lift again. Kate smiled and agreed and Reed suggested the girls ride up together. Kate glanced his way in surprise but Brittney was too excited to notice.

"Are you sure?" she asked. "I'd love to tell someone about what I just did."

Reed took the chair behind them, pondering what Kate had said. When they reached the top of the lift Kate made no mention of their conversation, but he wasn't sure if that was due to Brittney's presence, or her reluctance to speak further about his departure.

They continued boarding until it got dark and the lifts shut down. Loath to depart, Brittney begged the operator until he finally relented and let them ride up one last time. Illuminated by the light poles, they took their time during the descent, and Reed tried to enjoy the run, knowing it would be the last for some time.

When they reached the bottom they left their boards outside and entered the lodge. Jackson, Shelby, and Marta were already there. Ember and Tanner arrived soon after, with Ember's hand in a brace.

"What happened?" Reed asked, noticing first. "Did you fall?"

She scowled. "No I did not. Tanner thought a fall was funny and I hit him. Sprained my hand."

There was a round of laughter at Ember's expense, but Tanner shrugged sheepishly. "She flipped over and landed on her board. It was funny."

"You didn't have to laugh so loud."

"I promise I won't next time," he said.

Seeing the large Tanner with such a forlorn expression softened Ember's anger and she sighed. "You were right, it was funny."

He smiled and pulled her into a hug, but she winced when her hand hit his shoulder. "I'll get some ice," he said quickly.

"There's plenty outside," Jackson called.

Ember threw them a scathing look while Tanner departed, and then she sank into a seat. "How's the chili?"

"Delicious," Brittney said. "And I was freezing."

"That's because you begged the lift operator for one last run," Kate said with a smile.

"I didn't want the day to end," she said.

"I think you've fallen in love," Shelby said with a knowing smile. Then she glanced at Jackson. "We all remember our first day."

Jackson smirked. "I certainly remember mine."

"I'll always remember mine," Kate said quietly, her eyes on Reed.

He smiled, but sadness prevailed. He took her hand and squeezed it, their interplay going unnoticed as the others dived into stories of the day. As they ate dinner around a table by the fire, the conversation ranged across the mountain.

Tanner and Ember had spent most of the time on the bunny slopes, and they shared stories of their falls. The mounting affection between them was apparent, with Tanner being the most animated Reed had ever seen him.

Jackson and Shelby had spent the day on the upper slopes, opting for speed and racing each other down the mountain. While Jackson glowered, Shelby told of how Jackson had misjudged a jump and plunged into a snowdrift so far only his head poked out.

"He looked like a cabbage," she said, laughing.

"You didn't have to stand there laughing at me," Jackson said.

"Yes I did," Shelby said, pulling out her phone. "I needed time to take a few pictures."

All of them chorused to see the photo and the phone was passed around. Reed joined in the amusement when he saw the picture of Jackson's head atop a snowdrift, his expression furious, his goggles knocked askew. One hand was just coming free of the snow and raised as if in protest.

"It was beautiful," Marta said. "I passed them when Shelby was trying to dig him out."

Other pictures were shared and Kate praised Brittney on her newfound talent, her words eliciting a pink flush to Brittney's cheeks. Reed recognized her sincerity as an effort to make up for her jealousy.

They finished dinner well after dark and trudged through the snow to their cars. Tired and sore, it was nevertheless a happy group that climbed into the jeep and truck. Although Reed offered to drive Ember's jeep so she could ride with Tanner, she refused.

"No one drives Red but me."

"But the jeep is blue," Tanner said.

"It's got the spirit of a redhead," Ember said.

Unperturbed, Tanner leaned down and kissed her. "See you tomorrow?"

"I'd like that."

Kate leaned over when Ember strode around the jeep. "The last time she let someone drive, they scratched the bumper."

205

"Who was that?" Reed asked.

"Me," Marta said with a sigh. "I didn't mean to, but it's faster than I expected."

"Now she doesn't let anyone drive her jeep," Brittney said.

"She let Jackson last week," Kate said.

"She has a soft spot for him," Marta said. "He's like her big brother."

Ember turned back. "Are we going to stand here freezing or are we going to go?"

"Go," Kate said fervently. "But can we have hot chocolate when we get home?"

"I'm on it," Brittney said.

"Did I hear something about Brittney's hot chocolate?" Jackson called, poking his head out of the truck window. "Because I'm in."

"You weren't invited," Ember called, but her smile took the sting from her words.

"But I'm coming anyway," Jackson sang, and then backed out. "First one there gets the first cup."

"Don't be stupid down the mountain," Shelby's voice called.

"I won't," Jackson said, and then winked at Ember. "But it's on."

Laughing, he drove away as Ember turned to them. "Well? I'm not losing the first cup to him."

They piled in and Ember gunned it, sending them skidding through the parking lot to the exit. Reed gripped the armrest but Ember managed to correct and followed Jackson to the road. To Reed's immense gratitude, she did not attempt to pass him, and drove carefully down the snowy road.

The four of them lapsed into silence, the end-of-day fatigue getting to them. Kate put her head on Reed's shoulder and fell asleep, and he put his arm around her shoulders, holding her to his chest.

When they got to Kate's car he offered to drive and she agreed. Still tired, Kate tipped her chair back and fell asleep. It began to snow soon after and Reed drove them through the soft flurries, wondering if this was the night he would remember as the end.

He glanced to Kate, at her features relaxed in slumber, and his jaw tightened. Their lives might be pulling them apart, but he wanted to believe their relationship was stronger. There had to be a way he could show her how much she meant to him.

For the next half hour he wrestled over what to do, his thoughts continuing through hot chocolate and on his way home with Jackson. The question settled into his brain like an anchor that would not be dislodged, lingering with him through the next several days.

The next week he helped Tanner move into his room and set up temporary accommodations for himself in the living room. Much of his time was spent with Kate as they both fought the impending separation.

She was just starting classes and he had a great deal of preparation for the internship, the institute giving him reams of files to study up on so he'd be ready when he got there. He'd booked his ticket to arrive four days early but now regretted it, because it meant fewer days with Kate.

They talked very little of what they would do after his internship, and he sensed her reserve. Kate didn't want to talk about it because she feared the unknown. The few times he hinted at such a conversation she steered it to safer topics, and he realized she wanted time to prove what he could not.

Three days before his departure, as he got ready for bed, he pulled out his laptop and checked the times of his flight. As he stared at the screen a thought came to mind that made him smile. Sitting at the table, Jackson and Tanner, both eating cereal for dinner, noticed his expression.

"That's a devilish smile," Jackson said.

"I have an idea," Reed said.

"Looks like it's a good one," Tanner said.

"Trust me," he said. "It is. But I'm going to need some help . . ."

Chapter 6

The next three days passed in a blur of time with Kate. They were together so often it was difficult for him to put his plan into place, but he managed to work with the blondes until everything was set. Before he knew it, he was gathering his things and looking at his house for the last time.

He turned a slow circle, feeling a chill sweep across his skin at the sense of finality. Jackson had foregone his usual bowl of cereal for an actual dinner when Tanner had brought home Chinese, and the remains of the meal lay spread on the table. The absence of the nightly cereal made the kitchen feel like the future was already creeping into the present.

Would Jackson actually start eating dinner? Would Tanner change more of his habits? Like Jackson's penchant for bacon every weekend? Would he stop singing Celine Dion in the morning? But Reed couldn't expect his roommate and friend to stay the same after his departure.

"Ready?" Jackson asked.

"As I can be," Reed said. "Did you load the bags?"

"What do you take me for?" he asked. "I know how to get things done."

He grinned and nodded. "That you do."

"The girls are already on their way to the airport," he said. "We'd better hurry or you'll miss your flight."

Looking about the room one last time, Reed picked up his bag and shouldered the strap. Then he turned and left the house, resisting the urge to look back as he strode to Jackson's truck and climbed into the cab. He stopped to pat the hood of his aged car.

"Roman will take care of your car," Tanner said.

"She needs a lot of attention," Reed said.

Reed climbed inside the cab of the truck and shifted to the middle, allowing Tanner the window seat. On the way down the street he couldn't resist a look back. He recalled all the times he'd rushed out for dates with other girls, but those memories were dim and irrelevant. He recalled returning home the night he met Kate, the memory vibrant with a new spark. Then he recalled all the times he'd walked to Kate's car, the memories tinged with an unbreakable bond.

"I hope you're ready for tonight," she'd said on numerous occasions, her smile mischievous and inviting.

I hope you're ready for more, he thought.

Taking a long breath, he faced forward as they turned the corner and left the block behind. He'd expected to feel regret, but a slow smile spread on his face at the prospect of what lay ahead. His idea wouldn't stop them from having a long-distance relationship for a year, but it would prove exactly how important Kate was to him.

They reached the airport and parked. When they got out, Reed grabbed the handles of his two bags and Jackson pulled the third. They walked inside together and Reed spotted the five girls by an information kiosk.

"I can't believe you're leaving," Shelby said, stepping forward to embrace him first.

"You take care of Jackson, will you?" he replied. "His bowl needs to be filled twice a day, and don't forget to take him on walks."

She grinned and nodded, vacating the space for Brittney, and then Marta. He hugged each in turn, conscious of Kate hovering in the background. When he reached Ember the small redhead gave him a hug that nearly crushed the air from his lungs.

"Don't break her heart," she murmured. "Or I get to break your legs."

"I won't," he replied with a smile, and then turned to Jackson.

"Have fun in New York," Jackson said. "And bring me a t-shirt when you come back."

"I will," Reed said with a laugh.

Hugging Jackson broke the dam he'd set against his departure, and tears came into his eyes. When Jackson stepped back his eyes were wet as well and he complained loudly of the dust in the air. Shelby took his hand, and Reed finally turned to Kate.

"Call me when you land?" she asked.

"I don't think so."

His refusal caused her to blink in shock, and for several seconds she just stared at him. Her gaze swept over her friends but they did not appear surprised, deepening her confusion. Reed then smiled and took her hands.

"I want you to come with me."

"What?" she asked. "I can't just go to New York."

"You can for the weekend," he said.

"What are you talking about?" Kate asked. She glanced to her roommates for help, but even Ember was smiling.

"I want you to come with me," Reed repeated.

"When?"

"Right now."

"I don't understand," she said.

"I want you to be my date to New York," he said, pulling out his ticket. Then he used his thumb to slide the two papers apart, revealing a second plane ticket. "And this is your invitation."

"You bought a ticket for me?" she asked, her eyes lighting with a spark of hope. "But I don't have any—"

"—clothes?" Jackson finished, and rolled the bag he'd brought to her side. "Yes you do."

Kate's expression revealed her struggle to understand and she looked to the blondes. "Did you do this?"

"We packed your bag," Brittney said.

"It's got everything you need," Marta said.

"And a few things you *might* need," Ember finished with a smile and a wink.

Kate flushed and looked back to Reed, who shook his head. "There are two hotel rooms waiting for us, one with your name on it," he said. "But only until Monday morning."

"Waste of a room," Ember muttered, but Tanner shushed her.

"Are you going to go or not?" Tanner asked.

Kate met Reed's gaze, her confusion fading to a tentative excitement. "Did you really do this?"

"I didn't want to say goodbye," he replied. "So I decided you should come with me. It's only a few days, but it's more time together—and in New York City."

The knowledge that Reed had bought a ticket to New York—for her—just so they could spend more time together, finally seemed to settle in. She'd come to the airport expecting to part ways, but now she was being asked to leave with him, and tears welled in her eyes. She stepped in and kissed him, her lips crushing his.

"I can't believe you did this," she murmured.

"So you accept my invitation?"

She reached up and plucked the ticket from his fingers, her hands trembling. Then she turned to her roommates and embraced them, her gratitude tumbling from her lips. As Kate said goodbye Jackson sidled up and clapped Reed on the shoulder.

"Well played," he said.

Reed smiled. "I couldn't have done it without you."

"I know."

Reed laughed and stepped to Kate, extending his hand. Her eyes bright with excitement, she accepted his hand and they walked into security together. She clung to him as if afraid the moment was a dream, and he savored the thrill.

They removed their shoes and passed through security, where they paused to wave back to their friends. Then they made their way to their terminal. In all their dating they'd always returned to their separate homes, but this time they would be together in New York. Even if they were in separate hotel rooms, they were still alone.

"This is the best thing anyone has ever given me," Kate said.

He pulled her close and smiled. "It was a gift from me, to me," he said.

"Are we really doing this?" she breathed.

"We are," Reed said. "So I hope you're ready to start our next date . . ?"

Volume 25: The New York City Date

Chapter 1

Kate pressed her face against the window as the plane began its descent. The clouds were sparse but the smog smothered the city, the output from thousands of cars, busses, and taxis. She'd never seen something so big.

"I can't believe you've never been to New York," he said.

"I can't believe you have," she said, sparing Reed a glance before returning her gaze on the city.

"I told you, my mom wanted me to see more of the world outside of Tallahassee. For inexplicable reasons, she thought the capital of Florida was not the hub of the world."

"Are you going to tell me what the plan is yet?" she asked. "We've almost landed."

He didn't answer and she turned back to find his expression pensive. She recognized the chink in his resistance and dived in with a pleading look, causing him to smile and gesture to the city.

"We've got the weekend before you fly back," he said.

"Just three days?" she asked, trying to keep the disappointment from her voice. She'd expected more.

"My internship orientation starts Monday," he said. "After that you'd just be hanging out by yourself."

"A three-day date to New York City," she said. "I *guess* it will do."

He grinned. "To be honest I've only planned a handful of things. Since this is your first time and you didn't even know you were coming,

215

I thought it prudent to leave a little flexibility in case there were things you wanted to do."

"What's already on the schedule?" she asked.

"We'll have time to check in at the hotel and find dinner," he said. "I figured after that we could hit Times Square."

"Anything else tonight?" she asked.

"Not that I can share," he said with a smile.

"What about tomorrow?" she asked. Now that he'd started talking, she wanted to glean as much as she could.

"I have to drop my things off at the apartment," he said. "But after that, I figured you'd want to see the tourist places. Maybe the Statue of Liberty?"

"And Sunday?"

"You really don't want any surprises left, do you."

"Nope," she said blissfully. "I want it all."

He relented with a smile. "Tomorrow night we have tickets to Wicked."

Her heart jumped. "Really?"

"Your mom said you've always wanted to see it."

"I'll need to thank her later," she said.

"What else do you want to do?" he asked.

"Everything," she said. "I want to go to Coney Island and go to the top of the Empire State Building, take a ferry to Staten Island and see the New York Public Library and—"

"—you really want to go to the library?"

216

"Just to see the millions of books," she said.

"Anything else?" he asked with a smile.

"I want to ride the subway," she said.

"I think we can manage that."

She bit her lip as she considered her options but her memory had failed. She shrugged, content to let the city inspire new ideas. Then she realized there was one thing Reed had failed to mention.

"Where are we staying?" she asked. "A Fairfield or something?"

"Actually no," he hedged. "Tonight we will be staying at a different location."

"And where is that?" she asked.

"The Plaza Hotel."

"The what?" she asked, her eyes widening. "Isn't that expensive?"

"When I told Dr. Dickson I was bringing you for the weekend, he got me a discount," he said.

"Even with it," she said. "Just how much is this date costing you?"

"I try not to think about it," he said. "But since most of our dates have been inexpensive, my average still isn't too bad."

"Still," she said. "Between the ticket and the hotel, let alone the activities . . ."

He smiled and took her hand. "The blondes pitched in for the plane ticket. They said it's your next five years of birthday gifts."

"Wait, really?"

He smiled. "I'll promise not to go over budget if you promise not to worry about the expense. Deal?"

She hesitated but his easy smile was relentless. She remembered seeing it on their first date and thinking it wasn't fair, and after nearly a year together wondered how it had gained even more power.

"Deal," she said.

The captain's voice came over the intercom and the plane banked to the side, lining them up with the runway. Kate lifted her tray table and stowed her things, excitement making her hands tremble. Then she peered out the window.

Their landing in New York City was like a moment from a movie, like being whisked away on a weekend trip by a handsome boyfriend could not be real. Yet it was, and the tires skidded across the tarmac, slowing the plane on its way to the terminal. Before she knew it they were exiting into the packed airport.

They managed the labyrinth known as the New York airport and retrieved Reed's luggage before finding a taxi outside. From there the cab took them to the Plaza Hotel. Kate never took her eyes off the city and bombarded the cab driver with questions. The man answered like a city veteran. When they got out she stood and lifted her gaze to the stunning edifice, wondering when it would not be surreal. Reed collected his luggage and they walked into the lobby, where she came to a halt.

"I never expected this," she breathed.

Huge chandeliers hung from vaulted ceilings, their lights glittering off the polished floors. Tall windows, draped in red curtains, permitted light to grace the space, the fading twilight adding a touch of color to the glass. The sweeping staircase rose to a higher level and a woman in formal dress descended with a man in a tuxedo, their attire matching several others in the lobby. High backed chairs circled ornate tables, their softness formal yet inviting.

"How did you ever afford this?" she asked, turning to Reed.

"I raffled my snowboard," he said.

"You what?" she asked, swiveling to face him. She knew he had a nice snowboard, one that had taken him months save up for. But he'd sold one of his most prized possessions, just to make their date better.

"How?"

"Ember's blog," he said, a faint smile on his face. "The blondes had a hard time keeping you away from it the last few days. I will say I'm shocked by how many wanted to buy tickets."

She stared at him, struck by the sacrifice. "I can't believe you did that," she said.

"It's just a board," he said, and gestured to the check in. "Let's get you settled."

She wanted to press him for more details, but in the midst of such splendor she realized he'd sacrificed a great deal for this date. It wasn't about the money—he wanted her to know how much he loved her.

They checked in and then took an elevator to their floor. The elevator was no less ornate than the lobby, its walls a gorgeous wood paneling. She ran her finger along the molding, wondering if it cost more than her car.

A soft *ding* indicated they'd arrived and they exited into a long hallway. She'd expected an interior room, but Reed turned to a room with views outside of the hotel and gestured to it with a knowing smile.

"I hope you like your room."

"Walking me to a hotel room without supervision?" she asked, raising an eyebrow. "What are your intentions?"

"To show you how much I love you—at dinner," he said.

She laughed and unlocked the door. The interior of the room was just as spectacular as the lobby, with sheer curtains that allowed the fading light to grace the white bedspread and stunning artwork. It was small but not cramped, the space allowing for movement and visibility from the window.

She dropped her bags and strode to the window, peering down at the street far below. The height, the wonders of the hotel, and the fatigue from the long flight finally got to her and she giggled.

"What's that for?" he asked.

She turned away from the window and stepped to him, folding into his warm embrace. "No one has ever given me a gift like this," she said.

He leaned in and kissed her, the touch of his lips sending a shudder to her toes. She was highly aware of the bed just inches from them, of how easy it would be to fall into the soft blankets and five thousand thread count sheets. No one was there. No one would know.

Reed retreated and his voice was husky. "I think it's time to go now."

"Can't stand the temptation?" she asked, smiling as she leaned up and brushed her lips across his.

"Let's just say I'm hedging my willpower," he said, and then repeated, "Dinner?"

She smiled and nodded. "I'd prefer to eat in," she said. "But I could go out."

He laughed and led her to the door. "Then let's go. New York City awaits . . ."

Chapter 2

Since it was so close, they walked to Times Square and she gazed at the streets wonder. She'd been to big cities before, but none like New York. The towering structures and endless crowds of people drew her gaze, but there was always more. More buildings, higher buildings, brighter lights, thicker crowds.

"It's stunning," she breathed when stepped into the famous square.

Reed spun a circle, staring at the unique intersection at the heart of the city. Ads for drinks and other products were on prominent display, the lights as bright as the sun, the rays flooding the streets and illuminating the people.

The city smelled like bread and exhaust mingled with trash and pizza, a combination that repulsed yet also enticed. She caught a whiff of perfume and alcohol as a woman in a skirt and coat strode by, and the next moment rank sweat as a shabbily dressed man passed. Another man talked loudly on his phone, his clothing and language suggesting stock broker or banker. Three people from three worlds, all standing next to each other at the light, oblivious to each other yet somehow connected.

The light changed and Reed took her hand, keeping them together as they were swept across the street, the thudding of boots punctuated by a honking horn and a distant shout. The constant hum of engines and voices became a background of noise that swelled and faded in a melodic symphony of noise.

They stopped at a pizza place that claimed to have the best pizza in New York, and then got another slice at the one across the street, that also claimed to have the best pizza in New York. Then they took pictures in front of Times Square and sent them to Ember for her blog. Wandering across the square, they paused and watched a pair of street performers braving the cold to dance shirtless.

"Ice cream?" he asked, motioning to a small shop across the next street.

She shivered and leaned closer to him. "Too cold."

"They don't seem to mind."

She looked again and noticed the shop was packed with people, the mass blocking her view of the counter through the glass. She hesitated but ultimately shook her head again and pointed to a Starbucks.

"How about hot chocolate?"

"Much better," he said.

They crossed the street again and warmed up just inside the door, talking and pointing to the new performers that showed up on the square, a trio of nearly-naked cowboys that quickly drew a small crowd.

The coffee shop was packed with people, the press of bodies so thick it was claustrophobic. Baristas shouted orders to each other, the words a foreign language that the patrons seemed to understand. With shocking speed they made orders more complicated than the tax code, the steam of their machines rising in puffs of smoke.

Many were in a rush, their pace hurried as they departed on their way. Kate felt no such push and merely relished the bustle from her spectator's point of view. Thirty minutes after entering she got her vente macchiato and Reed had his hot chocolate in hand. Warmed from the steaming liquid, they ventured back into the frigid air and strolled down the street.

"I can't believe I'm here," she said.

"Me either," he said. "It's almost too much to take in."

222

"I keep forgetting you're going to be living in the city," she said. "Do you think you'll ever get used to it?"

"There's so much light I'll need sunglasses at night," he said, pointing to the Times Square billboards, which now showed a man casually standing in his underwear.

"I've never seen so many people," she said, watching the crowd of pedestrians pass the slow-moving cars.

"The institute is outside the main traffic areas," he said. "At least, that's what I've been told."

"Are you staying in a building like these?" she asked, sweeping her hand at the towering walls of concrete and steel.

"Actually it's an older house in Manhattan," he said. "The only thing that matters is that it's eight blocks from work, so I won't have to worry about transportation." He shivered. "At least when it warms up."

"And your roommates?"

"Three others," he said. "Clint, David, and Hannah."

"Hannah?" she asked.

"We each have our own rooms," he said with a smile.

"I didn't know there was going to be a girl," she said.

The knowledge set her on edge but she couldn't explain why. Reed was more than capable of keeping girls at a distance, and co-ed housing was common in Boulder. Still, the knowledge sapped her excitement for New York.

He stopped her and threaded his arms around her back. "Are you jealous?"

"What if I am?" she asked with a faint smile. "What are you going to do about it?"

"Kiss the doubt out of you," he said, and then did so.

"I think that's enough," she said, lightheaded from the contact.

"Let me know if you need another dose."

"I will," she said, and then swept her hand at Times Square. "Do you think we can go somewhere less packed?"

"I know just the place," he said.

He hailed a cab and then they joined the procession attempting to leave the area. "Where to?" the driver asked.

"The Empire State Building," Reed said.

Kate swiveled to look at him. "Really?"

"You wanted to get out of the crowd," he said with a smile. "Why not get above it?"

"Don't you have to buy tickets in advance?"

He reached into his pocket and withdrew two slips of paper. "You mean these tickets?"

She grinned and accepted one, examining it with interest. "How is it possible that you still surprise me?"

"I don't know," he said, mystified, "but I hope you don't figure it out. Once you do, our dating challenge isn't going to be as fun."

Mentioning their dating challenge elicited a smile. They hadn't spoken of it, but she felt a sense of finality to this date. She'd felt it on the last two dates. They'd managed to push back the clock, and Reed's surprise invite to New York had certainly done it again, but today was the first time the idea was not tinged with regret.

Inside the car, the sounds of the city were muted but no less vibrant, and she watched as the cab attempted to maneuver through the traffic. Reed was quiet and she wondered if he was thinking the same thing. But as the towering Empire State Building came into view her voice was filled with awe.

"It's like a mountain," she said.

"You should see the 102nd floor," the driver said. "It's incredible."

Kate looked to the ticket and found it included passes to both the 86th floor and the 102nd floor observatories. She smiled, pleased that Reed hadn't gone the slightly cheaper route. She lifted the ticket so the driver could see it in the mirror.

"It appears my date wants us to go to the top."

The man nodded and his eyes flicked to Reed. "A date who plans ahead? Sounds like a keeper."

Kate grinned and looked to Reed. "I certainly think so."

The cabbie came to a stop and gestured to the building. "Enjoy the view for me."

Reed handed him a bill. "Thanks."

They got out and she craned her head to look to the top of the building, but it seemed to stretch forever, piercing the clouds and reaching to the sky. The scattered clouds had cleared in the last hour, leaving just the dark expanse lit by the city lights.

"Ready?" he asked, taking her hand.

"Do you ever tire of being awesome?"

He laughed and led her to the doors. "I'm not as great as you think I am."

"Between the plane ticket, the food, and cabs alone you've spent a small fortune on this trip," she said. "All for me. That borders on legendary."

He shook his head, his easy smile returning. "Money has a purpose, and although rent and power and school are essential, they aren't the reasons I want a job. I want to have a job so I can do things like this—for the woman I love."

She leaned over and nudged him with her free hand. "And that's what makes you a legend."

He laughed again and led her to the line for the elevator. It was late and on a weekday, so the line was short, allowing them to board the large elevator within a few minutes. The elevator flew up the interior of the skyscraper but it seemed to take forever to reach the top. She swallowed against a surge of nervousness as she watched the numbers climb. A chill washed over her skin as the elevator slowed, and a moment later the doors swung open.

Chapter 3

The elevator exited into a large room. Windows lined the exterior, allowing a view of the exterior observation deck. Polished floors reflected the glow of lights. Kate advanced around the people waiting to go down and hurried to the door. A pair of teenage girls rushed past her, opening them to release a blast of cold air into the room. Reed reached the door and held it for her, allowing her to step onto the exterior deck.

A cold breeze ruffled her hair and she shivered, but not from the chill. As she approached the high fence she was shocked by the vastness to the city, the plunging canyons of concrete and steel, the currents of lights flowing in their depths.

She recalled someone in the elevator saying they were a thousand feet off the ground. She'd been that high in mountains but this was different. It felt like she stood on the pinnacle of an architect's imagination, as if mankind had lifted her into the sky to defy the pull of gravity.

"Breathtaking," she said.

"You took the word right out of my mouth," he said.

She noticed the trace of tension in his voice and looked his way. His jaw was clenched and he leaned away from the fence, the tension to his gaze palpable. She frowned, and then realized the source of his fear.

"Is superman afraid of heights?"

"Not usually," he said. He leaned to the edge and looked down, grimacing before retreating. "But this is *really* high."

She laughed and leaned up against the barrier, peering down into the city. Then she glanced back at him, smiling in invitation. He shook his head, keeping his distance.

"I like the view from right here," he said.

"Didn't you come up here on your last trip to New York?"

He shook his head. "I wanted to, but we didn't have enough time."

She knew she should feel bad that the height made him uneasy, but it was intriguing to find an aspect to Reed that wasn't perfect. She slapped her hand against the fence, causing the metal to rattle.

"Seems solid—ah!"

She pretended it gave way. His eyes widened and then narrowed, and he grabbed her hand, pulling her back with a rueful laugh. "You're a little devil, aren't you?"

"Maybe," she said, amused. "Or maybe it's just nice to find something you're not perfect at."

"We've been dating this long and you haven't discovered my other flaws?" he smiled. "I'm flattered."

She threaded her fingers into his and pulled him along the exterior of the observation deck. "I love seeing you like this."

"Mildly terrified?" he asked, and then grinned. "I'm glad my fear provides you with amusement."

"It does!"

"Does it not scare you at all?"

"Nope," she said.

His eyes narrowed. "Liar."

"A little," she admitted. "But I think I'm starting to get used to it now."

The initial euphoria of seeing the city had gradually been replaced with a quiet awe. In the stillness of the January night, the city seemed to twinkle as if the stars of the heavens had settled on the ground to birth the city.

"I've stood on cliffs and mountains," Reed said, "but never seen anything like this."

"Would you ever go skydiving?" she asked.

He shuddered. "Not by choice."

"I went with my brothers a few times."

"Really?" he asked, raising an eyebrow.

"The first time was terrifying," she said. "Looking out the door and seeing emptiness, I almost lost my nerve, but Bake told me he believed in me. I couldn't back out after that."

"They must do it often in the military."

"Quite a bit," Kate said. "Tyler too. Orin just does it for fun."

"Did Jason ever go skydiving?"

"He actually did," Kate said.

Reed gave a sour expression. "You know, he still irritates me."

"Really?" she asked, surprised. "Why?"

"He stole one of my dates with you," he said. "And right now, time with you is at a premium."

"I know how you feel," she said softly.

He grunted and swept his hand at the city. "We're standing on the top of the world, so why are we talking about what makes us sad?"

"Maybe because we're both worried about it."

"Our relationship is evolving," he said. "Not ending."

"Is that so?" she asked, unable to resist the smile.

"I think it is," he said.

"Then tell me what we're going to do when I'm in Colorado and you're here."

"Challenge accepted," he said with a smile.

She laughed at his tone. "The last time you accepted my challenge, it led to the dating challenge." She threaded her arm into his and they began to walk around the exterior.

"True," he said. "So maybe that's what we need. Maybe we need a new challenge."

"Call me intrigued," she said.

"Every Friday night," he said. "You and me, on Skype."

"What are we going to do, watch a movie together?"

"Does it matter? I can take a laptop bowling. That's not weird, is it?"

She laughed at the image of Reed going bowling with a computer for a date. People would think he was nuts—or brilliant. Then she imagined herself at a bowling alley holding a laptop to watch Reed at his lane, and smiled.

"We've really avoided this topic, haven't we?"

"Maybe we've been too attached to the dating challenge," he said. "Now that I think about it, it's become a large part of our relationship, and I think I was afraid of leaving it behind."

"I guess we just needed this to gain some perspective," she said, sweeping a hand at the view.

"So you agree?" he asked.

She came to a halt and looked into his eyes, to the sparkling blue that had captivated her for nearly a year. She'd been afraid of his departure for months, but now she found that fear had lost its power. Instead it was with a spark of excitement that she looked to the future.

"I'm in," she said.

He flashed a smile and leaned in for a kiss, but she reached up and put a finger on his lips. "But one condition."

"What's that?"

"You got the first date in the challenge, so I get the last."

"You didn't issue the challenge until our second date," he countered.

"Then our third date was the first, and I still get the last." Her voice carried a note of triumph. He laughed.

"You win. I guess that means you have a date planned?"

"Two weeks from today," she said. "On Skype, and you go where I tell you to go."

"How much of this do you have planned?"

"I can't answer that," she said.

He regarded her with an amused expression and then consented with a nod. "You get the last date. Then we start the new challenge."

"Deal," she said, and leaned into the kiss.

She marveled that she felt the same excitement she'd felt nearly a year ago when they'd gone on the very first date. The dating challenge was coming to an end, but it was time for a new beginning. And her smile would not be constrained.

They circled the building several more times and then ascended to the 102nd floor, where the crowds were nearly absent. Reed's initial tension had eased from his face, but she wasn't sure if that was due to time or the prospect of their new dating.

Reluctant to depart, they stayed on the observation deck until it closed at two in the morning. As they rode the elevator back to the ground she felt like her heart soared above, and not even gravity could bring her down.

They giggled and talked in low tones, their excitement drawing amused looks from the others in the car. Kate struggled to keep the smile from her face and failed, and one of the women smiled at her.

"How long have you been together?" she asked.

"Almost a year," she replied.

"When are you getting married?" her friend asked.

"Oh no," Reed said. "We're not engaged." They exchanged a look and grinned in unison.

"Sorry," the woman said. "You two just look like you are going to . . ."

"Don't worry," Reed assured her. "We're just dating."

Kate burst into a laugh and the two women looked confused, but Kate had no idea how to explain. Then the car reached the bottom and Reed politely wished them a good night. He managed to keep his laughter contained until they were on the street.

They got into a cab and laughed about the encounter all the way back to the Plaza. Then they ascended a much slower elevator to their rooms. Kate felt like she could go forever, but it was almost three in the morning, and they ended up talking in her room for another hour, sitting against the window and watching the city go by. Highly conscious of the bed just feet from them, she leaned against him on the tiny couch, yearning to be closer, and they talked until her eyes began to droop.

"We should go to bed," he murmured.

Her heart skipped a beat and she rotated to meet his gaze. He laughed and shook his head. "Don't get your hopes up."

"A girl can hope," she said, yawning.

They rose and she walked him to the door. "Call me when you wake up," he said.

"I will," she said, kissing him with all the passion in her heart. When they parted his eyes flicked to the bed and he swallowed.

"Goodnight, Kate."

He slipped away and she shut the door. Then she leaned against the cold wood and sighed, wondering if there would ever be such a perfect day again. Or perhaps, with Reed, there were many more in store.

Chapter 4

Kate woke to sunlight streaming through the window and groaned, reluctant to depart the incredibly soft bed. Then she recalled what Reed had planned for the day and stretched, a smile spreading across her features. She texted Reed and then stepped into the shower. Just as she was pulling on her shoes there was a knock at the door.

She swung it open and found Reed dressed in jeans and a long sleeved shirt. Her pulse quickened and she wondered if he'd always been that attractive. Or was it just the shirt? She invited him in and gathered her purse.

"Ready for today?" he asked.

"Are you?" she asked, flashing a teasing smile.

He grinned and took her hand on the way to the elevator. Once outside, they grabbed brunch at a café down the street, and then returned to the hotel to gather Reed's luggage. The trip to his new apartment was longer than the rides from the previous night, but the closeness remained, and she held his hand throughout the drive.

When the taxi came to a stop she exited and looked up in surprise. The building was a brownstone, a nice one. She'd expected a cheap apartment for the interns but the place was in an upscale portion of Manhattan, the neighboring structures neat and equally as attractive.

"It's nicer than I expected," she said.

"Dr. Dickson's family owns it," he said. "And they've lent it to the institute for years."

They climbed the steps to the large wooden door and Reed knocked. While they waited she looked down the street. Small trees were perfectly trimmed, and several joggers ran down the sidewalk. Unlike downtown, the air smelled fresh and clean, and even the concrete was pristine.

The door swung open to reveal a shockingly beautiful brunette. Her hair hung in ringlets past her shoulders, obscuring the strap of her sports bra. Her bare stomach was flat enough to inspire envy, while the tiny shorts revealed stunning legs. She unleashed a dazzling smile and Kate took an instant dislike.

"Sorry," she said breathlessly. "I just got back from a run. Can I help you?"

"I'm Reed," he said. "Moving in?"

"Oh," she said, opening the door wider and ushering them inside. "I'm Hannah."

"You live here?" Kate asked.

"I'm in the same program with Reed," she said brightly. "And you are?"

"Reed's girlfriend," Kate said, "Kate."

"Great," she said. "I'll show you around."

Kate hung back as Hannah showed the apartment, which was lavish and spacious. The main floor was reserved for the common area, and contained desks and comfortable couches. A large TV sat against the wall, and the kitchen at the back was well stocked, with expensive pans hanging from a rack above the island. The bay area at the front had been converted into a library, and she noticed most of the books were on psychology.

"We work long hours," Hannah was saying, "and when we're not working we study."

"How long have you been here?"

"Six months," she said. "I got here with Clint and we both finish in July."

Hannah led the way up the stairs, her hips swaying hypnotically and causing Kate to scowl. "There are four bedrooms on the second floor," she said. "I hope you don't mind, but I took the largest when your predecessor left."

"No problem," Reed said.

The second floor was all wood, the flooring an aged oak that reflected the lights on the ceiling. The rooms they passed were closed except for one, and Hannah paused to introduce the other two roommates.

Both were skinny and short, sporting glasses and button up shirts. They were leaning over a desk where books and paper were piled high, the notes suggesting the study time was a frequent occurrence. Empty cans of energy drinks filled the garbage can.

"This is David and Clint," she said.

"Clint," the blond, bespeckled intern said, rising to his feet to shake Reed's hand. "Glad you could make it."

"I'm excited to be here," Reed said.

"Your research is incredible," David said.

Even shorter than Clint, David was already losing his hair, the blond receding up his hairline like the surf at low tide. Reed was by far the best looking of the three, a fact Kate found disappointing. She would have preferred for someone else to get Hannah's attention.

"Research?" Reed asked.

"On dating and marriage," he said. "We've all read your thesis and watched your blog." Then he caught sight of Kate and fumbled his books as he stood. "Sorry, I didn't realize you'd be here. You're even prettier in person."

"Hi," Kate said, disconcerted by the attention.

"It appears you have me at a disadvantage," Reed said.

"Hannah found the blog," Clint said. "She's been following your challenge for a month."

"Clint," Hannah said, her tone gaining a warning edge. She flashed a smile that seemed to stun him. "It's not fair telling a girl's secrets."

"Sorry, Hannah," he said, swallowing and pushing his glasses up his nose.

"I'll show you your room," Hannah said to Reed, walking him to the end of the hall and pointing to the corner room. "I'm right next door, so if you need anything, I'll be here."

"I didn't realize you were all watching the blog," Reed said.

Hannah flashed her dazzling smile. "We share the same specialty, and my thesis was on women's power in the dating sphere. I look forward to working with you."

She reached out and touched his arm. Kate clenched her fist as Hannah smiled again and brushed past him to the door, leaving them alone. Reed put his bag down on the bed and gestured to the room.

"What do you think?"

"That your roommate wants you in her bed," Kate said.

"Hannah?" Reed asked. "She's just being friendly."

"A little too friendly," Kate said.

Reed laughed and wrapped her in his arms. "She may be interested, but I'm not. I already have the object of my affection in my arms."

She managed a smile and they set to unpacking Reed's things. While Kate hung the shirts in the closet, her thoughts dwelled on Hannah. The way her eyes had lingered on Reed's body, as if she was already watching him undress. Her hand had been on his arm a fraction too long, her smile just a shade too bright.

She recalled the moment they'd arrived and Hannah had acted like she didn't know Reed. But she had. Kate had seen it in her eyes, in the hunger of her gaze, the hunger of one fixated on an object to be desired, and nothing would stand in the way.

"Kate?"

She turned and looked at Reed, his amused expression suggesting he'd called her name a few times. Everything was already unpacked, including the two boxes he'd shipped ahead, all while she'd been occupied hanging his shirts.

"Sorry," Kate said. "Just distracted."

"About Hannah?"

"Maybe," Kate said, glancing to the closed door.

"You're worried about me?" he asked, his lips twitching. "I'm flattered."

"She likes you," Kate said. "A lot."

"You think so?" Reed asked. "I wonder what sort of date she would like."

"Hey!" she threw the last shirt at him.

"Sorry," he said, fending off the shirt. "It's not something to joke about."

Kate couldn't help but laugh at his expression. "You think it's funny? She's a hunter. I've seen her type before and she won't rest until she has what she wants."

"This prey has already been taken off the market," Reed said. "Have you forgotten that I kept my distance from girls for years while dating?"

"Not with one that hot right next door."

"You think she's hot?" he asked. "I hadn't noticed."

She scowled. "I know you're not blind."

"I'm not," he said. "I'm *blinded*. The moon may be pretty, but the sun makes it disappear."

She tried not to smile but it found its way onto her face. Reed grinned and stepped to her. He pulled her close enough to kiss but kept his distance, a teasing smile on his face, all but challenging her to smile.

"That was pretty smooth," she said.

"I do try," he replied.

Suddenly the door opened and Hannah appeared. She'd taken a shower and changed, donning sleek jeans and a top that accentuated her curves. Sexy and alluring, stunning yet attainable, she smiled and flipped her dark hair.

"I'm going to the store to grab dinner, you need me to pick up anything for you?"

"I'm good, Hannah, thank you." Reed didn't release Kate, and Kate tried to keep her smugness from her face.

"Okay, I'm here if you want anything," she said. She flashed her thousand watt smile again and left.

When she was gone Kate looked to Reed. "You're going to lock your door, right?"

"Yep," he drawled.

She grinned and tried to shove her doubt aside, but long after they left the apartment she couldn't shake the doubt that had wormed its way into her heart. It wasn't Hannah's beauty that worried her, it was the inherent connection she shared with Reed. Their interests aligned perfectly, and Kate could imagine Hannah wanting to study the topics every night, together. She trusted Reed, but every wall could be broken, and Hannah was a battering ram.

Chapter 5

After leaving the brownstone behind they spent the rest of the day touring the city, capping off the day in a Broadway theater. She'd listened to the music of Wicked for years and yearned to see it. The performance brought her to tears.

After the musical he dropped her off at the hotel and walked her to her room, but lingered at her door. His departing kiss left her breathless, and sparked a fire that made it difficult to sleep. It didn't help that Hannah was sleeping next door to Reed.

The next morning they continued their exploration of the city, visiting Central Park and Coney Island before taking a ferry out to the Statue of Liberty. As much as she tried to keep Hannah from her mind, the girl was pernicious, and every time Kate spotted a pretty brunette, her thoughts leapt to Reed's new roommate.

"Still thinking about Hannah?" Reed finally asked.

"No." She met his gaze and he raised an eyebrow. She sighed. "How can you tell?"

"Every time you see a pretty brunette you frown," he said. "It's actually kind of cute to see your forehead crinkle up like that."

"Don't patronize me," she said.

He laughed and gestured to the Statue of Liberty. "Are you jealous of her too?"

Kate eyed the statue with a critical eye. "Hannah has a better chest."

241

"And you think that's what matters to me?" he asked.

"I don't know," she said, turning a circle. "We've never talked about what kind of man you are. What do you like, legs, butt—"

"Are you trying to find out if I like your body?"

"Do you?" she asked.

His eyes glanced down her form and then away, and then flicked back to her. "More than I should admit."

The sudden nervousness in his tone drew a smile to her lips. "You *do* like my body."

"I think you're the sexiest woman I've ever seen."

She poked him in the chest. "A girl needs to hear it once in a while."

"I'll try to tell you more often," he said.

He grinned and caught her hand, leading her around the base of the statue. They'd already been inside, so they made their way back to the ferry and boarded with the rest of the crowd. The sun was bright but the air was cold, the wind pulling against her coat as the ferry carried them back to shore. Reed stayed at her side with his arm around her back, the pressure a warm presence that defied the wind.

"Today is our last day in New York," he said. "What else do you want to do?"

"Can we go to the institute?"

He raised an eyebrow. "We're in New York City and you want to go to my work?"

"When you call me, I want to be able to imagine where you're working."

"Really?" he asked. "This doesn't have to do with Hannah?"

"No." He stared at her until she flushed. "Not completely."

"If this is about you staking your claim . . .,"

"No," she said hastily.

"Too bad," he said with a shrug and a sly smile. "I would have liked to see that. But it's Sunday, so she probably won't even be there."

"So can we go?"

He regarded her for a moment and then swept a hand to the city. "Are you sure you want to go look at an office?"

"You make it sound so exciting," she said.

He laughed and then shrugged. She'd expected him to resist more, and wondered if Reed wanted to assure her that Hannah was not a concern. Taking her to the institute would go a long way toward doing just that.

When they reached the shore they took another taxi, into Manhattan and to the upper west side. The institute was just out of the residential towers and resided in the upper floors of a small skyscraper. Home to some of the best psychiatrists and psychologists in the city, its clientele included the rich and famous, many of whom were very protective of their privacy.

"There's a separate garage and private elevator access to the upper offices," Reed said as they entered the front doors. "I actually had to sign a confidentiality agreement when I accepted the contract."

"Really?"

He nodded. "If I break it, my life is effectively over, not that I would ever want to."

"How many doctors are here?"

"Five, currently," he replied. "But I've only met Dr. Dickson and Dr. Welsh. The interns rotate among all five, taking turns assisting each of them."

The main doors led to a small anteroom and a trio of elevators, each bearing gold embossed names for different companies. A receptionist and an armed guard were present and the woman greeted Reed as if he was an old friend.

"Mr. Thompson," the blonde said, rising to greet him. "I'm Sara, the agent for the building. We weren't expecting you until tomorrow."

"I know," he said, "but I wanted to stop by and show my girlfriend the office."

"Would you like to see Dr. Dickson?"

"He's in?"

"You're lucky to catch him," she said. "He stopped in to meet a client but should be finishing in a few minutes. I'll message him to meet you upstairs."

"Are any others in?"

"Only Dr. Pravesh," she replied. "But he's in a private session and won't be available for some time."

"Thank you," Reed said, and followed her direction to the elevator.

"Miss Williams?"

Kate turned in surprise when she called her name. "Yes?"

"Just wanted to say, I really liked your Magic Date."

"You know about our challenge?" she asked.

"We're required to know all about our interns," she said. "But I must say, investigating you was a pleasure."

"Thank you," Kate said uncertainly.

"I look forward to working with you in the future," she said to Reed.

"I do too," Reed said.

Sara stepped to the first elevator and used a keycard to open it for them. Then she reached in and pressed the button for the ninth floor. When the doors closed Reed threw Kate a curious look.

"What?" she asked, confused by the scrutiny.

"Are you threatened by her?"

Kate cocked her head to the side. "No," she said. "But she isn't attracted to you."

"You can tell?"

"A girl always knows," she said. "And I got the impression she already has a boyfriend."

"I got that too," he said.

The doors opened and they stepped into a lavish waiting room. Instead of the uncomfortable chairs one would expect, it contained couches and a television, even a few bean bag chairs. A separate room contained an enormous TV and multiple gaming systems, while another room contained a pool table, the balls perfectly racked beneath the soft light. Still another was a full office, complete with several computers, printers, and other equipment.

Persian rugs adorned the finely polished wood floors, and original paintings were on the walls. Even the lights were custom made, and a crystal chandelier hung from the vaulted ceilings. At the corner of the room, a spiral staircase curved up to a balcony, to a small library that overlooked the waiting room.

"Wow is an understatement," she said.

"You can say that again," Reed said. "The pictures don't do it justice."

A door opened and a tall man appeared down the hall. His suit was flawless but he had foregone the tie, giving him a more approachable look. His eyes had the softness that inspired instant trust, and his smile was warm without reserve. He approached and shook Reed's hand.

"Mr. Thompson," he said. "It's a pleasure to meet you in person."

"Sorry to interrupt," Reed said. "I just wanted to show Kate around."

"The famous Kate," he said, turning to her and shaking her hand. "You've got quite the following around here."

"Oh?" she asked.

"Your dates are legendary," he said. "There's even a pool going for who will win the challenge."

He leaned in to Kate, his tone turning conspiratorial. "My money's on you."

Kate smiled, unable to resist Dr. Dickson's warmth. "Smart money."

Dr. Dickson smiled and swept a hand at the office. "I'm glad you've loaned him to us. Don't tell the others, but he's the most talented candidate we've had in years." He glanced to Reed and winked. "Don't let it go to your head."

"I won't," he said, flashing his easy smile.

"That may be hard," Dr. Dickson said. "I have some big things in store for you."

"Oh?" Reed asked.

Dr. Dickson's eyes sparkled with anticipation but he dodged the question. "There's a lot to see," Dr. Dickson said, "but I'm sure you'll want to see your office first."

"I have an office?"

"Of course," he said. "You may not have a doctorate yet, but we choose interns because they will be the best."

Dr. Dickson nodded to Reed and then gestured down the hall, the motion bringing a startling revelation to Kate. She'd thought he would be a subordinate, but in this office, Dr. Dickson viewed him as a peer. At the end of his internship he would be fast tracked to any graduate program he wanted, with thousands of options at his fingertips.

As they walked around the offices Kate saw herself looking at Reed's future, at the clients he would inevitably bring because of his gift with relationships. The very reason she loved him was the same reason he would make a good doctor.

And she was just an engineering student from Colorado, a college girlfriend. As much as she wanted to refuse the thought, she couldn't help the insidious doubt. Reed was destined for great things. But was she part of his future?

She looked about the office and saw Reed working with Hannah, the two of them studying until late, sharing insights about their passion. It would be only too easy for that passion to escalate.

She'd landed in New York City and seen it for its myriad wondrous possibilities, but now she wondered if they city would tear them apart. She thought of Hannah and the job, her eyes sweeping across the office, and made a decision. Life may try to pull them apart, but she refused to accept that fate. Reed caught her eye and she straightened. New York might borrow him.

They couldn't keep him.

Chapter 6

Kate woke Monday morning to the distant sound of a car horn. She stood and stepped to the window. Her resolve from the last few days had solidified, and she nodded to herself. She turned away and gathered her things before descending to the lobby to check out. Other guests stood together and talked, their conversation unnecessarily loud, jarring with the peace she'd felt when she first arrived.

Reed was running late. He'd already texted that traffic was crazy so she waited outside, imagining Reed's morning with Hannah. She probably just got out of the shower, her hair wet and glistening on her bare shoulders, only a towel wrapped around her scintillating figure. But Reed was no normal man, and Kate imagined how Hannah would handle rejection.

She smiled as she realized a simple truth. Hannah knew how to get a normal guy, but Reed was not a normal guy. He had an integrity that would not be compromised, refused to be broken in the face of anyone and anything, even Hannah's ample assets.

A taxi pulled up and Reed swung the door open from the inside. Traffic was miraculously moving, so the taxi in the middle of the road elicited a chorus of honks. She ducked into the back seat with her bag in hand while the cabbie shouted at the cars behind.

"Hey," Reed said. "Sleep well?"

"I did," she said as the car began to move forward.

He raised an eyebrow. "You okay?"

"I am," she said, and meant it. "But it would have been nice to have you in the room next to me . . . or closer."

248

"I would have loved to," he said, his eyes light with humor, "but I've already strained my budget as it is, and New York is expensive."

"You got that right," the cabbie called back.

On the way to the airport they spoke of their new challenge, the Skype challenge, and the knowledge that they were parting lost its power. She marveled that the last three days had done the impossible, and prepared her for his absence.

They reached the airport and got out. Unloading their bags, they stood on the sidewalk while he paid the cab driver. Then he stopped and took her hand, turning so they faced each other. When he spoke his smile was soft.

"Kate." The softness to his tone was an invitation to speak, to trust him. "Are you sure you're okay?"

"I really am," she said. "I don't like it, but I'm ready."

He raised an eyebrow. "No worries about Hannah?"

"If you've kept your walls with me, she doesn't stand a chance."

He laughed lightly. "She might try to hold my hand."

She laughed with him. "That's the equivalent of sex for you—so remember, she's not going to be satisfied with holding hands."

Reed was a guy without peer, and standing on the sidewalk outside the airport, it seemed like he was a light in the midst of the city that wanted to corrupt him. Hannah was dangerous but she was by no means alone.

"Do you remember the Marathon Date?"

"I'm about to get on a plane," she said wryly. "I don't think I can sleep on your floor."

"We don't need to be together to be together."

"And how do we manage that?"

He gestured to her bag, to the outside pocket that had her tablet. "We already have the means. We just need a plan. When I'm not at work I'm with you."

"I like the sound of that."

"So it's a deal?"

Her lips twitched with amusement. "Did you have to ask?"

She wrapped him into his strong arms and for a moment she simply relished the sense of security. Then they stepped through the doors into the welcome heat and turned toward the ticketing counter. She noticed a guy dressed in all leather saying goodbye to a woman also in leather. Both of them sported shaved heads, tattoos replacing the hair.

"Just make sure the city doesn't change you," she said, lowering her tone.

"You think I'll get a leather jacket and a nose ring?" he asked. "Or maybe dreadlocks would look good on me."

She couldn't stop the laugh at the image. "Seriously. This isn't Boulder, and once the girls find out that you're a great guy, they're going to descend on you like it's Thanksgiving and you're a fresh piece of turkey."

"What if they're vegan?"

Kate burst into a laugh. "Even vegans will want you. So watch your back."

"I will," he promised, leaning in for a quick kiss. "And I'm counting on you to protect me."

"From Hannah?"

"From all the Hannahs."

"I think I can handle that," she said, collecting her ticket.

"But let's be clear," he said. "It doesn't make this suck any less."

It was the closest Reed had ever come to swearing, and she laughed, the one word revealing just how deeply Reed felt about the situation. The feeling of certainty she'd felt at the top of the Empire State Building returned and with it came clarity.

She reached up, putting her arms around his neck. "I'm really going to miss you."

"You too," he said quietly.

She held onto him as the mass of flyers rushed to and fro, moving around them like they were a stone in a creek. In minutes she would be among them, joining the throng of departures until she was on a plane flying away from Reed.

Abruptly she just wanted to leave, to be gone from the city that would be taking Reed. They walked to security and lingered in another hug. She kissed him goodbye and tried to convey every ounce of her emotion and need, fighting to make the connection last forever. Then she finally turned and got into line.

Her parents occasionally spoke of the era when people said goodbye at the gate, and watched their loved ones walk down the tunnel to the plane. The new security forced her to stand just feet from Reed, extending their goodbye each agonizing step toward the metal detectors. She looked to Reed and found a smile on his face. She reached the end of the line and rotated back, and still he was there, his easy smile on his face. She waved him away but he folded his arms and waited, making her laugh.

"I said goodbye," she called.

"And I made you a promise," he replied. "Every minute I'm not at work, I'm with you."

She shook her head and smiled, but as much as she wanted to keep him in sight, the line eventually moved through security. One moment he was there, smiling the slight grin she'd grown to love, the next he was out of sight. Then her phone buzzed.

"We don't have to be together to be together."

Her chest warmed to hear his voice. "I love you."

"And I you."

They talked all the way until she was on the plane and the attendants asked them to turn off their phones. She said a final goodbye and then stared at her phone, at the clock that had finally won. They'd fought the pull of time, but no one wins forever, and now her year had begun. She thought the parting would be filled with worry, but hope dominated her thoughts. Despite Hannah's presence, she and Reed were stronger than ever, a bond even New York City could not break.

"One year," she murmured aloud. "I can do one year."

Volume 26: The Distance Date

Chapter 1

The alarm sounded on Reed's phone, buzzing on the nightstand, the light reflecting off the dark ceiling. He'd set it to go off early so he could be ready for his first day, but it didn't wake him because he wasn't asleep.

Reed sighed and turned off the clock, sitting up to stare at the picture he'd set on the nightstand. Of all the pictures between him and Kate, it was his favorite, the one from their first date.

They were sitting on the cliff overlooking the valley in Colorado, the fading light of day illuminating their faces. There was an earnestness to her smile, an openness to her green eyes that he found incredibly attractive.

And he'd left her behind.

He shook his head and picked up his phone, dialing her number. It was early enough that he hesitated, but his desire to hear from Kate overrode his logic and he pressed the button. He half expected her to be asleep but she picked up on the second ring, her soft voice bringing a smile to his lips.

"Reed," she said, her voice betraying the smile.

"Are you awake?" he asked.

"Couldn't sleep," she said.

He smiled and sank back onto his bed. "We talked until two."

"That was five hours ago," she said. "We can't do this every night or you're going to fall asleep at work."

"Who needs sleep?" he asked.

His yawn betrayed him. She laughed. "Day one," she said. "Only a few hundred to go."

There was a knock at the door and Hannah's voice. "Reed? Care to join us for breakfast? We like to review the day's cases before we share a cab to the institute."

"I'll be right there," Reed called.

"Hannah calling?" Kate asked.

"Breakfast is calling," he corrected.

"Call me when you can?"

"I promise."

They said their goodbyes and Reed wiped his hand over his face. Then he rose to his feet and methodically got ready for his dream job. He showered and dressed before descending the stairs to grab a bowl of cereal with the others. Hannah made a point of sitting next to him, the conversation light as they discussed the upcoming day.

"Dr. Dickson wants you with him for the first week," Hannah said. "After that I think you'll jump into the rotation with the others."

Reed examined the list of clients, his eyes widening at the names. "Is this for real?"

Hannah leaned back and sipped her smoothie, a smile playing across her features. "The institute caters to politicians, billionaires, and celebrities, among other socialites."

He pointed to a name on the list. "Is he related to—?"

"Her son," Clint said, sipping his coffee. "Love her latest album."

"Will we see her?"

Hannah smiled and put her hand on his arm. "You have no idea what you're in for," she said. "And I can't wait to show you."

Hannah withdrew her hand before it would be inappropriate, but it was enough for Reed to feel her attraction. Ignoring it, he gathered his laptop bag and joined the others at the door. On the way to work he tried to keep Kate in his thoughts but he found himself excited about the upcoming day. He'd prepared his entire collegiate life for this moment and a nervous excitement threaded into his veins.

When they reached the building, Sara handed him his ID card, which allowed him into the elevator, and a key to his personal office. He expected some sort of orientation but instead he joined Dr. Dickson for a session with a rich couple having problems in their marriage. Prior to the session, he'd instructed Reed to sit back and observe.

Reed had studied psychology for years but learned more about behavior in ten minutes with Dr. Dickson. The man had a gift for knowing when to be serious and when to smile. Sometimes all it took was a steady look before an individual opened up, and Reed was impressed by the caliber of his talent and experience.

They took a break for lunch and Dr. Dickson took him to a five star restaurant that required six months to get a table. He walked in with a smile and a nod, calling the servers by name as they took their seats.

"Chef Skyler is incredible in the kitchen," he said. "And his Stromboli is to die for."

"Do you take all the interns out to lunch?"

"As a matter of fact, I do," he said with slight smile. "The office is a great place to work, but not ideal for connecting with the interns. Besides, I really wanted to talk to you about your research. Your thesis is fascinating."

Reed looked up from the menu in surprise. "You read my thesis?"

Dr. Dickson leaned back in his seat and regarded Reed with a bemused expression. "I meant what I said on Sunday, I haven't seen a candidate this gifted in years. Your ideas on relationships and family have the potential to be groundbreaking. Half our business is couples that don't know how to talk to each other—and I can only imagine what they would do if prescribed a date instead of a bottle."

"Is that why you let me come after I backed out?"

He smiled at Reed's candor. "I spoke to Dr. Caldin about you and Kate," Dr. Dickson said, nodding to the server as she filled his glass. "Thank you, Alisha, can you give us a moment?"

"Certainly," she replied, and disappeared after filling Reed's glass.

"Psychology as a science is always playing catch-up," Dr Dickson said. "We study and respond to the world and attempt to understand behavior, but technology has changed everything. The rapidity of its adoption by the collective consciousness has made our profession difficult, because we do not have time to develop practices that can respond effectively. And more often than not, we resort to pharmaceutical aid.

"Couples of every demographic are in turmoil," Dr. Dickson said. "The cell phone is undeniably one of the greatest tools of our modern age, but it has allowed the influences of the Internet to permeate the home. Pornography, games, and social media dominate the discourse until people forget how to make real romantic connections."

"It can't be that bad."

Dr. Dickson shook his head. "I have a sixteen-year-old patient that only knows how to communicate through Twitter—and she's by no means alone. I have couples that come in and want to use their phone *during* the session."

"What does my thesis have to do with this?" Reed asked.

"It answers the question psychologists are just beginning to ask," Dr. Dickson said. "How do we help those who have forgotten how to connect."

257

"Flattery will get you everywhere."

Dr. Dickson chuckled dryly and gestured to him. "I was going to wait until next week to tell you, but I want you to continue your research here, especially with couples. I want you to observe those we counsel and plan dates they can enjoy together. You'll get the credit, of course, but I will write the prescriptions."

A thread of excitement coursed through Reed at the prospect of seeing his theory put into practice. But could it work? He'd seen it work for those in college, but would it actually apply for adults in struggling homes?

"While I'm gratified by your faith in me," Reed said, "I'm not sure I'm ready for such an endeavor. My research in Boulder was effective, yes, but the data is still very preliminary, and the sample size was too small to measure a larger impact. I also knew the town, so I had more flexibility."

Dr. Dickson was nodding. "I assumed as much, which is why you will need time to discover New York City if you are to plan the best dates for our clients, all company funded, of course."

Reed settled back into his seat, for the first time understanding the full breadth of Dr. Dickson's idea, and the reason he'd presented it to Reed so early. It would take time to explore enough of the city to plan effective dates for clients, and more time to measure their impact. Reed's internship ended in a year, and in the terms of research, it wasn't much time.

"How soon do you want me to start?" Reed asked cautiously.

"Tomorrow," he said. "Each morning you will explore the city, and each afternoon you'll be assisting me. I've taken the liberty of scheduling my couple sessions during that time frame. Each Thursday you and Hannah can report on your results."

"Hannah?"

"Of course," Dr. Dickson said. "Family counseling is her focus as well, and we'll need a female perspective on the research. You'll get primary credit, of course, but Hannah's and my names will be part of the paper you'll write at the end of the year."

His tone bordered on apologetic, as if he knew Hannah's interest in Reed. Still, it made sense, and Reed didn't see an alternative unless he refused to do the project. While he doubted Dr. Dickson would remove him from the internship, the man had gone to great lengths to support Reed, and the project would be an enormous push for his career. Still, he knew exactly what Kate would say . . .

Chapter 2

"You're getting paid to date Hannah?"

Reed laughed. "I knew you'd say that."

"This isn't something to laugh about," Kate said. "I don't like the prospect of you spending so much time with her."

It was the end of their first day and Reed had waited until they were on Skype to tell Kate. He knew she would be upset—and rightly so—but he was torn. Dr. Dickson wanted to help his clients and thought Reed's research could do it, but Reed couldn't do it alone.

"The research needs a female perspective," Reed said. "Dr. Dickson is right about that."

Kate grunted in irritation. "So he's paying you to date her. Is he going to buy the engagement ring as well?"

"You're cute when you're angry, you know that?"

Her lips tightened. "I'm really worried, Reed. This is how relationships die. This is the story you'll tell your kids when you're married to her."

Reed sighed and gave up on the attempts to soften the situation. "I feel stuck," Reed said. "Dr. Dickson has gone out of his way and I really think he wants to help his clients. He also believes my theories can have an impact—not just in his practice, but on the field."

She chuckled sourly. "I knew the city would try to change you. I didn't realize it would happen so quickly."

"I want to help couples stay together, to help them fall in love—to stay in love. Like my parents couldn't." He grimaced. "I'm sorry Hannah is a part of it."

Kate looked to the ceiling and released a long breath. It was after midnight in New York and after ten in Colorado, her hair indicating she was ready to go to sleep. He'd worked late with Dr. Dickson and Hannah, talking about the research project, and hadn't made it back to the brownstone until an hour ago.

"One condition," Kate finally said.

"What's that?"

"You need to set me up with someone nice."

He blinked in surprise. "What?"

"If you're dating a hot girl, it's only fair I date a hot guy. I'm thinking someone with a plethora of abs." She scrunched her face up as if in thought. "Maybe an underwear model, but an intelligent one, like he's modeling to pay his way through school while volunteering at a soup kitchen."

"I'll see what I can do," he said with a laugh.

She grinned. "I'm not worried Reed."

"Really?" he asked.

She nodded. "I love you, and no amount of Hannahs can stop that."

"So you're saying you don't care?"

"I'm saying I don't have a reason to worry," she said with a crooked smile. "You've resisted plenty of hot girls before, so Hannah is no different."

Suspicious, he shook his head. "What's with the sudden confidence?"

261

"I talked to the blondes," she said.

Reed groaned. "Is Ember going to break my legs?" Then he had another thought. "Or is Hannah in danger?"

"Both are a possibility," Kate mused. "But they reminded me that I don't need to be afraid. And you're right, I do trust you."

"I like that thought," he said.

"Good," she said with a firm nod. "Because I'm excited for our date next Friday."

He winced. "Actually, I think we're going to have to hold off the last challenge date until next week. I'm working late every day planning our research, and next Friday is a big benefit for the New York Psychological Association. All the best doctors in the state are expected to come, and the institute buys a seat for each of the interns."

"Another date with Hannah?" she asked, but a smile took the rancor from her voice.

"I know this is hard, but can we put off the last date?" he asked. "You said you already had a plan for a final date and I'm really looking forward to seeing how you end the challenge."

"You should be," she said. "Just make sure Hannah doesn't tag along."

"That would just be awkward," Reed said.

"I know," she said, her expression amused. "And I'd have to bring your model friend to balance the scales."

"Maybe we can set them up," Reed said. "I think they'd get along."

Kate laughed. "Probably. Now, no more about Hannah, I want to hear about your first day."

Grateful for the change in conversation, Reed described the events of the day, leaving out only the specific patient information. Kate didn't seem inclined to end the call and they talked until both were yawning before finally saying goodnight.

Exhausted, Reed slept like a stone and only woke when there was a knock at the door. He rushed to get ready and skipped breakfast, calling Kate briefly before jumping into the cab with the others.

He arrived at the institute and received a company credit card with an exorbitant daily expense budget. After checking in with Dr. Hahn, who Hannah was doing another research project with, Hannah joined him outside the building.

"We have until lunch," Hannah said, smiling brightly. "Where to?"

Reed managed a smile and gestured to the city. "Everywhere."

Starting online, they researched eateries and activities, cataloging those they intended to visit throughout the first week. Dr. Dickson wanted them to experience everything so their recommendations would be more prepared. As much as Reed wanted to dislike Hannah, she was funny and intelligent, and equally as excited about the research excursions. But throughout it all, he kept his heart firmly locked. Only Kate had the key.

Chapter 3

The week at the institute became a blur of exploring the city and sessions with Dr. Dickson. He saw multiple couples each day and Reed sat in for most of the sessions. A handful refused to allow anyone else to be present, and Reed didn't even know their identities. When he was not with Dr. Dickson, he was with Hannah.

He escaped during lunch to call Kate each day, but the demands of his time quickly mounted, and their calls grew progressively shorter. He made up for it at night, staying up until after midnight each day to talk to her.

The other interns studied most weeknights, doing research for the various doctors. Clint was the most widespread and was currently working for three separate doctors. David and Hannah were both working with two, while it appeared Reed would be working exclusively with Dr. Dickson.

Although Reed struggled with the distance to Kate, he relished the first few days. School had been filled with classes and theory, but in the institute he got the chance to see theory put into practice, witness the very real challenges faced by families. He felt like he'd been learning about the ocean for years and now he finally got to feel the surf on his feet. When Saturday came he was actually disappointed they wouldn't be going to the institute, but there was another reason to look forward to the day.

"Happy Birthday," Kate said.

"It's six in the morning."

"I wanted to be the first to tell you," she said.

"You mean before Hannah."

The video call on his phone was grainy but her smile was clearly visible. "I don't know what you're talking about."

He laughed and then stifled the amusement before it could wake the others. Each day he spoke to her in the morning and talked to her before falling asleep at night, her face the first and last things he saw. Each was a moment to be treasured.

"I love waking up to see your face," he said.

"Me too," she replied. "Are you ready for today?"

"I need a few minutes to get ready," he said. "Can I call you when I'm walking out the door?"

"Before you go," she said. "I want to watch you open your birthday present."

"Birthday present?" he asked.

"It's under your bed."

"How did you get it there?" he asked, dropping off the bed and leaning down to look under. To his surprise there was a small package just out of sight.

"When we unpacked your things," she replied. "I didn't want to mail it so I left it there."

He sat on the bed and propped the phone against the pillow. "I can't believe you did this."

"You taught me to plan ahead," she said smugly. "Now open the present."

The package was small, no larger than a few inches, which explained why she'd been able to carry it in her purse without him noticing. Bright red wrapping was tied with yellow ribbon, the corner torn as if she'd hastily stashed it out of sight.

265

Abruptly seized with a desire to preserve the paper, he undid the ribbon and unfolded the paper, revealing a small, flat box. Soft, black velvet covered the wood, and a brass clasp held it shut. Curious, he opened the box and smiled.

"Cuff links?" he asked, raising them into the video.

"I didn't figure you one for jewelry," she said. "But when you were showing me the website for the internship there was pictures of fancy benefits and charity events."

He held them up and admired them. "Your timing is excellent," he said wryly. "I just learned the benefit next Friday is formal. One of my errands today is to get a tux."

"I'll want to see a picture of that," she said with a smile.

"Will do," he said, and looked to the phone. "And thanks. These are very thoughtful."

"Call me when you're on your way to the store," she said. "It might sound stupid, but I miss shopping with you."

"Why don't you go with me?" he asked.

"To the store?"

"Why not?" he replied. "I have to buy groceries and its Saturday, so you're probably out of milk."

She brightened at the prospect and nodded. "Give me a half an hour to get ready."

"Deal," he said.

They hung up and he headed to the bathroom. Just as he knocked, Hannah exited with a towel around her body. Water glistened in her hair and on her bare shoulders but she gestured to the shower.

"You're up early," she said. "Do you need the shower?"

266

"I have a few errands to run," he said.

"Aren't we getting your tux later?" she asked.

"This afternoon," he said with a nod.

She vacated the bathroom. "It's all yours."

"Thanks," he said.

"Oh," she said with a smile. "And Happy Birthday. I'll have to find you something when we go shopping."

"You don't have to do that," he protested.

"What are friends for," she said, flashing a brilliant smile before disappearing.

Reed frowned but she was already gone. He shut the door and made sure to lock it before stripping and stepping into the shower. Irritated by the exchange, he kept it brief and then dressed in dirty clothes rather than walk down the hall in a towel. When he was back to the safety of his room he changed. Then he picked up his wallet and phone, and noticed he had a missed call from his mom.

He called her back as he strode downstairs and waved to Clint and David, who were eating a leisurely breakfast while watching TV. Passing them by, he exited onto the street and turned toward the nearest grocery store, a small shop just two blocks away. His mom wanted all the details of New York and when he finally managed to shake her, Kate called.

"What's taking so long?" she asked, the background noise indicating she was in her car.

"My mom called," he said.

"I'm just pulling in now," she said. "You ready to shop?"

"Very," he said fervently, eliciting a laugh.

He walked through the doors into the small grocery store. It wasn't a Target or a Walmart, but it was large enough to have everything he would need. The familiar practice of hunting for edible favorites was surprisingly enjoyable on the phone with Kate, and they laughed and talked about times they'd cooked and succeeded. And times they'd cooked and failed.

"Remember when we tried to make that dinner from Pinterest?"

He grinned as he recalled a messy soup of meat, cheese, and spices. "I think that goes under the fail category."

"You know, if you include our non-challenge dates, we've been out a lot," she said.

He picked up a package of cottage cheese and swerved around a mom examining a package of meat. He looked to his list as he considered her comment.

"I bet we've been out a hundred times," he said.

"Really?"

"The last six months we've been eating dinner nearly every night," he said.

"True," she replied. "But not all of those were out."

"You don't have to eat out to go on a date," he said. "Look at us now. We're doing our grocery shopping together even though we're on opposite sides of the country."

"I don't think that counts," she said.

He turned down the cereal aisle. "How else would you count it?"

"Not like that," she said.

"Whatever way you record it, we've certainly been on a hundred dates," he said.

"I'll allow it," she replied. "But you don't get to count next week."

"The benefit? I thought we talked about putting you on my phone so you could be part of it."

"I've changed my mind," she said. "I want you to focus and then I want to hear about it after."

He came to a halt in the aisle. "You won't think I'm going with Hannah?"

"I already think that," she said with a laugh. "She's your work girlfriend."

"She says you get all the attention," Reed lamented.

Kate laughed lightly, and he was grateful there was no hint of strain. He'd been worried about her response, but she'd proven remarkably unfazed by the whole situation. Then again, he'd fallen in love with her courage.

"Bake is calling me," she said. "Can I talk to you later?"

"Sure," he said. "Love you."

"Love you too," she replied.

Although Kate seemed to be handling his working with Hannah, he found that he still disliked the situation. Hannah went out of her way to entice him. Most of the actions were subtle, but some were more obvious.

He grunted and released his irritation by dropping a pair of cans into his cart. He couldn't blame her, the girl knew what she wanted. But perhaps it was time he had a frank conversation with Hannah. Satisfied at his plan, he finished his shopping and headed back to the apartment.

Chapter 4

Reed stared at himself in the mirror, shocked at the dashing figure staring back at him. He considered himself handsome, but clad in the black and white of a tuxedo he looked muscular and trim, his dark hair complementing the black material that brought out the blueness of his eyes. So why was he so uncomfortable?

"You look stunning," Hannah said, stepping into view of the mirror.

That's why.

"Thank you," Reed said. "Can you take a picture for Kate?"

She readily agreed but her smile lost a few watts. As she stepped back he offered a casual pose, eliciting a laugh from the other two interns. Clint shook his head in chagrin and rose from the plush couch to join them.

"You look better than I do."

"The *mannequin* looks better than you do," David said.

Clint grinned and ran his hand through the bald spot on his head. "I have his lack of hair."

David laughed. "I hate to tell you, but most girls like the hair."

Clint groaned like he'd been wounded. "Is that true?" he asked, looking to Hannah.

"Sorry," she said apologetically.

She smiled and reached up to ruffle Reed's hair. He ducked away so they wouldn't see his flush and escaped into the dressing room, and from the safety of solitude he admired the view. He didn't consider himself vain, but dressed in formal clothes, the pride was quick and powerful. Then his phone buzzed.

"You look *hot*."

He smiled and turned in the mirror. "You think so?"

"If I was still there, I'd be taking it off you."

In the mirror he flushed bright red. As if she recognized the impact of her statement, Kate laughed, the sound that of a Disney villain that had cornered the hero. Reed shook his head and sat down.

"I really wish you were my date to this," he said. "I may look good, but I've never worn a tux, so I feel really out of place."

"What about prom?"

"Never went," he said. "It was back when I had a crush on Aura and she was going with someone else."

"I can't believe you've never worn a tux," she said.

"How many formal events have you been to?" he asked, lowering his voice as he heard the door to the next changing room open and shut.

"Plenty," she replied. "Tyler even took me to an Air Force function and I got to wear a really nice dress." Her tone was wistful.

"I'd like to see a picture of that."

"It was a couple of years ago," she said, "so maybe I'll just wear it for you."

"Then it would be my turn to take something off you."

He froze in surprise, the words escaping his lips before he could stop them. Kate too seemed shocked and the silence hung on the call as

271

his brain registered what he'd said. What was wrong with him? Then Kate began to laugh.

"You must be *really* distracted," she said.

"I'm sorry," he said. "I shouldn't have said that."

"Yes, you should," she said, her tone pleased.

He gave a wry chuckle and resumed changing. "Being apart from you is wreaking havoc on me," he said.

"Is that all it took?" she asked smugly. "If I knew that I would have sent you away months ago."

He laughed again and leaned back against the wall. "It's been a week and I can't stop thinking about you."

"Me too," she said, her tone amused. "Now go get ready for your date with Hannah so we can be together."

"Only because you said so," he replied.

"But no hand holding," she warned. "Just a few more weeks and those hands will be all over my—"

"*Okay*," he said hastily. "I think I need to go now."

"See you soon," she said brightly.

He grinned and hung up. As he dressed in his regular clothes he kept thinking about what she'd said and realized the barriers to his physical walls had eroded more than he realized. They'd protected him for so long that he wasn't sure what to think if they were gone.

He exited the changing room and made his way to the counter, where he paid for the tux rental. Hannah appeared at his side and placed a sleek, red dress wrapped in plastic on the counter. She'd donned several but it appeared she'd made her choice.

"You're lucky," she said. "One tux and you're set. We have to have a different dress for every event."

"Amen," the girl behind the counter said fervently.

"You should buy the tux," David said.

"I can't afford to right now," he said, handing his card to the girl. "I spent a lot the last few weeks."

David shrugged. "Don't say I didn't warn you."

They finished paying and exited the store, which was somewhere downtown. Reed found it disconcerting not to know where he was, but the cab drivers always knew. On the drive home, Reed listened to his roommates' conversation and wondered when he could have a conversation with Hannah about boundaries.

The cab took them back to the brownstone and he spent much of the remaining Saturday Skyping with Kate. She was delighted with the extra time, and again they talked until deep into the night.

Sunday he spent most of the day with Hannah, reviewing their notes of the week and planning what to do for the next week. Hannah had lived in the city for six months but spent most of her time working, so she was exploring the city with him.

"Check this out," Hannah said, shifting her laptop to show him the screen. "This restaurant is called The View, and it's the only revolving restaurant in New York City."

"Put it on the list," Reed said.

They were sitting across from each other at the kitchen table, papers scattered across the surface with notes and ideas. Reed would have preferred for Hannah to not have a talent for creative dating, but her insights were smart and innovative.

"You guys up for dinner?" Clint asked, descending the stairs dressed to go out. "Dave and I want to hit the sushi place around the corner."

Reed shook his head. "What about Chinese?"

"You guys have fun with sushi," Hannah said. "We'll order in."

"You sure?"

"Yeah," she said. "We've got a lot to plan tonight."

"Have fun," David said, descending the stairs and donning his coat.

They walked out the door, leaving Reed alone with Hannah for the first time since he'd moved in. Reed would have liked to think that it was simply coincidence, but he suspected she'd taken advantage of the moment to gain some time alone.

"What do you want to eat?" she asked, putting her phone to her ear.

He guessed she was ordering from the place they'd ordered from on Wednesday, so he reached to the nearby fridge and plucked the menu from beneath the magnet. A quick glance and he nodded.

"Sweet and sour chicken, and chow mein."

She ordered and then put her phone down. "Isn't that what you got earlier this week?"

"They're my favorites," he replied.

"Ever had the Peking roasted duck? It's to die for."

"I wouldn't mind," he said. "I just haven't had the chance."

"Most of the guys we're dealing with have already picked their favorite places to eat," she said, her golden brown eyes turning thoughtful. "Part of our job will be to instill a desire to try something new. They could easily fall in love with the dinner spot right across from their work." Her gaze settled on him, a slight smile bending her lips.

"Perhaps," he said. "And with food, they will certainly need to acquire a sense of adventure."

She agreed with a nod and then stretched, leaning her curvy body back in the chair as she yawned. "My last boyfriend would never have done anything like this," she swept her hand at the table.

"How long were you together?" Reed asked.

"Six months," she replied. "We met through Tinder and one night became every night. After a few months I realized that's what he saw from our relationship, and tried to go on an actual date. He wanted to have sex in the theatre and I broke it off."

"Right there?" Reed asked.

"I wanted more than a physical relationship," she replied, and then shrugged. "I don't think he understood."

"Any other boyfriends?"

"One serious," she said, "early college."

She talked about her first serious relationship that lasted two years, and he talked about Kate. He'd steered the conversation that way so he could focus on Kate, but she did not seem to mind. However, her questions were more about their challenge dates.

The doorbell rang and they took their dinner into the library to eat, the conversation shifting to college, families, and past relationships. He looked for an opportunity to talk about boundaries but it never came. Hannah was easy to talk to and funny. She was also brilliant, and Reed found himself admiring her perceptive mind. As much as he would have liked to stay coworkers, he sensed the start of a friendship, one that left him uneasy.

Chapter 5

The next week passed in a cycle of exploring New York City, sessions in the institute, and evenings split between research with Hannah and calls with Kate. With all the demands on his time, he had to fight for time where he could talk to Kate.

Friday came and the interns were permitted to leave early to get ready for the benefit. Hannah left shortly after lunch, while Reed remained behind to finalize the report of their week's activities. Reed stared at the list of their first two weeks' activities, disturbed by the sheer amount of time he'd spent with Hannah. He and Hannah had eaten together at expensive restaurants and obscure pizza places, discovered helicopter rides and near secret clubs, even ascending to the rooftops and an underground tour.

"You ready?" Clint asked from the door.

Reed nodded and hit send before walking out of his office and shutting the door. Then he joined Clint and David on their way down in the elevator. Within minutes they were back at the brownstone and he retreated to his room to get ready.

Reed donned his tux in a hurry to FaceTime Kate for a few precious minutes before they left, but she didn't answer. Instead she replied with a text to say her Friday class would not be out for another half hour.

He grunted in irritation and sent a message back that he would try to call later, and included a picture of him in his tux. Then he descended the stairs and waited for the others. David and Clint arrived first and a moment later Hannah appeared.

Dressed in a red and black dress that hung off one shoulder and showed her cleavage, Hannah veritably floated down the stairs. Her hair was pulled to the back, the ringlets tied into artful twists, revealing her shoulder and her diamond necklace.

Clint whistled. "You put us to shame."

"And then some," David said.

Hannah flashed a self-deprecating smile as she swept by them to the door. "Says the men who look like gods." Her eyes flicked to Reed and gained a glint of desire.

"You flatter us," Clint said, and then his smile turned smug. "Even if it's true."

They walked outside and caught a ride to lower Manhattan. The hotel hosting the benefit was new, the structure all angles of glass and steel. The lights and red carpet guided the guests up the stairs. Actual paparazzi were present, snapping photos of the handful of celebrities in attendance.

Caught up in the surreal moment, Reed strode up the stairs and entered the marbled lobby, slowing as he viewed the decadence. Tuxes and designer dresses were worn by the doctors and their spouses, and the social elite that had come to donate and mingle.

Grand staircases rose to a second floor, where more richly dressed men and women talked, the hum of conversation occasionally broken by tinkling laughter. Signs for the charity were posted in discrete locations, a reminder that proceeds from donations and the purchased seats would go to the Foundation House.

At the back of the hall, large doors led to the banquet hall. A server, dressed in burgundy vest and matching bow tie, opened the door, allowing a glimpse of tables draped in white and adorned in crystal glasses. A small stage lined the rear of the banquet hall and a podium held the center.

A string quartet in the lobby added a soft melody to the voices and laughter, while crystal chandeliers bathed the chamber in light.

Diamonds and other gemstones sparkled on necks, ears, and cuff links, a counterpoint to the security roaming the room.

"First benefit?" Hannah asked in aside.

"Do I look as out of place as I feel?"

She swept her hand to the group. "It gets easier. We have one of these ever few weeks, so you'll get lots of practice."

Reed looked down at his tux. "I should have bought my tux."

"That's what I told you," Clint said, clapping in the shoulder. "And look, an open bar."

He smirked and disappeared, taking David with him. Reed remained in place, trying to get comfortable in the setting and the clothes, and wishing Kate was at his side. He wasn't usually unsettled by social situations, but the sheer amount of money in the room left him uncertain.

"Relax," Hannah said with a smile. "I promise it gets easier."

"I'm fine," Reed said, straightening and gesturing an invitation toward the room. "Shall we?"

She gave an approving nod and they worked their way into the crowd. Reed had never met the people present, but he did recognize some. He spotted a pair of doctors whom he'd quoted in his research, and a woman he'd only seen in a movie. It was odd and strangely exhilarating to be thrust into such a different world.

Hannah caught his arm and pointed. "Do you see the girl in the white and green dress by the bar?"

Reed craned his neck to look through the crowd and nodded. "She doesn't look like a doctor."

"That's Elaina," Hannah said. "She and the guy next to her are interns at the Theodore Institute in Jersey."

278

"They're students?"

"Rivals, of sorts," Hannah said. "But Elaina is Dr. Dickson's niece and lives in another brownstone close to us."

Elaina caught sight of them and waved, and Hannah returned the gesture. She was short, with black hair and dark eyes. Her clothing and jewelry screamed wealth but her smile was genuine and sincere, much like her uncle, in fact. She separated herself from her companion and crossed the floor to join them.

"Hannah," she said, giving the taller girl an embrace. "It's always good to see you."

"You too," Hannah said.

Reed couldn't be certain if the girls liked or disliked each other, but smiled as he stepped forward. "Reed Thompson," he said. "Elaina . . ."

"Vanderbilt," she replied.

"I hear you chose a rival institute," Reed said.

She lowered her voice and leaned in. "Maybe I *like* a long commute through smog infested streets."

Reed nodded sagely. "We all do, but you beat us out for the job."

She laughed, a high, unfettered sound that Reed immediately liked. The girl reminded him of Natalie when they were younger, and he sensed the start of an easy friendship. She was confident but not arrogant, and Reed fleetingly wished she and Hannah had traded places.

"I'm at the table next to you," Elaina said, "so we can pass notes if it gets dull."

"It's always dull," Hannah said.

The girl laughed again. "I know," she replied, and winked before turning and making her way back to the guy at the counter. Their subsequent kiss made it clear their relationship was more than professional.

"Her specialty didn't line up with Dr. Dickson," Hannah was saying, "So he helped her get into the other program. It's good, but not as good as ours."

"Reed," Dr. Dickson called, drawing their attention to a nearby group. "I'd like you to come over here and meet Dr.'s Billingham and Manchester." He then spotted Hannah and summoned her as well.

"Mr. Thompson, Ms. Parker," he said introducing them as they approached. Then he turned to his companions. "Their research on familial relationships and time is very intriguing."

Dr. Billingham, a short, balding man with ready smile, raised an eyebrow. "*Reed* Thompson, your intern?"

"I hope there isn't another one," Reed said, eliciting a laugh.

"James won't shut up about you," Dr. Billingham said, using his champagne glass to point to Dr. Dickson.

"Why are we talking about work?" Dr. Manchester said. "I didn't come to a party with my office in tow."

"Don't mind him," Dr. Billingham said. "He chose the wrong specialty." He flashed an amused smile.

"Too late to change now," Dr. Manchester said dryly, raising his glass.

A woman approached and Dr. Manchester was suddenly all smiles, the expression eliciting a spark of memory, and he recognized him from his picture. Reed had read a few of his papers on addiction recovery. His practice focused on chemical and drug addiction, many of his clients coming from the children of rich families. His research and papers were well respected in the community.

Dr. Manchester excused himself and strode away with the woman. Reed caught snippets, enough to hear that she had a question about her son, who was apparently acting up in school. He noticed other such conversations and realized the benefit was not just for charity, it was a place for the doctors to find new clients.

His perspective suddenly shifted. Beneath the glitz and opulence it was just a networking event. In Boulder the men would have been in suits and ties and the women in dresses likely bought from a mall. The venue would have been at a hotel or convention space, the walls a dull brown instead of a marble and glass.

Reed smiled to himself and for the first time felt comfortable. Dr. Dickson was just like Dr. Caldin, a mentor and a friend that believed in him, while the institute was just a job. The other interns were colleagues to be learned from, students just like him.

He could do this.

His nervousness melted away and he responded to Dr. Billingham's comment, eliciting another laugh. Hannah spoke with equal wit. When they moved into the banquet hall Reed no longer felt out of place, and for the first time since stepping into New York City, he felt like he belonged.

Chapter 6

The banquet ended late and Reed and Hannah shared a cab back to the brownstone. Clint and David had been too free with the open bar and gone home earlier, so it was just Hannah and Reed. Both were excited with the connections they'd made, and Hannah spoke of meeting prestigious alumni from her dream school.

"I'm glad you were here tonight," Hannah said.

"Why do you say that?" he asked as they reached their stop.

They got out and Reed paid the driver, and he departed, the sound fading in the empty street. The air was crisp, the breeze chilly, but with a hint of spring. Hannah breathed in the night air and pulled her wrap tighter about her shoulders, her smile one of admiration.

"You just have a way of impressing everyone you meet." She flashed a faint smile. "Myself included."

"I think that's a bit of an exaggeration," Reed said.

"It's not," Hannah said. "This was your first social function and you turned heads."

"I wasn't the only one," Reed said.

He'd said it in an attempt to turn the conversation away from himself, but immediately regretted it. To another girl it would have been seen as a compliment, but to Hannah it would be viewed as flirting. Hannah's smile revealed that was exactly how she interpreted his praise.

Her hair was still flawless, her eyes an intense golden brown that was attractive, and conveyed an engaging warmth. Her dress highlighted her shape, and even after a night of dancing and talking, she still looked breathtaking.

But Reed did not feel the attraction.

What he did feel was the spark of friendship. She'd been at his side for many of the conversations in the evening and she spoke with grace and intelligence, her thoughts on relationships very similar to his own.

Being Hannah's friend would have been fine—but he knew how such a connection could build, especially with Hannah's obvious feelings. The only way to prevent a future conflict would be a frank conversation now, so Reed steeled himself for what needed to be said.

"Hannah," he said, his tone serious. "I need you to understand that I love Kate, and there will never be anything between you and I."

She regarded him for a long moment, a trace of surprise in her gaze. Reed's candor bordered on bluntness, but he'd grown tired of always dancing around her obvious attraction. Then her eyes lit with amusement.

"I can wait."

She smiled and strode up the steps, leaving Reed by the street. Her response was brief but spoke volumes. Reed's choice to address her attraction had not fazed her, and merely confirmed her intentions.

"Coming to bed?" she cast over her shoulder as she unlocked the door.

Reed frowned, and realized that acknowledging her attraction may have been a mistake. With no reason to hide, she was free to flirt whenever they were alone. Choosing not to respond, he went up the stairs and followed her into the brownstone.

"Good night," he said as he went up the stairs and retreated to his room.

The clock on the nightstand said it was after three in the morning, so he stripped his tux and donned a pair of shorts and a t-shirt. Finally comfortable, he sank onto the bed and pulled out his phone. After a moment's hesitation, he sent a text to Kate.

Just got back. Call me when you wake up. Love you.

He plugged his phone in, but as he lay down it buzzed. A smile spread on his face as he answered the FaceTime call, and watched Kate's face resolve into focus. She was in bed, her hair tied back and her pillow in the background, but her eyes were clear.

"What are you doing awake?"

"My boyfriend was on a date to a ball," she said, the smile evident in her voice. "I couldn't sleep."

He stifled a laugh. "It wasn't a date," he said.

"But it was a ball," she countered.

"I can't deny that," he said.

"How was it?" she asked, yawning.

"Do you want to hear about it now or in the morning?"

She paused and he could imagine her considering his question. Then she yawned again. "Give me the highlights now and you can tell me the rest tomorrow."

"I met Justin Timberlake."

"What?" she asked, jerking upward. "Really?"

"No," he said. "I just wanted to make sure you were awake."

"That's not fair," she grumbled.

He grinned and started with who he did meet, alumni from the best psychology programs in the country, many of which he knew only by

284

name. She smiled at his obvious excitement while he shared the details of his conversations.

During the banquet he'd been seated with the rest of the institute and he'd sat between Hannah and Dr. Dickson, who'd murmured to him details of individuals during the speeches, helping him know who to talk to after the meal.

"What was for dinner?" she asked.

"Best chicken of my life," he said. "I don't know what was in it or on it, but I want more."

"Did Hannah behave?"

"Of course," Reed asked, and shared what he'd said to Hannah outside the brownstone.

"I can't believe you said that," she said, clearly pleased.

He grimaced, and then revealed Hannah's response. Kate's expression soured and she shook her head in irritation.

"The girl is relentless, I'll give her that."

"I can handle Hannah," he said.

"I know exactly what she wants to handle," she said. She then wiped a hand across her face. "I'm sorry. It's late and I know you had a good night. I don't want to ruin it for you."

"You're not," he said. "I may have gone to a ball, but I came home to you."

She laughed lightly. "That girl is too close for comfort."

"You're closer," he said, and tapped his chest.

She shook her head. "I want to be."

He frowned. "What are you saying?"

285

"Nothing," she said. "I'm just tired. We can talk tomorrow."

He sighed and shook his head. "I'm beginning to think I don't deserve you."

"Hannah doesn't deserve you," she corrected.

He grinned. "Date tomorrow night?"

"Promise?"

"I promise," he said.

She yawned and nodded. "Then I'm saying goodnight. I love you."

"I love you, too," he said. "Sleep well."

"You too."

He hung up and the screen went black, plunging the room into darkness. Sighing, he leaned against the headboard and stared at the dim ceiling. Two weeks into his internship he'd hoped to find a rhythm of work and distance dating with Kate. Instead he was more worried than ever.

He plugged his phone in and reclined on his bed. The clock numbers stared back at him, a reminder of just how much time lay between him and Kate. His love for Kate was as bright as ever, the gap creating an ache in his heart. As he stared at the clock he resolved again to talk to Kate throughout each day. As long as he stayed close with Kate, Hannah would be powerless. Smiling at that thought, he closed his eyes and fell asleep.

And dreamed of Kate.

27 Dates: The Series

The Dating Challenge

The Dating Secret

The Dating Game

The Christmas Date

The Valentine's Date

Author Bio

Originally from Utah, Ben has grown up with a passion for learning. While still young, he practiced various sports, became an Eagle Scout, and taught himself to play the piano. As a teenager he began creative dating and continued the practice into college, where he took a break to do volunteer work in Brazil. After school, he launched his first series, The Chronicles of Lumineia, and has since published over 20 titles across multiple genres. He loves to snowboard, build treehouses, and play board games, especially with his family. His greatest support and inspiration comes from his wonderful wife and six beautiful children. Currently he resides in Missouri while working on his Masters in Professional Writing.

To contact the author, discover more about 27 Dates, or find out about the upcoming sequels, check out his website at 27Dates.com. You can also follow the author on twitter @27Dates or Facebook.

www.ingramcontent.com/pod-product-compliance
Lightning Source LLC
Chambersburg PA
CBHW021950170626
46808CB00001B/90